PRAISE FOR T.R. RAGAN

Her Last Day

"Intricately plotted . . . The tense plot builds to a startling and satisfying resolution."

—*Publishers Weekly* (starred review)

"Ragan's newest novel is exciting and intriguing from the very beginning . . . Readers will race to finish the book, wanting to know the outcome and see justice served."

—*RT Book Reviews*

"Readers will obsess over T.R. Ragan's new tenacious heroine. I can't wait for the next in the series!"

—Kendra Elliot, author of the *Wall Street Journal* bestsellers *Spiraled* and *Targeted*

"With action-packed twists and turns and a pace that doesn't let up until the thrilling conclusion, *Her Last Day* is a brilliant start to a gripping new series from T.R. Ragan."

—Robert Bryndza, #1 international bestselling author of *The Girl in the Ice*

DERANGED

Other Titles by T.R. Ragan

Jessie Cole Series

Her Last Day
Deadly Recall

Faith McMann Trilogy

Wrath
Furious
Outrage

Lizzy Gardner Series

Abducted
Dead Weight
A Dark Mind
Obsessed
Almost Dead
Evil Never Dies

Writing as Theresa Ragan

Return of the Rose
A Knight in Central Park
Taming Mad Max
Finding Kate Huntley
Having My Baby
An Offer He Can't Refuse
Here Comes the Bride
I Will Wait for You: A Novella
Dead Man Running

DERANGED

A
JESSIE COLE
THRILLER

T.R. RAGAN

THOMAS & MERCER

Text copyright © 2018 by Theresa Ragan
All rights reserved.

Published by Thomas & Mercer, Seattle

www.apub.com

Amazon, the Amazon logo, and Thomas & Mercer are trademarks of Amazon.com, Inc., or its affiliates.

ISBN-13: 9781503904293
ISBN-10: 1503904296

Cover design by Kirk DouPonce, DogEared Design

Printed in the United States of America

Jesse, Joey, Morgan, and Brittany
So many memories, so much happiness
So grateful to have you in my life

One

Dean Crawford

Dean Crawford, psychologist and guidance counselor at Folsom State Prison in California, made his way through a series of gates, the steel doors clanking shut behind him. After the guard identified him and checked his appointment list, he waited for the next door to open. He had two offices—a small shared office on the top floor and one windowless room below, situated between the cellblock where inmates were housed and a cafeteria. It was there, surrounded by the body odors of too many men, where loud noises and voices bounced off concrete walls and violence hovered in the air, that he met with his clients.

"Hey, Dr. Crawford, where are my meds?" someone called from inside a cell, prompting laughter. The inmate knew he couldn't prescribe medication and liked to taunt him about not being a "real" doctor. Hands reached out through steel bars. Dozens of inmates shouted obscenities along with "quack, quack," a habit they couldn't seem to kick. It gave them something to do.

A large percentage of the inmates he met with were locked in their cells. Others roamed free in the dayroom. He tended to work with some of the most challenging inmate-patients, the ones who might have suicidal or homicidal tendencies. As he walked toward his office, he tried not to breathe in. The place smelled like unwashed bodies mixed with chlorine. The stench alone should have been enough to deter most prisoners from ever coming back, but it didn't. Ninety percent of these guys had been released at one time or another.

They talked a good talk, but they always came back.

This was their home.

Standing in front of his office, he unlocked the door, flipped on the lights, and took a seat behind his desk. Before he could settle in, a longtime inmate, Michael Bowker, stuck his head inside the office. "I've been rehabilitated," Bowker told him. "When do I get out of here?"

Dean glanced at the clock. "You're supposed to be at work, aren't you?"

"I'm thinkin' of quittin'."

"If you do, you'll spend all day locked in your cell instead."

Bowker scratched the open sore on his chin. "You sure about that?"

Dean nodded.

"My daughter never showed up to see me the other day."

"I know. I'm sorry."

"I told you she was a selfish bitch."

Dean sighed.

"When's my next appointment?"

"I don't have my calendar with me. You'll have to check with the officer down the way."

Bowker looked to his left. "Mean son of a bitch. I don't like him." His shoulders drooped. "Listen, man. I'm rehabilitated. When do I get out?"

"You took a razor to a guard's head. Remember?"

Bowker's face crumpled. For a second he looked as if he might cry, but then he smiled instead. "Yeah, I remember. He didn't die!" He shrugged. "I better get to work."

"Good idea."

Five minutes after Bowker left, a guard ushered in a grizzly bear of a man, a top-of-the-food-chain predator, who had to stoop to get through the door. He had dark, shifty eyes and a permanent scowl that had left deep grooves in his forehead.

Dean glanced at his list of appointments. His new patient's name was Lou Wheeler. After a fellow psychologist had suffered a heart attack, Dean's caseload had doubled. Lou Wheeler was one of ten inmates recently handed over to him. Although Dean preferred to follow an inmate's journey from the day of incarceration to the date of their release, many of his clients, like Lou Wheeler, remained locked up long after serving their sentence due to bad behavior.

"Come on in," Dean said.

Twenty-two years ago, Lou Wheeler had raped and strangled a twenty-five-year-old woman before burying her on his property in Clarksburg. It was believed he'd also killed his wife, but there hadn't been enough evidence to convict him for her death.

His chains clanked as the guard ushered him to the chair in front of Dean's desk. Dean looked at the guard. "Remove his cuffs."

He wasn't sure who looked more surprised, the guard or the prisoner, but the uniformed man did as he asked, then stepped outside the office and shut the door. According to his last counselor, Lou Wheeler was easily angered. But being shackled caused most inmates to shut down, and the whole purpose of his being here was to get him to open up.

Lou Wheeler squinted at him. He looked older than his sixty-nine years. Scars from acne had left deep craters on his face.

"I'm Dean Crawford. How are you doing?"

Lou stared him down, as if assessing the situation. "I could use a smoke."

Dean opened the bottom drawer of his desk to his right and pulled out a cigarette, lighter, and ashtray and set the items in front of Lou.

Lou lit up, took a long drag. As smoke rolled slowly out of his nostrils, he said, "So what do you want?"

"Standard evaluation, just like Jacob Harrison used to do."
Lou chuckled.

Dean scratched his head. "It says here in your file that you haven't been attending group therapy."

Lou leaned over and blew smoke at Dean's face. "I don't need therapy."

There was a long pause before Dean asked, "Aren't you curious to know what happened to Jacob?"

A scar ran through the corner of Lou's upper lip, making him look as if he were snarling at him. "Did someone finally take the son of a bitch out?"

"Heart attack."

"Hmm."

"Now that Jacob Harrison is gone, I'm the guy who will be doing your evaluations."

Lou's laughter came out as a snort.

"You find that amusing?"

"Yeah. I do." He took another long hit until his lungs were filled to the brim with carcinogens and toxins.

Dean looked back at the folder on his desk and leafed through his records. Harrison's scribblings were difficult to read, but not impossible.

"Lou Wheeler has maintained his innocence since day one of his incarceration. Can't seem to keep his hands to himself. Raised in a string of foster homes. Angry. Doesn't talk much. Hates just about everybody and everything. Likes to provoke other inmates. Fond of pushing people's buttons."

Dean turned his attention back to the man. "You have two dozen disciplinary offenses to date."

Lou eyed the ashtray and tossed his cigarette butt to the floor. Then he looked around the room as if he was bored.

Dean stood, picked up the cigarette butt, and stubbed it out in the ashtray. He sat down again and continued to skim Harrison's scribbly notes. *"Inmate has failed to make progress since his incarceration. Antisocial and uncooperative with staff. Disciplinary action recommended if Lou Wheeler continues to skip anger management meetings. Parole will not be recommended at this time or in the foreseeable future due to poor behavior."*

Dean shut the file and leaned back in his chair. "You were sentenced to twenty-five years, and now it's more than double that. You were recently placed in lockdown for threatening the guards. All you had to do was keep your head down and your hands at your sides, and you would have walked out of here years ago. What's the deal?"

Silence.

"Why did you kill her?"

Lou looked at him then, eyes dull and unblinking. "I never killed nobody."

"Tell me about your wife and kids."

Lou rubbed his chin. "Never should have married the worthless, no-good bitch. She didn't know how to shut the fuck up."

"And your kids?" Dean asked.

"What about 'em?"

"Do you have a relationship with them?"

"They're dead to me."

Dean looked back at the file and the Post-it note he'd found stuck to the front. "Your son called. It says here that he wants to meet with you."

Lou leaned forward, his chest pushing against the stacks of files on his desk. "Tell him I said to fuck off."

"Aren't you curious to know what he has to say?"

"Nope."

"Did you know your son's car accident ten years ago left him with amnesia?"

"Don't care."

"He doesn't remember anything about his life before the accident, including his childhood."

Lou reached over his shoulder and scratched an itch. When he looked back at Dean, his gaze was piercing. "That the truth?"

Dean nodded.

"I'm in this fucking shithole 'cause of him."

Dean hadn't yet read all of Harrison's notes, but Lou Wheeler's statement fascinated him. "You're in here because of your son?"

Lou waggled a finger at the file in front of Dean. "It's all in there somewhere. Ben killed that girl. Not me." He scratched his chin. "Wouldn't surprise me if he killed his mother, too. And yet I'm the one sitting here talking to you."

Many patients professed their innocence. Nothing new there. But the majority of them, no matter how violent or evil, usually showed some semblance of affection for their children. "Ben was seventeen at the time. This is your son you're talking about."

"That kid ain't normal. Never was."

"He's a journalist," Dean read aloud. "Married with two kids." Dean looked up and said, "He's about as normal as it gets—a regular family man."

Lou slouched back in his seat, his meaty arms crossed over his chest. He kept shaking his head as if Dean were talking out of his ass.

"If you don't believe it, maybe you should meet with him."

"Maybe I should," Dean said. "What would have motivated your son to kill the young woman?"

"His mother was Satan. If you sucked Satan's titties, you'd be fucked up, too."

"What about your daughter? Was she messed up?"

"Not like Ben. Don't get me wrong, though; she could be a cunt like her mother."

"What was it about Ben that makes you think he was capable of killing? Did you see him kill the girl?"

"I said all I needed to say about that in court."

Dean made a note to get the transcripts. Lou Wheeler was unusual, and Dean wanted to know more about him. Contrary to popular belief, most inmates eventually admitted to guilt. But after decades, Lou Wheeler had remained steadfast when it came to his innocence. As the man talked, Dean could feel his sense of betrayal when it came to his only son.

"Ben was strange," Lou added without prompting. "Fucked-up, crazy-ass strange. Never said much, neither. There was a black soul inside those eyes of his, and they seemed to look right through you. As he grew older, bigger, even I stayed clear of him."

Two

Jessie Cole

Jessie Cole, Sacramento PI, sat at her desk in her office and tried to ignore the sinking, depressing feeling she always got when she finished paying the bills. She scrolled to the bottom of the spreadsheet on her computer and stared at the balance. Less than $1,000 in her checking account. How was that possible? Her stomach turned.

She scanned the two columns of numbers looking for anything unusual, like large withdrawals or accidental repeats. When she'd first glanced at the balance upon logging on to her bank account, she'd been sure the bank had messed up. But that wasn't the case. She clicked into her savings account, her emergency fund: $5,250.

Last month she'd canceled all their television subscriptions. This month she might have to cancel the pet insurance she'd gotten after Olivia brought home Higgins, a stray dog that had been hit by a car and left to die.

Business had slowed to a crawl over the past month. Maybe it was time to look into doing some advertising. Rent for the house and the office space alone would take a big chunk out of the balance. And then there was car insurance, gas, food, electricity, and Olivia to consider.

The door to her office swung open, and her fifteen-year-old niece walked inside. Jessie had been Olivia's guardian for the past eleven years.

Jessie looked at the clock, surprised to see that it was already three.

"What's wrong?" Olivia asked.

"Nothing."

"Ahh," Olivia said as she approached. "You're paying bills."

Jessie signed out of the online bank account. "How was school?"

"You'll be happy to know I got a B-plus on my math test."

"Good job." Jessie put her checkbook away, propped her elbows on the desk, and looked her niece square in the eyes. "So what's going on?"

"I'm glad you asked." Olivia dropped her backpack on the floor and took a seat in the chair in front of Jessie's desk. "Bella will be getting her driver's permit next week."

Jessie held back a groan and then quickly began sorting through her mail. "That's nice."

"Her parents bought her a car."

"Wow," Jessie said, her stomach turning over. "Very nice."

"You're not listening to me."

"Yes, I am." Jessie met her gaze.

"I got an idea, and I wanted to talk to you about it."

"Okay. Shoot."

"I know we're not exactly swimming in money, so I thought it would be a good idea if I started saving up for my own car. I have a thousand dollars saved up already, but I need to get serious. Obviously, the car will have to be used." Her eyes widened. "It really just needs to run."

Olivia continued on before Jessie could chime in. "A long time ago, you told me I could start babysitting once I had my driver's license."

Jessie sighed.

"I also want to start walking dogs after school. I have a friend who makes two hundred dollars a month walking the neighbors' dogs!"

"What about homework?"

9

"I have a B-plus average. I'll be able to study and babysit at the same time. Do you think I could babysit for Ben and his wife?"

"I don't know," Jessie said. "I need to think about it."

"I already called Andriana, and she said, with your permission, I could babysit on Friday night."

Jessie rolled her eyes. *Damn it, Andriana.* Andriana was a well-respected lawyer in the community. They had been friends since high school. But she never should have agreed to having Olivia babysit until she talked to Jessie.

"So? Is that a yes?"

"I need to think about all of this," Jessie said as she turned toward the window overlooking J Street. There was a car parked across the street. Nothing unusual about that except that the driver wore sunglasses and a baseball cap and appeared to be looking at them. When Jessie stood, the car drove away.

Olivia looked in the direction of Jessie's gaze. "What?"

"Nothing."

"There's one more thing I need to talk to you about," Olivia said.

Jessie didn't like the shift in her tone. Whatever it was, it couldn't be good. "Go on."

"I talked to Grandpa the other day."

Jessie's dad, Ethan Cole, lived a few miles away. He was a fix-it man who got paid for a wide range of tasks that included anything from drywall repair to electrical work. He was also a drunk, which was why she tended to keep her distance. "Is something wrong?" Jessie asked. "Did he call?"

"He's fine. I called him to see if he wanted to join us for Thanksgiving."

Jessie took a breath. "You should have talked to me first."

"I'm sorry." She raised a brow. "I'll help with the cooking. It'll be great."

"Olivia . . . ," Jessie said.

"I know Grandpa has problems, but we can't just cut him out of our lives. It's not right."

For the past two years, Jessie and Olivia had enjoyed Thanksgiving on their own. Just the two of them, cooking and prepping, then eating leftover turkey and pie for days. There'd been a time when Olivia was much younger that Jessie had attempted to include Grandpa, but the day had always turned out to be about him, ending with his drinking too much and passing out on the couch. She'd finally given up. The holidays were so much more enjoyable without her father around to complicate things.

"Go home," Jessie said, waving her niece away. "Let Higgins out for a bit, and then do your homework. We'll talk about this later."

Olivia stopped at the door. "I need to call Andriana about Friday night. Can I tell her yes?"

"Yes. Fine, but she'll have to bring Dylan to our house."

"That defeats the whole purpose since you would be there," Olivia said, arms spread wide in exasperation. "All my friends have been baby-sitting for years. Andriana doesn't even live far from here. I'll lock all the doors and update you every hour." Olivia straightened and presented Jessie with the sweetest, most innocent expression Jessie had ever seen. "Please?"

"Okay. Okay. Go. I have work to do."

"Thanks. It will be great. I'll be able to buy my own car, which means you won't have to take me to school."

As soon as her niece walked out the door, Jessie's head fell back. Besides the worry of her niece driving around with friends and not paying close attention to whether everyone put on their seat belts, Jessie knew Olivia had no idea how much it cost to maintain a vehicle. And she probably hadn't considered the cost of gas and insurance.

If business didn't pick up, Jessie might have to go back to serving cocktails.

As she straightened in her chair, she thought back to the time when she'd first moved out of her dad's house and into the rental down the street with her sister and niece. It had been important at the time that her sister, Sophie, stay home to take care of Olivia, who was only a baby, so Jessie had quit college and worked as a barista during the day and a cocktail waitress at night. The tips alone had kept food on the table.

When Olivia was four years old, Sophie had disappeared. Only recently had her body been discovered in a ravine in Auburn. It still haunted Jessie to think that her sister would never be coming home. She missed her every day.

Olivia waved, smiling and happy, as she walked passed Jessie's office window. Seeing her looking so content reminded Jessie how lucky she was to have Olivia in her life.

Jessie smiled and waved back.

THREE

"Slow down!" he called after her.

The woman running through the field in front of him ran even faster. Either she didn't hear him, or she was having too much fun. He wasn't sure. Her long, lithe legs were tan and muscular. It was like watching a wild and exotic creature. She wasn't anything like the other girls he usually conned into believing he was a well-known photographer.

This girl was different.

She wanted to be a model, and she knew she had the goods. "It's only a matter of being discovered," she'd told him. And what better way to jump-start her career than by being on the cover of a magazine?

As she ran, she glanced over her shoulder at him and smiled, revealing straight white teeth. Her shiny, blonde hair moved over her back like a silk cape. In his forty-two years on earth, he'd never set eyes on a more beautiful female. She had great skin and a curvy body, and best of all, her blue eyes were bright and alive.

In the distance was the faded-red barn with a weather vane that leaned too far east. Outside the wide-open doors sat a rusted Ford Crown Victoria. The car was Pepto-Bismol–pink speckled with brown rust. The back tires were low on air.

The barn, the car, and the thirty acres of damp green grass surrounding the one-story ranch house belonged to Mr. and Mrs. William Matthews. Bill and Marie were older than shit. They had no idea he often used their place to do "business." Bill could hardly move without help, and Marie couldn't hear a gun blast, let alone a woman's scream, from five feet away.

Already out of breath, he slowed to a walk and lifted his face to collect a ray of sun through the trees. It wasn't especially warm, but by the time he found the girl sitting on a bale of hay inside the barn, sweat trickled down the middle of his back. He didn't like the idea that perhaps he was getting too old for this line of work.

"What's your name?" he asked.

"I already told you. It's Lavinia."

She was leaning back, her fingers splayed on the hay behind her. She raised both legs and wiggled her sneakers at him. Her head tilt was meant to beguile. It didn't. "Where's everyone else? I thought you said you had a team of people?"

"They'll be here soon. We'll take some pictures first, and then Jared will work on the lighting."

The smile disappeared. She pushed herself to her feet and brushed straw from her legs. She wasn't nearly as pretty when she wasn't smiling. "I'm not stupid. You're not really a photographer, are you?"

He sighed as he made his way to the corner of the barn. From beneath an old crate he pulled out a stack of periodicals. Mostly farming magazines. He carried them back to her and tossed them on top of the hay where she'd been sitting. "Every cover was shot by me." He gestured his chin toward the pile. "Go ahead and take a look."

She grabbed the magazine on top, examined the girl on the cover, then flipped to the next page to read the credits. After inspecting two more magazines, she said, "Okay. But if nobody else comes in the next ten minutes, I'm leaving."

"Understood." *She might be beautiful,* he thought, *but she's dumber than fuck.* The fact that she was here told him that much. *But still, best to hurry.* He grabbed hold of the thick rope dangling from a high beam above his head and tugged at it until the end of it reached his waist. Then he made a noose.

"I'm not into posing for any kinky stuff," she said, lifting her nose into the air.

He stopped to explain. "Nothing kinky going on here. We've got a unique idea for this month's cover. We're going back in time, back to the day when a rope and pulley hung over the haymow. Back then, they tied one end of the rope to the fork over there, and the other ran outside where a man on the—"

"Okay," she said. "Enough with the hicksville lingo. Your team better show up in the next five minutes, or I'm outta here."

A beautiful bitch, he thought as he unraveled the other end of the rope piled on the ground. Pulling the end of the rope to the car outside, he tied it to the front bumper. With that done, he readied his digital camera—an oldie but goodie. When he turned back toward the barn, he was more than stunned to see her put the noose over her head and make a funny face—eyes wide, the tip of her pink tongue sticking out at him.

"Hold that pose," he said.

Click. Click. Click. "Brilliant!" And he wasn't shitting.

Appearing to enjoy herself, she turned her back to him so that all he could see were long legs and an amazing ass peeking out from denim shorts. Just as she'd done earlier, she looked over her shoulder and smiled.

Fuck.

She's perfect.

"You should be in the pictures," he told her.

"That's the whole idea." Her eyes rolled heavenward. She was in her element, being playful, turning and posing, smiling and showing off, dazzling him with her moves.

His breathing accelerated. "You're doing great." He looked to his left. "There they are. I just saw my crew's car pull into the driveway." Another lie. "We'll be finished in no time. If you could tighten the noose a bit. But keep having fun with it."

"Which magazine is this for?"

"The *Progressive Farmer*," he said. "A million subscribers. When they see the issue with your face on it, everyone will be asking about the girl on the cover."

She pulled too tight. Frowning, she struggled to loosen the rope around her neck. "I don't know about this," she croaked.

"Almost done."

Her fingers slipped between the noose and the soft flesh of her neck, which must have helped her relax because she was back to her playful self, smiling and kicking up hay.

"Where are you going?" she asked when he turned his back to her and went to open the car door.

"Nowhere. This old thing doesn't even work. A few more shots from the car, and then we'll move to the tractor."

"You won't be able to see my face clearly from way over there."

Just keep talking, you disloyal bitch. Nobody gives a rat's ass about your face. If you hadn't betrayed your brother, you wouldn't even be here.

He jumped in and turned the key, pleasantly surprised when the engine roared to life on the first try. He put the gear into reverse and hit the gas.

Through the windshield he watched her body lurch upward, her feet leaving the ground so fast he would have missed it if he'd blinked.

He slammed on the brakes.

With the rope tight around her throat, she swayed in midair. Her arms and legs flailed about.

16

He jammed the gear into park and jumped out of the car in time to see her clawing at the ropes, her eyes bulging in fear, the tips of her sneakers five feet from the ground.

He ran toward her. *Jesus.*

Click. Click. Click.

She squirmed and kicked.

He was as hard as a fucking rock—a rarity these days since nothing turned him on anymore.

The only sound besides the low rattle of the engine outside was the squeak of the rafter above their heads. He stepped closer and got smacked in the face with her left foot.

Fuck! He jumped away and wiped his nose. No blood, but that would leave a mark for sure. He grabbed hold of one of her ankles, then pulled a pocketknife from his pocket and made his signature mark. Then he let go and watched her struggle, wondered how long it would take for her to die.

"Who's in there?"

His heart skipped a beat as he whipped around. Ten feet behind the old Crown Victoria, old Bill Matthews hung tight to his walker. Shoulders hunched forward, the old man peered their way, straining to see out of grayish, rheumy eyes.

Lavinia's feet dangled less than a foot from where he stood. Her right leg twitched. The blonde wasn't giving up. *Jesus. She should have died already.*

Seconds felt like minutes as panic set in. He needed to get out of here. There was no way Bill Matthews could have seen him from that far away, but if Matthews came any closer, he might be in trouble. His gaze darted around the inside of the barn. He couldn't leave behind any evidence that he'd been here. He tucked the knife and the camera into his back pockets.

Fingerprints.

He grabbed the magazines. What else had he touched?

The rope.

Nothing he could do about that. He wouldn't be able to dispose of her body like the others. Bill was as blind as a bat, and it was dark inside the barn. But still, when he looked back toward Bill, he was more annoyed than surprised to see the old man pumping his shotgun.

For half a second he considered killing him. Instead, he decided to make a run for it. He ran to the corner of the barn, grabbed an old gunnysack, and stuck the magazines inside. He darted from the barn, his arms pumping at his sides as he tore through the high grass.

A bullet whizzed by his left ear.

Too close.

A lucky shot. He went to the ground and army-crawled his way through the grass until he was out of sight. Only then did he dare look back toward the barn just as Matthews disappeared inside.

It wasn't until he skidded down a slope of dead leaves and dirt to his flat-bottom Jon boat that he remembered he'd left his fingerprints on the key in the ignition.

Shit. Shit. Shit.

Nothing he could do about that now. He plunked down on the rough wooden seat, reached for the oar handles on both sides of him, and started rowing.

Damn. He should have taken the old geezer out.

FOUR

COLIN GRAYSON

Homicide detective Colin Grayson looked around the property surrounding the barn where a young woman had been murdered only
hours ago. Tall green grass, shrubs, and a few gangly oak trees dotted
the nearly thirty acres. Perimeters had been secured: The barn. The area
in and around the car. And the path the killer took to run away—a
straight beeline to Folsom Lake.

He looked up at the darkening sky. They needed to work fast. Rain
and wind could and would undoubtedly mess with evidence, washing
away DNA and blood spots or moving fibers. An aerosol spray was
being used to harden and preserve shoe impressions, from the barn
where Colin stood all the way across the field and down a dirt slope to
the water's edge.

At the moment the scene looked like organized chaos, everyone in
their allotted space, working fast, always under pressure. Their only witness, Bill Matthews, had been isolated, escorted back inside his house
to sit with his wife.

Photographs had been taken of the scene and the body a few feet
away.

As the ME examined the woman's body, crime scene technicians worked in tandem on the perimeter surrounding the barn and house, collecting any discarded materials, including wrappers, bottles, cans, and papers. A line of police cars made a path down the gravel driveway. An ambulance waited by the house, lights still flashing.

Colin walked back to the body and bent down close to the ME as she worked.

The pressure on the dead woman's jaw had caused her tongue to stick out. It was dry. The indentation around her throat was a raw dark-purple color. Petechiae were visible on face, legs, and feet. "Died from asphyxia," Colin stated rather than asked the ME, Brenda Parsons, a forty-year-old woman he'd known for years.

She didn't look up at him, merely nodding as she placed paper bags over the hands to preserve trace evidence under the fingernails. "Ischemia, to be more exact," she said as she worked. She pointed to areas on the face, especially around the eyes and nose. "Burst capillaries. The blood from her carotids had nowhere to go. It was a slow hanging . . . ten minutes would be my guess. It was just a matter of which organ would give up first: the heart, the lungs, or the brain. In this case, I'd say it was the brain, but you didn't hear any of this from me."

Hours of lab work still needed to be done before anything went on record. Colin had been in the business long enough to know the drill.

"Not a drop hanging," Brenda went on. "No sign of damage to the spine."

He noticed a couple of spots of blood on the victim's thighs just below the end of her denim shorts. *Wearing shorts in the winter.* The thought caused him to pull his collar closer around his ears. "What is that from?"

"I took samples. Her clothes will be fully removed at the lab, but my initial thought would be angel lust."

"Angel lust?"

"It's fairly common in hangings. The noose causes pressure to build up, and it has nowhere to go. So oftentimes the genitals become engorged. Not only are her labia swollen, the immense amount of pressure caused her to have a bloody discharge." She finished her examination and gestured for the EMTs to help her bag and transport the body.

Colin left her to finish her work and approached Ren Howe, a young rookie investigator whose heart wasn't in his work. He almost always looked distracted or annoyed, as if he had other places he'd rather be. Ren's dad, an agent with the FBI, had pulled some strings to get him the job. Most of the guys in the station stayed away from Ren because they thought he believed he was better than everyone else. He came across as lazy, unmotivated, and disconnected. The usual complaint was that he had a chip on his shoulder and a stick up his ass.

But Colin did his best to ignore all of it. As long as Ren was on payroll and under his watch, Colin was going to make him work. If Ren didn't like it, he could quit. And maybe, just maybe, there was something else going on with the kid, and Colin could help him.

"Did you talk to Bill Matthews?" Colin asked.

"I did." Ren glanced at his watch. "I talked to the wife, too."

"Let me see your notes."

As if it were a chore, Ren retrieved his notebook from his inside coat pocket. As he flipped pages, Colin saw something odd. He took the notebook, turned the pages until he came to a pencil drawing of the woman hanging from the rafters. The likeness was uncanny. "What is this?"

Ren's face turned a shade of red.

Colin flipped through the pages of the notebook, finding more sketches of macabre scenes. "What the hell is this?"

Ren shrugged. "I enjoy drawing."

"A dead woman hanging from a rope?" Colin took a breath, counted to two. "Look around you. Everyone here is working their asses off to collect evidence before it rains. Do you have any idea why they're working so hard?" He didn't wait for Ren to answer. "Because they—we—want to catch the bastard who did that," he said, pointing to the body bag being lifted onto a stretcher.

"She was a topless dancer."

Colin had no words. It was worse than he thought. Ren's attitude was going to affect the rest of his team. He was going to have to write him up.

"I don't know why you're so upset," Ren said. "I did what you asked. I talked to the Matthewses. Marie Matthews suffers from macular. She can't see, and she didn't hear a thing, so there was nothing to gain from talking to her. But Bill is another story. He says he saw plenty." Ren took back his notebook and quickly found the pages he was looking for. "Bill Matthews was at the back of the house when he heard the sputtering of the car's engine. When he looked out the window, he saw a man in the driver's seat. Bill uses a walker, but he said he made good time getting outside. He grabbed the shotgun he keeps near the door, shouted at his wife to call 9-1-1, and then headed outside. By the time he approached the barn, the man was no longer in the car, but the engine was still running. According to Matthews, the intruder was inside the barn, taking pictures of a woman dangling from a rope. He thought he might be seeing things and that maybe whatever was hanging from the beam was a life-size doll. But then the woman kicked the intruder in the face. That's when Bill Matthews knew he needed to do something quick."

"So he fired a shot at the man?"

Ren shook his head. "For an old guy, he's smart. He didn't want to risk hitting the girl, so he called out to him. When the intruder took off, Bill Matthews fired off a couple of shots. He thought maybe he hit him on the first go, but he's not sure. He got behind the wheel of the car and drove close enough to the barn so that her body was lying on the ground. He said the rope around her neck was so thick and so tight he couldn't loosen it, so he used a pair of bolt cutters to remove it. He felt a pulse, too—thought she had a good fighting chance until thirty seconds before the ambulance arrived when he said she took her last breath."

"Any ID found on the body?"

"Yes. Her name is Lavinia Shaw. I've already looked her up online. She's a looker, and she's everywhere, as far as social media goes. A dancer by night and a college student by day. California State University, Sacramento. Her family lives in New Jersey. She's the oldest of three."

When he finished, Colin said, "Put on some gloves, and then go talk to Clayton over there, and see what else needs to be done."

"You're not going to tell anyone about the sketches?"

"I can't make any promises."

Ren shifted his weight. "I'd appreciate it if you didn't."

"Why are you doing this?" Colin asked. "Why are you here?"

"I think you know why."

"If it's to make Dad happy, you need to get out. Life's too short." He watched the ambulance drive off. "Lavinia Shaw is proof of that."

FIVE

JESSIE

No sooner had Olivia headed for home than Jessie's phone buzzed. It was Colin, her on-and-off-again boyfriend, who happened to be on again. "Hey there," she said when she picked up. "Still on for dinner tonight?"

"That's what I'm calling about."

Damn. He was calling to cancel. Again. She could hear it in his voice . . . a serious tone lined with sorrow. He was at a crime scene. "What's going on?"

"A woman in her twenties, found hanging from the rafters of an old barn set between Folsom Lake and Auburn-Folsom Road."

"Suicide?"

"No. I'll fill you in later. I've got to go, but I wanted to let you know I wouldn't be coming. Sorry about tonight. I know this seems to be happening a lot lately—"

"No worries. Some other time."

After saying goodbye, she thought about Colin and how they didn't have the sort of relationship very many people could handle since they hardly saw each other, but long hours and hard work were in their blood. It was what they did; it was who they were.

Her phone buzzed again, and she picked up the call.

"Is this Jessie Cole?"

"Yes, it is."

"My name is Nikki Seymour. I heard you were in Clarksburg recently, asking about Ben and Nancy Wheeler."

Jessie opened the top desk drawer and pulled out her file on Ben Morrison. He'd moved from Clarksburg to Sacramento when he was eighteen and had changed his name from Wheeler to Morrison. He was a crime reporter who suffered from amnesia. During their search for Jessie's sister, he had become her friend. When he asked her for help in digging into his past, she hadn't been able to say no. She was doing all she could to find out more about his childhood but so far was hitting a dead end. His sister, Nancy, wouldn't answer her calls, and nobody in the small town of Clarksburg would talk. They either didn't remember the Wheelers or had private reasons they weren't willing to share for why they refused to talk.

Jessie had visited schools and knocked on doors in Ben's old neighborhood, handing out business cards along the way. She'd even returned to Holland Market in hopes of striking up another conversation with a couple who had known the family, but she was told they had moved.

"You knew the Wheelers?" Jessie asked.

"Yes. I grew up next door. My mom said a detective had come by, asking questions. After a lot of badgering on my part, she finally gave me your name and number."

Excited by the prospect of finally catching a break, Jessie sat up straighter. "Your mother doesn't want you to talk to me?"

"That's an understatement. She never liked the Wheelers. In fact, she abhorred them."

"Why is that?"

"The family was considered dysfunctional, offensive, and evil. Most people who've been living in Clarksburg choose to forget the Wheelers were ever a part of their community."

"I have a long list of questions," Jessie said, glancing through the notes in front of her. "How much time do you have?"

"I'm in Clarksburg now. I'll be staying with my mom for a few more days at least. She sprained her ankle and needs help getting around." There was a pause before she added, "I'd rather not meet here at the house, but I have some time today if you'd like to meet me at the Old Sugar Mill."

Jessie glanced at the time. "I can be there in forty-five minutes."

"That will work. Look for the woman with red curly hair. I'm hard to miss."

After saying goodbye, Jessie hung up and jotted down the woman's name in her file.

A few minutes later, the door opened, and her assistant, Zee Gatley, marched right in and slapped a large manila envelope on Jessie's desk.

"What's this?"

"Another workers' comp case done. Closed. That's three in two weeks. Not bad, huh?"

Jessie smiled. "Good job."

"So what's next?" Zee looked at all the papers scattered across Jessie's desk. "What are you working on?"

"I just got a call from a woman who used to be Ben's neighbor. We're meeting at the Old Sugar Mill to talk."

Zee brightened. "Mind if I tag along?"

Jessie thought about Nikki, figuring the woman might not be as forthright with two people instead of one. She stood and began gathering her things. "I think it's best if I meet with the woman alone. Besides," she added, looking around, "I would really appreciate it if you could stay here to answer the phone and help me get things organized."

Zee muttered a string of curse words under her breath.

"Did you say something?" Jessie asked, although it was nothing she hadn't heard before. Zee had been diagnosed with schizophrenia at a young age. The medication she took stopped her from seeing or hearing things that weren't there but didn't completely eliminate her habit of thinking out loud.

"I didn't say anything," Zee said as she made her way to the file cabinet and began going through the box overflowing with papers and assorted mailings.

Jessie slipped on her coat and then stopped at the door. "You're doing a great job, Zee. Thank you."

"Sure. Okay. See ya later."

———

Zee Gatley

Zee grabbed a handful of papers from the to-be-filed box. Her mind usually drifted when she did this type of work, and today was no exception. This morning, her horoscope had said, *Someone you see most days suddenly becomes irresistible.*

She'd been racking her brain all day. Other than her father, his girlfriend, Jessie, Ben, and Olivia, she didn't see too many people on a regular basis. She did see the postman every once in a while. She wrinkled her nose. He was in his forties, had a big belly, and he was definitely easy to resist.

Boredom set in quickly. She yawned. She could go home early, but her dad's girlfriend would probably be there, and the woman had a habit of talking too much. Instead, Zee headed for the coffee shop upstairs to get a soy chai latte.

"I haven't seen you in a while," the barista behind the counter said.

Zee glanced at the name tag pinned to his shirt: Tobey. "Yeah, well, I've been busy," she said.

"The usual?"

"Yep." She tossed the exact amount needed on the counter and went to the window that overlooked the tree-lined street. Clouds dotted the sky. She wondered if it would rain. She could see Jessie's house from here.

A tap on her shoulder startled her. She jumped, and the tea Tobey had brought her flew across the room, raining hot liquid on a couple of tables. *Damn.*

"Don't worry about it," he said. "I'll get you another."

She knew she should feel guilty or bad or something, but those emotions weren't normally a part of her DNA. Zee suffered from a mental disorder that led to a breakdown in the relationship between thought, emotion, and behavior. She hadn't even known she was sick or different from anyone else until her therapist told her. Without medication, she heard people calling her name when no one else was around. She would also have full-blown conversations with imaginary people. And there were always bugs—giant black flies and flying beetles.

As long as she remembered to take her medication, she did okay.

Zee grabbed some napkins and dabbed at the tea on her shoe. Then she headed for the bathroom. When she returned, Tobey was mopping up the mess.

"I made you another," he said. He pointed to the to-go cup on the counter, making it clear he wasn't going to try to hand it to her.

She picked up the tea and was about to leave when she realized she needed to say something . . . anything. "Thanks."

He straightened. His expression was one of confusion. Had she said the wrong thing? "Sorry," she added. But he appeared too dumbstruck to answer, so she left.

Zee wondered what Tobey's problem was, but she forgot all about him when she returned to the office and found a man standing inside by the window, looking out.

"Can I help you?"

He turned around. He had wiry reddish-brown hair. He was tall and reed thin. "Jessie Cole?" he asked.

She thought about saying yes. This was her chance to be the boss. But her goal was to find normalcy in her crazy life, so she said, "No. I'm Zee, Jessie's assistant. Can I help you with something?"

"Maybe I should wait until she returns."

Zee shrugged. "It's up to you."

He fidgeted with what sounded like a bunch of keys inside his coat pocket. "You work with Jessie on cases?"

She tried not to look or sound too eager. "Yep."

"Then I guess it wouldn't hurt to run something by you and see what you think."

Excited at the prospect of doing something other than filing, Zee straightened. "Sure." She gestured toward the chair in front of Jessie's desk before hurrying around to the other side, where she took a seat, focused her attention fully on the man with the pale skin and thin face, and waited.

It took him a moment to get situated. His long legs weren't helping matters. She found herself wondering what sort of work such a gangly guy might do. Why was he here?

She needed to be patient and give the man a chance to tell her what the deal was.

"It's about my wife."

Despite all the thoughts running through her mind like the images in a flip-book, Zee said nothing.

"I believe she's seeing another man."

"Did you ask her?"

"No. I want to be sure before I confront her. It could be my wild imagination getting the best of me."

She could relate. "Do you have a picture of her?" Zee asked before she could take it back, since they didn't handle infidelity cases. Jessie wouldn't like her discussing the man's wife with him for no reason other than to fill time. But Jessie didn't have to know, Zee decided as she watched the man reach for his wallet and pull out a photo.

As Zee stared at the picture he'd handed her, she tried to freeze-frame her expression, not wanting her face to reveal what she was thinking, which was, *Hell yes, she's having an affair. Have you looked in the mirror lately? I mean, come on.* The woman was gorgeous. And this guy, with string beans for legs and a bird's nest for hair, was not. His suit was disheveled, and if she were him, she'd shave the little bits of hair struggling to grow above his thin red lips.

"What is it?" he asked, pushing a wiry curl out of his line of sight. "Something there?" He blindly brushed his hand over his face.

It took her a second to realize he was reacting to the way she was looking at him. "Oh no. Nothing wrong with your face. I mean, nothing out of the ordinary happening there."

He looked doubtful.

"I was only thinking that it's a shame that the agency doesn't handle infidelity cases."

"Why not?"

"Hmm. That's a good question. I don't really know why."

"I'll pay good money. This agency has a good reputation, and I'll top whatever you charge to handle your other cases around here. My only request would be that everything we talk about be kept between the Jessie Cole Agency and me. I don't want anyone to know of my concerns about my wife. For all I know, she could be taking dance lessons after work."

"I understand." Although she didn't understand at all. Zee had never been in a relationship. She'd had a crush on one lunatic who'd ended up locking her in his basement. Needless to say, it hadn't ended well. And what reputable PI agency would talk about their clients' personal business? It seemed odd that he would bother to mention that his being here would need to be kept a secret. Paranoid, maybe?

Zee cleared her throat. "If you don't mind, I'd like to ask you a few questions, take down your name and phone number, and then discuss your case with Jessie when she returns."

"Do you think she might take me on?"

"We'll see." Zee grabbed a notebook and pen. "Your name?"

"Easton Scott."

"Twenty-nine?"

"Pardon me?"

"Sorry. I took a guess. Your age?"

"Thirty-eight."

"Did anyone ever tell you that you look much younger?"

"All the time."

And judging by his clipped tone, he didn't care what people thought one way or another. Zee tapped the end of the pen against her chin. "What is it exactly that makes you wonder about your wife's—"

"Hang-up phone calls at all hours," he spat out. "She recently started wearing lipstick to work and spending more time with her friends." His face reddened. "I am an extremely jealous person. Please don't," he said when Zee started to jot down some notes. "I just need to get a few things off my chest."

Zee set her pen down. "Go on."

"For most of our married life, I've tried to keep certain things to myself. For instance, I merely grit my teeth when she gets too bossy or opinionated. It sucks, and she can really piss me off sometimes. But I love her, and more than anything, I want our marriage to work." He raked long fingers through his hair. "I've said too much already. If your boss agrees to take on my case, perhaps we'll talk again." He quickly rattled off his phone number. Then he pulled out a checkbook and wrote out a check in the hefty sum of $3,000 that he slid across the desk. "I'm going to go now. Have your boss call me if she's interested."

Zee held up the check and was about to tell him that there was no need to leave such a large deposit, but he'd put those long legs to good use and was already gone.

SIX

JESSIE

A chilly November breeze found its way through Jessie's jacket, sending a wave of goose bumps over her arms and legs as she entered the Old Sugar Mill. It was a beautiful historic building that had been partially restored. There were doors on both sides of her that led to wine-tasting rooms.

A minute later, Nikki Seymour walked through the main entrance, bringing a rush of cold air along with her. Just as she'd told Jessie on the phone, she was hard to miss. The red hair would have been enough to easily find her in a crowd, but she was also quite tall. And the place was practically empty.

"Jessie Cole?" Nikki asked.

Jessie nodded.

They shook hands.

"Sorry I'm a tiny bit late. Mom had a long list of things for me to do before she'd let me loose."

"No problem. I'm grateful you could get away for a few minutes."

"If you're hungry, this wasn't the best place for me to pick. It's just that it's close to Mom's house."

"I'm not hungry," Jessie told her.

"Let's go this way. I know the owners." Jessie followed Nikki into one of many wine rooms.

Nikki took off her coat and hung it on a chair in the corner. "I'll be right back."

She returned with cheese and crackers and two small glasses of white wine. "The cold weather is scaring people away. Usually the lines for a tasting go clear out the door."

"It's a beautiful building," Jessie said.

Nikki nodded. "Best if I get right to it," she said, "since I'll only be home for a few days."

Jessie pulled out her notebook and pen. "If you don't mind, I'd like to start at the beginning. When did you first meet Nancy or Ben?"

"Nancy and I were in the same kindergarten class. Mrs. Kilpatrick. Nancy was extremely shy. That's all I remember about her until fourth grade."

"But you were neighbors," Jessie said. "How close was your house to the Wheelers?"

"They lived directly across the street. All I had to do was open the front door to see their front lawn."

"But you and Nancy weren't friends?"

"No, not at first. Nancy kept to herself. Eyes down. Mouth shut. I wouldn't have noticed her at all if I hadn't overheard a group of kids giving her a hard time."

Nikki took a sip of wine, and then there was a long pause while she seemed to think about what she wanted to say next. She looked troubled. "I'm sorry. I didn't realize this would be so uncomfortable for me to talk about, but the truth is, the more Nancy Wheeler tried to disappear, the more she stood out. Sort of like my red hair."

"It's okay. Take your time."

"Let's see . . . how do I explain . . . ? Nancy's clothes were always stained. Her hair was stringy, and her body odor was hard to take for very long. Nobody wanted to sit next to her, let alone talk to her. But once I saw what was happening, I knew I had to do something."

Jessie made notes every time Nikki paused.

"The bullying occurred during recess. Nancy was sitting by herself on one of the many benches on the playground. A group of kids had surrounded her and were calling her names and poking her with sticks. I was horrified. I squeezed my way between Nancy and the bullies, and I told them to leave her alone. I was already tall for my age, and it really didn't take much to get them to back off. I walked home with Nancy that day and every day afterward." Nikki smiled. "We hit it off. In fact, I thought she was very nice, and funny, too."

"But?"

"But her parents were a different story. Her mom was unlike any-one I've ever met in my life. Everything and everyone made her angry. She wore a permanent scowl on her face. I think it was maybe my third visit to their house when she accused me of eating the leftovers from dinner the night before. I told her it wasn't me and that I hadn't eaten a thing since I'd been there, but she didn't believe me. Suddenly she was in my face, and when she raised her hand, I was shocked to see that she meant to strike me with a leather belt. I still remember thinking, Where did she get the belt? I covered my head, cowered, and waited for the blow."

"That's horrible."

"It was, and it would have been much worse if Ben hadn't shown up. After a moment, when nothing happened, I looked up and saw Ben and his mom playing tug-of-war with the belt."

"And that was when you met Ben?"

"Yes. Of course I would see him from my house occasionally, com-ing and going, since he lived across the street, but that particular day was the first time I met him face-to-face. Although Nancy and I were a year apart, we were in the same grade. He was four years older than

Nancy and three years older than me." Nikki thought for a moment. "I believe he would have been attending junior high school at that time."

Jessie made a note. "So you were how old?"

"I must have been nine at the time of the belt incident."

"Did you ever go to the Wheeler house again after that?"

"I did. Nancy would make sure nobody was home before I entered the house."

"Did you and Nancy ever hang out at your house?"

She shook her head. "Not ever. Mom wouldn't allow it. She made it clear she thought the Wheelers, every single one of them, were trash, and she didn't want me anywhere near them. So I would tell her I was playing with one of the other kids down the street and then sneak through the Wheelers' backyard since they didn't have a fence surrounding the property."

"Did you ever meet Nancy's dad?"

"I did." Her body quivered as if the thought of him gave her chills.

"How would you describe Mr. Wheeler?"

"Absolutely frightening, everything about him—his sausage-like fingers, his dark eyes, his thick neck. He was a big man, and he always sounded as if he was having difficulty breathing. For that reason I always knew when he was close by."

"But you still went to their house?" Jessie asked, perplexed.

"I did." She shrugged. "Lou Wheeler didn't get home until late on the weekdays. And the truth is, by the time I was fourteen, I had a crush on Ben, so I didn't even think about running into his father."

"Interesting."

She chuckled. "Well, besides the fact that he saved me from his mother, Ben was bigger and taller than most guys his age. Being tall myself made his height a big plus. He was also muscular and really cute, in my opinion. When I was in ninth grade, he was a senior in high school, and that's when I noticed that the girls seemed to be into him. The funny thing is, I swear to you I don't think he even noticed."

Jessie frowned. "I was told that Nancy and Ben went to live with their grandmother when Ben was thirteen or fourteen, but you're saying they were still living across the street from you?"

"They never went anywhere. Ben was around eighteen when his dad went to prison for murder."

Jessie made another note. If Nikki was telling the truth, then that would mean much of what Nancy had said about her family had been false, as if she'd desperately wanted to lead Jessie down a rabbit hole. Jessie looked at Nikki. "After their father was arrested, did you get a chance to talk to Ben or Nancy?"

She shook her head. "Shortly after Lou Wheeler's arrest, their mother was found floating facedown in the slough. It was a horrible time. My mom kept me out of school. She was freaked out—wouldn't let me out of her sight. I never saw any of the Wheelers after that. Years later, I tried to locate Nancy and Ben on social media, but I didn't have any luck."

"It makes sense that your mom would be worried after everything that occurred. She probably just wants to forget any of it ever happened."

"Yes, but at the same time, the way she reacts—the fear in her eyes when I bring up the Wheelers—it just seems strange considering the Wheeler house has been empty for so long."

"Do you think your mom saw something?"

"I think she would have told me if she had. I have a niggling sense she's convinced Lou Wheeler is going to come after her."

"He'll be spending the rest of his life locked up. But even if he were to be set free, why would he go after her? Did they ever talk to each other?"

"Not that I know of."

"What about your dad?" Jessie asked. "Where was he during all of this?"

"He died of cancer when I was five."

"I'm sorry."

"Thanks. It's been a long time."

Jessie sipped her wine. "Would you say, in your opinion, that Nancy and her brother got along?"

She shrugged. "I don't remember the two of them ever talking, let alone hanging out." She snapped her fingers. "I do recall Nancy telling me once that Ben scared her." She sighed. "I don't remember if she told me why, though. Sorry."

"That's okay. I heard a story about a neighborhood boy being hurt by Ben when they were left to play together."

"Yes. Chris Hardwick. He was in the hospital for a long while. I forgot about that."

So not everything Nancy had told her was false. "Did you ever notice Ben being cruel to animals or violent in any way?"

"No. Never. He was quiet and sort of different, but I was never—" She stopped midsentence.

"What is it?"

"There was one thing."

Jessie waited.

Nikki rested the tips of her fingers on her throat. "I can't believe I'm telling anyone this, but it happened right before Ben's dad was taken away. I had gone to a party. I was fifteen, rebellious, always wanting to get away from my mother's hovering ways. Anyhow, I got a ride from a girl who lived around the corner to a party across town. I had drunk a beer or two, but never hard alcohol. After my friend disappeared, I was offered a drink from a punch bowl. It tasted like Kool-Aid, so I drank way too much. It wasn't long before the room began to spin. I found a seat on the couch, and the next thing I remembered, I had a boy on each side of me, and they were talking and leading me down a hallway. Then Ben showed up, seemingly out of nowhere. There was a scuffle. I was wobbly on my feet, and everything was hazy, but I remember Ben pushing the boys away. He looked furious as he informed them I was his sister's age. Ben dragged me out of the house and into his car and then proceeded to lecture me all the way home." Nikki frowned. "He told me that the two boys had bad intentions, I was a naive little girl, and I might have been lucky this time but maybe not next time.

"I started laughing. I was tipsy. I thought it was all sort of romantically heroic that he cared so much. When he pulled into his driveway, I leaned into him and tried to kiss him. I even told him I loved him. Everything changed in that moment. I swear he transformed before my eyes. His jaw hardened, and his brow furrowed as he grabbed hold of my shoulders. Despite all of this, I wasn't afraid. He told me I didn't know him. That he was not a good person. When I told him he was wrong, again leaning toward him, he wrapped his hands snug around my neck, his thumbs pressing inward, and said I was foolish and much too trusting and that he could easily snap my neck like a twig."

"What did you do?"

"I couldn't breathe and that scared me. I pushed him away, jumped out of the car, and ran home. To this day, though, I think he was only trying to teach me a lesson."

"A lesson?"

"Never be too trusting."

"And did you talk to him about it the next day?"

Nikki shook her head. "Days later, the police found Aly Scheer buried in the Wheelers' backyard."

SEVEN

BEN MORRISON

Ben's work as a crime reporter had brought him to more than a few prisons over the years, but never Folsom Prison, and never to visit an inmate whom he knew or was related to. In a way, he would be meeting his dad for the first time.

Ben was a reporter. He'd interviewed his share of criminals, and yet this was different. He had no idea what to expect. He didn't feel apprehensive or fearful. Mostly, he was curious.

After being processed for visitation, Ben followed the guard past the room reserved for families of lower-security inmates and down a corridor to a space containing three small booths with glass partitions separating visitors from prisoners. The guard pointed to the stool at the far end. Ben sat as he was instructed. The guard said he'd be back in a few minutes, then walked away.

Ben stared through the glass partition. It wasn't long before a large barrel-chested man was led through a steel door and to the chair on the other side of the glass. The guard took off the inmate's cuffs, leaving the chains around his ankles. The man shuffled forward and took a seat directly in front of Ben.

For the next twenty seconds, they merely stared at each other. Ben had no recollection of the figure sitting across from him. The crooked mouth and menacing eyes shadowed in dark circles did nothing to inspire old memories to come forth.

Ben picked up the phone, held it to his ear, and waited for his father to do the same. When he did so, Ben said, "So you're my father."

Lou Wheeler's expression remained unreadable. "Why are you here?"

"I wanted to meet you."

Lou leaned back in his seat, knees wide apart and head tilted, as if he didn't know what to think about this little reunion. After a few seconds, he sat forward a bit and scooted his chair closer so that his nose nearly touched the window. Into the receiver he said, "You pulled the wool over all their eyes, didn't you? They all fell for your little amnesia trick. Everyone except me. You don't fool me. You never did."

The conversation had quickly taken an unforeseen turn. His father's words struck him as surreal. For the past ten years, he'd thought his parents were dead because that's what his sister had told him. But then Jessie had begun her search into his past and learned that his father, Lou Wheeler, had been incarcerated and was still alive. And now here Ben was, talking to a man he didn't recognize—his father—a convicted murderer who pegged him as a liar. "Why would I want to trick anyone into believing I have amnesia?"

Lou smiled, a snakelike, unfeeling grin. "Because you don't want anyone asking too many questions. If they did, sooner or later they might discover the truth about you."

"And that is?"

"That *you* should be sitting in this chair," his father said, "instead of me."

"You were convicted by a jury," Ben reminded him, his voice calm. "All the evidence pointed to you."

Lou Wheeler lifted a brow. "Why would I kill her?"

"Why don't you tell me?"

He sneered. "She was your girl, not mine. Why would I care about the bitch? I had my hands full with your cunt of a mother. Don't tell me you don't remember that mongrel?"

"I have no memory of either one of you."

His dad snorted.

"If she was my girl, as you say, why would I kill her?"

"Two reasons. One, it's who you are. And two, she wanted to break up with you."

"I've seen the police reports and court—"

"It doesn't matter what you've heard or read. I know the truth. I was there when you took the slippery slope right out of your mother's cunt. The minute you opened your eyes, I knew."

The look on his father's face and the dark timbre of his voice warned Ben not to take the bait, but he couldn't help himself. "Knew what, exactly?"

"That you were born this way—deranged. What many would call a natural-born killer. And we both know that Aly Scheer wasn't your first kill."

Ben's hands were shaking. It took every bit of self-control he possessed not to jump up and leave.

His father was wrong.

Everything Ben had read about his case pointed to his father's guilt. The man was a compulsive liar. He made things up as he went along, repeated what he believed to be the truth until that's all there was left for him to hold on to. He was cruel, violent, and quite possibly insane. He blamed others at every turn.

"You killed her," Lou said again with authority, with certainty.

Ben took a few seconds to calm down. "Everyone who knew you back then says you always refused to take responsibility for your actions." Ben looked around to make sure nobody was close by before he lowered his voice. "Your hairs, your blood, and your semen were found on the woman."

Lou Wheeler shook his head. "You didn't know I was home. Your mother and sister were just leaving for the store when I got home that day. From the kitchen window I overheard the two of you arguing. You called her a few choices words, and she slapped you across the face. And you just lit up, pal."

Pal. Something zapped and popped inside Ben's brain, electrifying him. His stomach turned.

"You strangled her with your bare hands. Made it look easy. And then you grabbed a shovel, dragged her into the woods toward the slough, and buried her. When I saw you coming back toward the house, I got in my car and pretended to be pulling into the driveway. You came out of the house, jumped into your van, and took off." Lou leaned closer to the glass, his dark eyes piercing. "Want to know why they found my hair and semen on her?"

Ben said nothing.

"Because I ran back to the spot where I'd seen you with the shovel, and I dug her up and fucked her while she was still warm."

Ben stared him down. "You sick bastard."

"I ain't the one who killed her."

The rage bubbling inside Ben made him nauseous.

"Next time you come for a visit, we can talk about how your cunt of a mother ended up facedown in the slough. Bring your sister, too, will you? I'd love to see how she's grown." When he laughed, a severe pain pulsated behind Ben's eyes as streaks of light flashed within his head like lightning in the horizon.

Lou Wheeler hung up the phone. His chains rattled as he stood and gestured for the guard.

Despite the throbbing ache in his head and the bright lights, Ben didn't move or look away until Lou Wheeler was out of sight, and the door clicked shut behind him.

Pressing his temples, Ben closed his eyes and tried to will the images of Aly Scheer away. But they were right there in front of him. The same ones he'd been seeing for a while now—images of a dead woman lying in the middle of a field.

His heart pounded against his ribs.

He stood, didn't wait for the guard. Just walked back the way he came, collected his possessions at the front desk, and then made his way out the door, where he drew in a lungful of fresh air.

He hadn't killed anyone.

Lou Wheeler was a liar.

From that moment onward, Ben refused to think of him as his father. As far as he was concerned, his father was dead.

EIGHT

After paddling two miles downriver, he saw the pine tree that leaned far to the right, its branches nearly touching the water. As he dragged the boat from the water, he kept thinking about the girl in the barn.

The boat felt extra heavy. His muscles were tense and overworked. He couldn't stop to catch his breath. There was no time. Once he got the boat into the thick of the trees, he kicked leaves and tossed branches and handfuls of soil all around the sides. He used the bigger branches to cover the top of the boat.

When that was done, he used a leafy branch from a pine tree as a broom, sweeping the dirt back and forth all the way to the edge of the lake to cover his tracks.

As sweat dripped from his face, he reviewed his work. Leaves and branches and all matter of vegetation made it look untouched. The tracks were gone. It would be a while before someone uncovered the boat.

No doubt Old Man Matthews had called the police, which meant the search was on. With that in mind, he turned away from the lake and headed for his car.

He drove cautiously on Greenback Lane, his hands firmly on the wheel, attentive as he made sure to obey all speed limits and road signs.

His pulse was still racing, his heart ready to jump out of his chest. He'd had a few close calls in his day but never this close. It upset him to think he wouldn't be able to use the Matthewses' barn in the future. It would be months, possibly years, before he found such a perfect setup again. Two old people, living on acres of unused property that sat right next to the water. It had been too good to be true.

He kept his eyes on the road. *All good things must come to an end.*

As he relaxed, the corners of his mouth turned upward.

Everything happens for a reason. He hated that saying. What reason was there that Lavinia Shaw had to die today?

He pulled at his hair. What if she hadn't died at all?

She'd still had life in her when he'd been forced to run.

Nah.

He bit his lip.

She was dead. She had to be.

There was no way the old man could have moved fast enough to get her down from the rafters and save her. No possible way.

Movement to his left caught his eye—an older kid wearing a red T-shirt and jeans bolted across the street. No streetlight. No crosswalk. He slammed on the brakes, screeching to a halt. The car behind him did the same, very nearly bumping into him.

Shit!

The kid looked at him and flipped him off.

Ignore him. Move on. His adrenaline soared as he put his foot on the gas and continued on. The kid deserved to be pinned under his tire, skull split open, blood spilling out. *But I guess it wasn't fucking meant to be,* he thought bitterly.

It wasn't until he was nearly home that he gave himself permission to think about Lavinia. *Pretty, pretty girl.* What a shame he hadn't had the chance to take her down from the ropes, position her at just the right angles, the light hitting her face just so as he took proper pictures.

He glanced in the rearview mirror, eyeing the bag sitting on the back seat. His camera was inside. Later tonight after he was sure his mother and aunt were asleep, he would look at the pictures.

A siren sounded, and he pulled to the side of the road.

The police cruiser sped past.

Once the flashing lights disappeared, he slouched back in his seat and let out a bark of laughter.

What a rush. All of it. The planning. The kill. The narrow escape.

He could never stop.

Taking another person's life was like riding a roller coaster. The slow build of energy going up the hill, the thrill of the drop, and then the acceleration and g-forces on the loops. When it was over, all he could think about was getting back on the ride again.

NINE
BEN

Ben took the last bite of juicy chicken cacciatore on his plate, savoring the flavor of a homemade meal as he chewed. Across the table, his wife, Melony, smiled at him. Only a hint of a smile, really, but it was there. And it did something to him—sent a fire through him, warm and satisfying. He loved her. He'd moved out a little over a week ago. And he wanted nothing more than to be back home with his family where he belonged, but he also knew it was still too soon.

"When was the last time you ate?" she asked him, cutting into his thoughts.

"I've been eating," he said. "Just not anything as tasty as this."

She gave him the side-eye. She still loved him, he could see that, but she was wary of him, didn't trust him like she used to. And he couldn't blame her. From the moment he'd first met her, she'd been his savior. After the accident that had left him with amnesia, she'd been the only person in the hospital who had seemed to understand what he was going through. She'd nursed him back to health. She hadn't cared that he had no memory of his life before he'd met her.

None of that had mattered.

Until he'd begun having flashbacks—grisly images of bloodied scenes he couldn't bring himself to talk about. It wasn't just the flashbacks, though, that had sent his marriage veering off course. It was him. He was changing—the mood swings, the inability to talk to Melony about his frustration with the unknown, the disturbing memories.

He had so much going on. His sister refused to talk to him about their past. And now Lou Wheeler, his father, blamed him for the murder of Aly Scheer. Ben had no plans at this time to tell Melony about his visit with Lou. But she was smart, and she knew he wasn't being as open with her as he used to be.

It was the altercation he'd had with Abigail's soccer coach that had been the final blow. He didn't trust the man, didn't like him throwing his arms around the girls during their huddles. But Melony and the other parents loved the guy and his family. Melony insisted Ben was being paranoid and stubborn and wanted him to apologize to the coach for making a scene at the end of a soccer game.

Ben sighed. He knew he could weasel his way back into her heart and her bed if he simply told her what she wanted to hear. But he also knew that she wanted the old Ben back, the man she'd married.

That man, Ben worried, might never return.

"Can Sean and I leave the table now?" Abigail asked.

Melony eyed the kids' plates. "Take your dishes to the kitchen, and then get started on your homework."

Sean frowned. "Can I play thirty minutes of video games first?"

"Not until your homework is done."

His seven-year-old son groaned and headed off.

Ben missed all this—the silly drama and the humdrum life with small children. Waking up to the alarm and hitting "Snooze," showering and dressing, hearing his son and daughter downstairs, the clanking of cereal bowls and silverware, the smell of coffee, everyone running for the door. Ten hours later, he would return to hug the kids, kiss the wife, watch some news, eat dinner, and head upstairs to bed. Monotonous. Boring. Ordinary. And he wanted this life more than anything.

Once the kids had left the dining room, Melony looked across the table at Ben and said, "I read your story the other day about the little boy who went missing and was found in the woods five days later. Alive." She smiled wistfully. "Those are the kind of stories you should do more often."

"It's not often those types of stories end up with a happily ever after."

She sipped her wine, her eyes looking over the rim of the glass, meeting his.

"Abigail mentioned Career Day coming up soon and needing one of us to go to her school to talk about what we do. Can you go?" Melony asked. "I'll be training a new round of nurses, and I won't be able to get away from the hospital."

"Let me know when, and I'll be there."

Silence lingered once again.

Ben was afraid of saying the wrong thing. Afraid she might realize she didn't love him any longer, afraid she enjoyed having time to herself. "I miss you," he said.

"I miss you, too. But I need you to stop keeping things from me. We used to talk about everything."

Unfortunately, Ben wasn't ready to tell her everything. There were too many blanks in his life, too many horrible images flashing through his mind on a daily basis. Images that made him question not only *who* he was but also *what* he was.

"I talked to Coach Willis and his wife the other day at school. I told Roger that you were deeply sorry for what happened."

"I wish you hadn't done that," Ben said.

Just hearing the name of Abigail's soccer coach sent a crackle of electricity through him. Nobody knew the guy. Not really. All the parents of the girls on the soccer team thought they did because they had befriended his wife and two daughters. Surely, they thought, a man raising daughters of his own was a decent man. But Ben had done some research. He wasn't ready to share his findings until he had more information.

Roger Willis had moved his family three times in the past five years—from Washington to Oregon to California. Social media revealed that Willis appeared to have a good relationship with his elderly parents, who had lived within a few miles of him when they were in Oregon. And the man had not been fired from his job at the high school where he used to work. So what was the deal with this guy?

Melony wouldn't like it, but everything about Willis pointed at him being a pedophile. In Ben's opinion, he had many common characteristics. Child molesters came from all walks of life. Level of wealth, status of employment, religion, education—none of that could rule out a predator. Many of these sickos hid behind a mask of respectability within the community. They were usually adult males, married, with work that involved children. For this reason, Ben had made some calls and talked with a detective in Washington, who'd told him that keeping track of sex offenders was a daunting task. They were masters at manipulating people and slipping under the radar. Sex offenders were supposed to report any change of address, but many never did. In some states, convicted rapists could serve their time, and if the act was committed before a particular date, they could lawfully and freely walk on school grounds.

"I know you've been watching him," Melony said.

His wife's words took him by surprise. "I drove by his place on one or two occasions."

"I have it on good authority that you spent an entire Saturday parked outside his house."

"He can't be trusted, Melony."

"Abigail's school did a background check on Roger Willis. He wouldn't be working there if he hadn't passed."

"I've been around men like him. I'm asking you to trust me."

Melony set her wineglass to the side. "Do you think I don't want to protect our daughter? I love our children as much as you do. You aren't the only one with an overactive imagination and parental instincts. I would never do anything that I thought would harm either of our children, and I'm telling you you're making a mistake."

Ben sighed. Melony had always had faith in humanity. It was who she was. Ben, on the other hand, held fast to his innate sense for identifying people who were up to no good. It was in their mannerisms.

There was darkness inside of Willis, a certain look when he met Ben's gaze. And yet Ben wasn't ready to fight Melony on this. Not yet. He would find a way to prove to his wife that Roger Willis should not be trusted, and then he would work on mending their marriage.

"Last week I invited his daughter Paige over after school," Melony said. "She's a normal, sweet, well-adjusted little girl. His wife thinks very highly of her husband. I like her." Melony stood and began gathering the dishes from the table. "Just promise me you'll stay away from Roger Willis." She stopped to look at Ben. "I don't think that's asking too much."

He was tempted to say the words whether he meant them or not, but he refused to do it. "I'm sorry," he said. They were both quiet as they cleared the table. Once the dishes were put away, Ben made his way down the hall to Abigail's room and poked his head inside. "I'm heading off."

"I was hoping you were back for good," she said.

"Soon," he said as he stepped inside. "I do have a favor to ask of you."

"What is it, Dad?"

"Coach Willis."

"Dad. Not this again."

"It's my job as your father to protect you. I know you like your coach and his daughters. I get that. I just want you to be aware of your surroundings, okay?"

"I know. I know. Don't talk to people I don't know. Don't take candy from strangers or get into the car because they have a cute puppy."

"Exactly. I want both you and Sean to always be prepared." His daughter nodded, but he could tell by the bored expression on her face that he was losing her attention. "Remember when there was a small fire in the kitchen, and your brother ran to his room to hide?"

She nodded.

"For weeks after that we practiced fire drills so we would all know, as a family, what to do and where to go."

"I remember. That was fun."

"Well, this is sort of the same thing. I don't ever want you to be alone with your coach or any other adult without me or Mom there with you."

Melony joined them. "What's going on?"

"Nothing," Ben told her. "I'm just saying goodbye before I head out." He leaned low and planted a kiss on Abigail's forehead.

"You'll come to school for Career Day, right?" Abigail asked.

"I'll be there."

"Thanks, Dad. And don't worry . . . about anything. I'll be fine."

Melony walked him to the door. Sean chased after them and quickly latched on to his leg, begging him to stay. Ben picked up his son, surprised by how heavy he was getting. "You be good. Help your mom out when she asks, okay?"

"I will. Love you, Dad."

"I love you, too."

TEN
COLIN

Flashdance, the strip club on Vista Avenue, had seen better days. Colin knew this for a fact. Before marrying his ex-wife another lifetime ago, the guys had brought him here. The stage was warped, and the mirrored walls were smudged with fingerprints. The staff and the customers used to be young, and the bartenders and the two girls working the poles looked worn down by life and broken dreams.

He looked over his shoulder. Ren had stopped midway, a smile on his face as he enjoyed the show. Colin gave a little whistle to get the kid moving again.

Up ahead he could see the private rooms with all their red velvet upholstery. Cheesy but classic.

"How about a lap dance?" one of the girls asked him. She had thick makeup around her eyes, lots of curly blonde hair reminiscent of the eighties, and an outfit that didn't leave much to the imagination. "Oh," she said when Ren joined them, "is this a father-son party?"

Colin bristled. "What's your name?"

"Willow," she said, ending with pursed lips.

He showed her his badge. "We'd like to talk to your manager about a girl who used to work here."

All the enthusiasm left her body. "What's her name?"

"Lavinia Shaw."

"Poor Lavinia."

"Did you know her?" Ren asked.

"Yeah. Everyone knew Lavinia. Or wanted to know her, if you know what I mean."

"Not sure I do," Ren said.

Willow looked Ren over as if trying to figure out his age. "Long legs, big smile, bigger tits. She had the whole fresh-faced-schoolgirl look going on," she said. "Does that help?"

"Sure. Thanks for clarifying."

She looked at Colin and rolled her eyes. "Stay here. I'll go find Leo."

"Before you run off," Colin said, "mind telling me if you ever saw Lavinia with the same guy more than once?"

She laughed. "They all came back to see Lavinia. Some of them returned every night that she worked. I'll be right back."

"I've only been to one strip club before," Ren told Colin after she walked away. "It was nothing like this."

Colin couldn't imagine the kid sitting in a strip club. "Did you sketch the girls while they danced?"

"As a matter of fact, I did."

Colin shook his head. Before he could say anything more, Leo, a short, stalky man with a bad comb-over, introduced himself and quickly led them into one of the private rooms.

Leo shut the door behind them and said, "It's bad for business if the clientele sees a couple of detectives hanging around."

Colin nodded and then winced when Ren took a seat on the velvet couch.

"Have a seat," Leo offered.

"I'll stand. Thanks," Colin said. He didn't need to hit the black-light switch to see that the couch was covered in body fluids.

Leo went to the portable refrigerator in the corner and grabbed a water bottle. "Water?"

They both declined.

Leo twisted off the top and took a swallow. "Willow said you had questions about Lavinia. How long will this take?"

"Not long," Colin said. "Can you tell us how long Lavinia has been working here?"

"Less than a year, which is a shame. She brought us a lot of business. God rest her soul, of course."

"Of course."

"Did she have any problems with any characters in this place?"

Leo shrugged his shoulders. "Sure, yeah, I guess so. The customers aren't exactly high class around here, but she never filed a complaint or talked to me about any stalkers or anything."

Ren looked at Leo. "So you never noticed anyone unusual hanging around Lavinia?"

"No."

"How many nights a week did she work?" Colin asked next.

"One and a half. Tuesday and every other Thursday because she only had those two days off from school, and she'd made it a habit of visiting her brother in prison every other week." He scratched his arm. "She was a nice girl. We're going to miss her around here."

"Any idea why her brother was doing time?" Ren asked.

"No. I never asked."

"Do you keep security cameras in this place?"

"Are you kidding me? Nobody would come. No pun intended."

Ren chuckled.

"I mean, I have cameras in my office and out in the parking lot. That's it."

Colin said, "I'd like to have a look at the outside videos. Can you get those for me?"

"It'll take a while. If you want to leave me a number where I can reach you, I'll have Penelope see what she can put together and then give you a call."

"How soon?" Colin asked.

"Tomorrow good?"

Colin nodded. "Was Lavinia close to the other girls here?"

"Yeah. Definitely. You spoke to Willow, and Danika's not here tonight. But I'd be happy to give you her number since my main concern is to keep the girls safe."

Colin believed Leo was genuinely protective. They exchanged information, and then he thanked Leo for his cooperation. As he and Ren walked past the stage, heading for the exit, a douchebag customer began harassing a stripper as soon as she started to walk off the stage. The man grabbed the woman's arm and demanded a kiss. Spittle hit her cheek as he reminded her of all the tips he'd given her.

Ren shoved his badge in the guy's face. "She's done dancing. Let her go."

The customer did as Ren said, but he wasn't happy about it. "The bitch owes me."

"Sit down and shut the fuck up," Ren said, "unless you'd rather spend the rest of the night down at the station talking to me."

The man sat down with a grunt.

Ren caught up to Colin, and the loose gravel crunched beneath their feet as they walked to the car.

"Good job, kid," Colin said. The rookie was turning out to be full of surprises.

"Yes, sir. You haven't seen nothin' yet."

ELEVEN

JESSIE

The next morning, Jessie arrived at the office as Ben was rolling up his sleeping bag. He'd been bunking there ever since his wife had kicked him out of his house. "I take it Melony hasn't agreed to let you move back home?"

"It's complicated. But mostly she wants me to stay clear of my daughter's soccer coach."

She eyed him curiously. "And I guess that's a big *N-O.*"

"My instincts tell me this guy is bad news. I've made some phone calls, but so far, his trail leads nowhere. Not only does he have gaps in employment, he also moves around a lot."

"Where did he live before moving to California?"

"Washington and Oregon, as far as I can tell."

"Mind if I hand this over to Zee? She's quick and her mind won't stop. Sometimes she's up all night trying to work things out. She has access to databases I've never heard of."

"Sure," he said. "Why not? As long as it doesn't take away from her duties here."

Jessie saw that Zee had left her a note. She pushed it to the side for now, then grabbed a pad of paper. "What's the coach's name?"

"Roger Willis."

She wrote down the name and the states where he'd once lived. Once she was done, she looked back at Ben. "It's not easy being a parent, is it?"

"It's a balance, and it's not all fun and games, that's for sure. It's tough saying no when you really want to say yes because you love them and want them to be happy."

"I hope you can get this all figured out."

"Yeah, me too."

"There is something else I wanted to talk to you about," she added when Ben set about putting his things away.

He placed the sleeping bag in the closet and started working on folding up the cot. "What's going on?"

"I got a call from Nikki Seymour." She waited. "Recognize the name?"

"No. Should I?"

"She used to be friends with your sister," Jessie said. "She and her mom lived directly across the street from where you grew up. Her mom still lives there, though her dad died when she was very young."

Ben stopped what he was doing and gave her his full attention.

"Apparently Nikki used to have a crush on you."

The name meant nothing to him. "And?"

"I still need to talk to her again, but in a nutshell, her mother was and still is afraid of your father. Nikki believes that her mother is scared Lou Wheeler would come after her if he ever got the chance."

Ben frowned.

"Nikki told me your mother was an incessant complainer and, overall, a very angry person. She seemed certain that you and Nancy never went to live with your grandmother."

"Why would my sister lie about that?"

"She obviously didn't want you to know that your father is still alive. You had lost all memory of your childhood, and she's made it clear she thinks it best if the past is left in the past."

"So the few things Nancy has ever told me were lies."

"Not everything. She did tell you that your parents weren't good people. According to Nikki, that certainly seems to be the truth."

He put the cot away, then turned back to Jessie. "I went to Folsom Prison and met Lou Wheeler face-to-face."

"You talked to your father?"

"Lou Wheeler is beyond heartless and cruel, and he blames me for the death of Aly Scheer."

Her heart went out to Ben.

"What if he's telling the truth?" Ben asked, his tone earnest. "What if I am responsible for the woman's death, and that's the real reason my sister won't have anything to do with me?"

"Ridiculous." Jessie didn't like it when Ben talked like this. "Unless you can look me in the eye and tell me that your memories have returned and you are one hundred percent sure that you killed her, then *no.*" She shook her head. "You didn't do it, Ben. Between the amnesia, the sudden onslaught of flashbacks, and now everything going on at home, you're feeling vulnerable. You're way too hard on—"

"I have too many questions to let this go. I think I'm going to pay my sister a surprise visit," Ben cut in. "I'm going to tell her everything I know, and then I'm going to make her talk."

Jessie didn't like the ominous tone of his voice. "How can you force her to talk?"

"By promising never to contact her again if she does."

———

It wasn't until a few minutes after Ben left that Jessie noticed how tidy the office looked. Not only had Zee finished the filing, she'd also swept the floor and cleaned the window. Papers once scattered across Jessie's desk had been neatly stacked. Next to her computer was a check written out to Jessie Cole's Investigative Agency in the amount of $3,000. Just as she picked up the note lying beneath the check, Zee walked through the door.

Zee spread her arms wide. "So what do you think? The office looks pretty good, doesn't it?"

"It looks great. Thanks."

Zee pointed to the check she was holding. "Isn't that exciting?"

"I just got in." Jessie read the note.

Zee crossed the room and hovered over her. "Easton Scott showed up after you left for Clarksburg. I told him we didn't do infidelity cases, but he really, really wants our agency to handle this."

"Did he say why?"

"Just that he wants the whole affair handled quickly and quietly by an agency with a good reputation. He seemed confused, though, as if he was worried that his imagination might be getting the best of him. He acted more upset with himself for being here than he was about the possibility of his wife cheating on him."

"Strange."

"Definitely. He gave me the impression that he really loves her but that he's too trusting and needs to know for sure what is going on, if anything."

"Why does he think she's cheating? Has he seen her with another man?"

"No. He said they've been getting quite a few hang-up calls at home and that his wife is suddenly dressing up before work—you know, lipstick and other stuff. But even with all that, he doesn't want to confront her without proof."

When Jessie first opened her PI business, she'd been adamant about not handling infidelity cases. Cheating spouses kept many investigative agencies afloat. But for her it was personal. After spending seventeen years listening to her parents fight only to have her mom up and leave, abandoning them all, she wanted nothing to do with breakups and cheating spouses. There were plenty of other things to focus on: skip searches, preemployment and tenant screenings, cold cases, and missing persons. And yet, at the moment, she was short on clients, and the deposit alone would give her a few more months to figure things out.

"What are you going to do?"

"I'm going to give him a call and see when he wants us to start." Jessie grabbed her cell phone and dialed the number Zee had written down.

Easton Scott picked up right away. She told him who she was and why she was calling. When she mentioned she'd take on his case if he was still interested, he released what sounded like a sigh of relief.

Jessie could hear traffic. He was in his car, probably on his way to work. He repeated everything Zee had told her.

"Have you checked your cell phone bills, Mr. Scott?" If his wife was seeing another man, Jessie could almost guarantee that his number would show up as one that was dialed more than once.

"I did. There was nothing unusual. Please, call me Easton."

"Okay, and feel free to call me Jessie." From the sounds of it, Easton had done his homework. But there was always the possibility that his wife had a second phone that he didn't know about.

"My wife is incredibly smart. If she is seeing someone, I'm going to have to stay one step ahead of her."

If that were true, Jessie thought, then his wife definitely had a second phone, a throwaway. "How will you do that—you know—stay one step ahead of her?"

"I'll have to act as if nothing is going on whenever I'm with her. Bring her flowers every week, take her to dinner, pretend everything is great."

"You bring her flowers every week?"

"Of course. I want her to know she's loved."

Jessie had no words. "If she is having an affair, Easton, why would she stay with you? Why not just pack up and move out?"

"Money," he said flatly. "She likes all of the things money can buy. Nice clothes, spa days, flowers, and dinners out. I believe she'll do anything to keep this lifestyle."

"I'm curious. Is it your wife you're afraid of losing or the money you would have to pay her in the event of a divorce?"

"I love her," he said without hesitation. "I've loved Diane since the sixth grade." He cleared his throat. "I'd like to get this taken care of as soon as possible."

"Well, we'll do what we can, but it will really depend on the circumstances."

"Yes. Exactly. That's why this is so urgent," he explained. "I'm going to Vegas on business. I leave tomorrow and won't be returning until Sunday night. That will—at least, it should—give Diane ample opportunity to meet with her lov . . . someone else, if there is anyone else."

"The only way to know for sure would be for my agency to keep your wife under surveillance 24-7 while you're gone."

"Yes."

"Surveillance is not cheap. I charge by the hour, and that price doubles after midnight."

"I understand. I left you a deposit. If that's not sufficient—"

"It's fine. I just want to make sure we're clear."

"I'd like you to get started right away."

"I'll need to have you fill out some paperwork first. All standard questions about your wife: where she works, her hobbies, her daily routine. I will also need you to sign an agreement stating everything we've talked about."

"I left my email address with your assistant, Zee. If you could email me the forms, I'll fill them out and send them back to you."

"That will be fine."

"When can we talk again to discuss your findings, if any?"

He was definitely in a hurry, she thought. And he didn't seem to grasp that these things took time. "It's unlikely we'll have all the answers when you return from your trip, but either way, I'd rather discuss this with you in person. Can you come by first thing Monday morning?"

"Yes. I'll see you then."

She ended the call. Zee was looking at her expectantly, waiting.

"Looks like we handle infidelity cases," Jessie told her.

"Cool."

Jessie didn't quite see it the same way. If she weren't in need of some extra cash, she might have turned Easton Scott down. Infidelity cases weren't that easy to prove. On the other hand, most people didn't think they were being followed, which made it easier to keep track of them.

"When do we start?" Zee asked.

"We?" Jessie turned on her computer and waited for it to boot up.

"You have to let me help."

Zee was definitely an asset. Her quick handling of workers' comp cases had helped keep the business afloat. But she couldn't afford to pay someone to do surveillance. It wasn't cost effective.

"What's that look on your face?" Zee asked. "I'll go crazy if I have nothing to do. The voices will come back full force. I'll have to up my medication. My dad's girlfriend will try to cheer me up by feeding me strange, lumpy muffins made from oats and applesauce, and she'll want to drag me to all the garage sales around—"

"Okay. I get it," Jessie said with a laugh. As long as Zee took her medicine, she tended to get through her day without any trouble. She had a knack for PI work. "You're acting as if I was going to let you go."

"You weren't?"

"Of course not. You've been a great asset."

"So does that mean I'm getting a raise?"

"No. It's not in the budget. But you can watch Easton Scott's wife during the day. I don't think your dad would like the idea of you sitting in your car overnight."

"I'm twenty-eight years old. I can make my own decisions. Dad knows that. I'll bring things to do. I have a Kindle with a backlight and plenty of books to read. I haven't worked on an infidelity case before. The more I learn about the business, the better. That way, if your agency goes under, I can buy you out or get a job with another agency."

"So you're using me," Jessie stated, missing the days when Zee tended to keep to herself.

"Sure. If that's what you want to call it."

Jessie chuckled as she picked up the note she'd made earlier and handed it to Zee.

"What's this?"

"Ben could use some help finding out more about Roger Willis. Ben thinks the man is up to no good."

"In what way?"

"Willis is a teacher and a soccer coach, and Ben doesn't like the way Willis interacts with the young girls."

"Just a gut feeling at this point?" Zee asked.

Jessie nodded. "Ben has found some gaps in the man's employment. As far as he knows, Willis used to live in Washington and Oregon before he moved to Citrus Heights, California. If you get bored, I offered Ben your services."

"I'll see what I can find." Zee gave her a look. "Sometimes I wonder how you ever got along without me."

"Yeah," Jessie agreed. "Me too."

He glanced at his cell phone to get the time. He'd been watching the two women through the window for ten minutes. It would be another twenty before he'd have to head back to work. He didn't know what the dark-haired girl's role was within Jessie Cole's detective agency, but he knew she wasn't Jessie Cole because he'd seen dozens of images on the internet. Jessie was the one sitting behind the desk. Light-brown hair and petite, which in his opinion contrasted with the stories that had been written about her.

Obsessed with finding her missing sister, Jessie Cole had become a PI and apparently realized she had a knack for solving missing persons' cases. She'd definitely had her fifteen minutes of fame and then some. *Tenacious* was the adjective often used to describe her tactics. Her eagerness to pull the trigger too quickly had earned her the nickname Quick Draw McGraw. According to the records he'd managed to get his hands on, her license to carry had been revoked.

His online research had also brought him to a subreddit on serial killers that connected Jessie to the Heartless Killer. One of the discussions was a chat about how thorough the Heartless Killer had been when it came to researching his victims. Which sounded eerily familiar, he thought, since he, too, was meticulous when it came to studying his prey.

The Heartless Killer's fans talked about him as if he were some sort of a god. And there was one interesting tidbit he thought might be good to know in the future: apparently the Heartless Killer had known that Jessie Cole had a blood phobia. The mere sight of a drop of blood could cause her muscles to seize, sort of like a fainting goat that suffers from an uncontrolled stiffness when panicked.

No gun and an aversion to blood.

That little tidbit had been frosting on the cake.

The purpose of today's visit had to do with his newfound interest in all things Ben Morrison. And he knew Jessie and Ben had worked together to find her sister, but why? What was the relationship between Jessie Cole and Ben?

The mere thought of Ben Morrison made his teeth clench. The man had gotten away with murder. Ben Morrison had a wife and two kids. He was a family man. Such bullshit. For too long, Lou Wheeler's son had been enjoying the freedoms of everyday life, a life he didn't deserve.

Ben would pay. It was only fair.

But the PI might need to go first.

After narrowly escaping his last kill at the barn, he'd watched a press report on TV and had been relieved to learn that Lavinia Shaw was dead. Homicide detective Colin Grayson was leading the investigation. Without much digging, he'd been surprised to see Jessie Cole's name come up for the second time. Apparently she and the homicide detective had a thing for each other.

Colin Grayson had no suspects at this time. Nice. Because that would give him time to have a little fun with Jessie Cole, maybe mess with her head a bit.

It was interesting to see that Ben, Jessie, and Colin seemed to be interconnected. If he fucked with one of them, it would be sort of like getting three birds with one stone. Although Ben was his main attraction, Jessie Cole and her ability to stick her nose into other people's business intrigued him.

A cold but invigorating November wind swept across his face. About to head off, he remained still when he saw Jessie stand. Both she and the dark-haired girl put on their coats and left the office. He watched as they exited the building. Jessie walked the younger woman to her car, and after she drove off, Jessie proceeded to cross the road and head off by foot.

What is she up to? he wondered.

He followed her, surprised when less than two blocks away, she walked through a rickety gate and approached a timeworn house. The roof had bald spots where shingles used to be, and half the gutter was missing. A dog barked inside as she worked a key into the lock. He hadn't known she lived so close to her office. An idea struck him. While she was out, he may as well take a tour of her office. He rushed back the way he came, crossed the street, and made his way into the building where Jessie Cole worked.

A blonde wearing ripped jeans, a red visor, and a white tee with a colorful appliqué advertising a coffee shop smiled at him as she passed.

She was young—not yet twenty, was his guess. He wondered if she could possibly be as happy as she looked. One thing he'd learned from the work he did was that everybody had a story. He had one, too, and it was a doozy.

While growing up, he'd shared a one-room house with his mother, Susan, a prostitute who engaged in sadomasochistic acts with her clients while he slept. Of course, he never got much sleep. He spent most of his childhood hiding under the covers and praying the screaming and groaning would all stop. He still couldn't get the tortured, orgasmic sounds that arose from his mother while she was being whipped and brutalized out of his mind.

At night it was his mother who was tortured.

But during the day, she became the abuser.

Every day with his mother had been a new adventure.

She would remove his socks and shoes, then hold his ankles tight between her thighs and whip the bottom of his feet with a wooden spoon. Another favorite pastime of hers was dunking his head in the toilet and holding it there until he passed out. Sometimes she would dress him up like a girl and take him for a stroll through the mall, just to humiliate him.

Once a week, she left him alone so she could focus on baking brownies for her customers. The ingredients were never exactly the same but always included shit left on the front lawn by one of the neighbors' dogs. To this day, the thought of watching those men gobble up her homemade brownies made him gag.

Man, oh man, how they loved her baked goods!

Thoughts of his mother always brought him back to one question: Were serial killers born or raised? That was the question he often asked himself.

By the time he found the door marked with a simple sign, JESSIE COLE DETECTIVE AGENCY, he'd gotten himself worked up thinking about the fearful, scared little boy he once had been. His muscles quivered.

He knocked before turning the knob.

Locked.

Reaching into his coat pocket, he pulled out two bobby pins and made quick work of picking the lock. The second he was inside, he shut the door, rolled up his right pant leg, and used the blunt end of the bobby pin to repeatedly stab at his shin.

Serial killers were fucking raised.

He kept stabbing until drops of blood appeared. Only then was it possible to take a calming breath.

After a moment, he found a box of tissues, a tape dispenser, and a stapler on top of the file cabinet. He used tissue and tape to bandage his leg before rolling his pants back in place.

Feeling better, he walked around the desk and took a seat in Jessie's chair. That's when he noticed how neat and organized everything was. Nothing like his aunt's house, where he and his mother lived. His mother suffered from Alzheimer's—couldn't remember if she was coming or going half the time. Her twin sister was a hoarder. They made a delightful pair. He couldn't get to the bedroom at the back of the house without kicking through garbage. If his aunt weren't receiving a big Social Security check every month, he would have taken her out already.

He glanced outside. No sign of Jessie Cole. Better hurry, all the same.

On the desk, front and center, was a check made out to the Jessie Cole Detective Agency for $3,000. Underneath the check was a note about Easton Scott wanting to hire the agency to keep an eye on his wife. Additional notes were scribbled in the margins. *Out of town this coming weekend.*

Interesting. An idea came to him, and he pulled out his phone and took a picture of the check with Easton Scott's address. If Jessie ended up following this guy's wife, it might be fun to watch her in action, especially if he could find some way to make things exciting.

He laughed as he opened the file drawer on the bottom right and flicked through rows of manila folders—old cases stamped CLOSED. He pulled out the file labeled SOPHIE COLE, riffled through it, and then left it on the desk as he stood and went to check out the closet.

Stacked inside were plastic bins. Also, a cot, a pillow, and a blanket. As he sifted through the clothes inside a duffel bag, he realized Ben Morrison was actually sleeping here. Interesting. He'd been watching Ben off and on for about a week. The crime reporter spent long hours at the *Sacramento Tribune*, where he worked. On the second day, he'd followed Ben here to Jessie's office but hadn't stayed long enough to keep track of when Ben had left since he'd promised his aunt he'd pick up some groceries.

Outside, a police car pulled up to the curb.

His pulse kicked up a notch as he shut the closet door, grabbed the file from atop the desk, and made a quick exit, careful to lock the door behind him.

TWELVE

BEN

Ben had arrived in Tampa a few hours ago. He'd been sitting in the rental car in front of Nancy's house for fifteen minutes, going over in his mind what he wanted to say. He needed to get it right, didn't want to scare her away. More than anything, he needed her to tell him everything she knew about their childhood.

Strange to think he didn't know his own sister. He'd seen her once in the hospital more than a decade ago when he was recuperating from his accident. And then again, recently, when she'd spent the day with his family getting to know his children, Abigail and Sean. At the beginning of that visit, he'd thought maybe his sister had been offering an olive branch—*you're my brother, let's be friends.* But by the end of the day, he'd known otherwise. Despite the perfect day they had shared, she'd told him flat out that although his family was lovely, she wanted nothing to do with him. She would not be back.

How long has she been living in Florida? he wondered.

The house was a charming English cottage with arched windows and a white picket fence lined with greenery. A house you might see in a fairy tale. He saw movement in the kitchen, but he couldn't tell by the silhouette if it was Nancy.

He climbed out of the car. A tiny bell tinkled when he opened the wooden gate. He followed the stone path to the front entry and knocked on the door.

"Who is it?" she asked from within the safety of her home. *Smart woman.*

"Is that you, Nancy? It's me, Ben. Your brother."

The door swept open, wide enough for him to see the shocked expression on her face. Wide enough to see a small baby bump beneath her cotton shirt. His gaze moved from her stomach to her face. "Are you pregnant?"

She nodded.

"You were pregnant when I saw you last?"

Another nod.

"Congratulations," he said. Why hadn't she told him? What was going on?

Nancy stuck her head outside and looked around as if she were afraid the neighbors might be watching. "Well, come on inside."

He followed her down the hallway.

"Have a seat while I get you a glass of water."

He didn't protest. He walked ahead into the sparsely decorated living room while she took a right into the kitchen, with its granite countertops and stainless-steel appliances. The living area consisted of lots of built-in shelves, and tile accents framed a small fireplace. Hardwood floors and custom light fixtures made the place look like a model home.

At first he heard cabinets opening and shutting in the kitchen, but then all was quiet. What was she doing?

By the time she brought him a glass of water, but had nothing for herself, he knew her intention was to keep this meeting short. He wondered if she'd grabbed hold of her cell and called the authorities or maybe her husband. Perhaps she had a weapon hidden somewhere on her person.

Either way, he'd lost track of what he'd planned to say first.

After setting the glass on the table in front of him, she remained standing, her back ramrod straight. Her eyes were deeply set, circled with exhaustion and most likely endless, dark secrets. Despite all of this, she did not look frail. She looked sturdy, ready to fight if she needed to. She looked like the kind of person he'd want as a sister. The thought that he might never see her again made his chest tighten.

When she finally took a seat in the cushioned chair across from him, years of unspoken words along with the awkward silence hung heavy in the air between them. If only he could remember his past. Something told him Nancy had once been a solitary flicker of light in a world of darkness.

"I saw Lou Wheeler the other day," he blurted out. "The meeting did not go as I had hoped or expected. It was short and unfortunate. The man said nothing worth repeating, except for one thing."

She stared at him, unblinking, her bottom lip trembling. It was difficult for him to tell if she was going to cry, scream, or maybe both.

She was terrified. That much was clear, but of what?

"Why didn't you tell me our father is alive and in prison? Why do you tell me lies when all I asked of you was the truth?"

"I can't do this," she said, her voice almost a whisper. "How many times do I need to tell you I don't want to talk about the past?"

"But you came all the way to California to see me. Why?"

Still nothing.

Ben tried to relax. "I came here today to make you a proposition."

She waited.

"You're the only one I can talk to about my childhood—my parents, my friends, the people I hung out with growing up." He sighed. "If you answer a few questions and tell me what you know—the good and the bad—I promise to stay out of your life forever."

Her eyes slowly closed as she gave a subtle shake of her head. "Please."

She rested both hands on her baby bump and finally lifted her gaze to meet his. "You'll never come back?"

"Never."

"What do you want to know?"

"Everything."

All it took was a promise to stay out of her life to get her talking.

"We were born into a hell house," she began. "Our parents were psychopaths." She raised her chin as if she were doing everything she could to stay strong while she talked. "Mom never had a kind thing to say to either one of us. Never. She dished out punishment like it was her job. I slept with a sharp knife under my pillow. Dad was gone a lot. He did odd jobs around town, but mostly he was a fisherman. When he was home, he drank too much. Whiskey made him violent. Too many times to count, he left Mom with a black eye and you with a split in your lip."

"What about you?" Ben asked. "Did he hurt you?"

"He rarely hit or kicked me. He saved me for other things. But this isn't about me, Ben. It's about you. That's why you're here."

He nodded. *He saved me for other things.* Enough said.

"As you grew older, Dad tended to leave you alone because you were big and muscular, and you were beginning to fight back. Besides, he was satisfied with using Mom as his punching bag." She raised her hands, palms up. "Simply put, it was a shitty life for all of us. I can't remember one good thing about those days. Not one, except, I guess, those nights when Dad was gone, and I slept soundly and dreamed of growing up and moving away—far, far away."

"I'm sorry."

Another shrug.

"And what about our relationship? You and me?" he asked. "Were we close? Did we play, talk, conspire against our parents, do anything at all together?"

Nancy fidgeted in her seat. "You were painfully quiet. You never said much to anyone, including me. Mostly you kept to yourself, locked in your room or out in the woods somewhere close to the slough."

"What about friends?"

"You didn't have any."

"What about Nikki Seymour?"

A glint of surprise showed in her eyes. "She was *my* friend, but I guess she did develop a crush on you close to the end."

"The end?"

"Right before Aly Scheer was found buried on our property and Dad was taken to prison."

"Was Aly my friend or yours?"

"Not mine. I was only fourteen. She was too old for you, too. If I remember correctly, she was twenty-five and you were eighteen. She came from a well-to-do family, and I remember Mom constantly talking about the Scheer family money and how she might be able to get her hands on some of it if you two hooked up. Anyhow, Mom believed you were dating her, but I wasn't so sure."

"Why not?"

"I just never saw you with anyone before. It was hard for me to imagine you having a friend, let alone a girlfriend. You only brought her to the house on two occasions that I know of, and I never saw you kiss her or hold her hand."

Before he could ask her why it would be so difficult back then to imagine him having a girlfriend, Nancy said, "Despite the woman's well-to-do family, Mom hated her, of course. Called her all sorts of ugly names and told me Aly only liked you because you drove her wherever she needed to go."

"Did you ever meet Aly, talk to her?" he asked.

"No introductions were ever made." Nancy shrugged. "Aly never seemed interested in meeting me or anyone else in the family."

"Our father blames me for his arrest and imprisonment," Ben went on. "He says I killed Aly Scheer and that I'm the one who should be locked behind bars."

"You've changed," she said.

He wasn't sure what that had to do with anything. "Are you saying Lou is telling the truth?"

"Possibly." Nancy seemed to have a difficult time keeping eye contact. "I don't know."

"But it wouldn't surprise you, would it?"

Her shoulders tensed. "No."

Ben swallowed. Nancy thought he was capable of murder. No wonder she wanted nothing to do with him. "Thank you for your honesty, but I need to know why you feel this way and what it was about me that frightened you."

"Everything," she blurted out. "You were awkward and just . . . different. Like I said, you mostly stayed to yourself. But sometimes I would try to have a conversation with you, and you always had a faraway look in your eyes. The first time I saw a zombie movie, I thought of you. And it was all because of the eyes—the blank, empty stare."

His sister wouldn't stop fidgeting as she talked. She kept curling and uncurling her fingers. He was thankful when she continued talking without further prompting from him.

"I witnessed you and the neighborhood boy playing outside once. I thought it was fascinating to see you interact with another human being. Although the boy provoked you, once you jumped on top of him and put your hands around his throat, you were relentless. I screamed and knocked on the window, but you either didn't hear me or didn't care. The boy was in the hospital for a very long time, but he survived."

It was quiet for a moment, the awkward tension between them thick. "I'm sure there's more," he said, prompting her to continue.

She nodded. "A couple of kids at school used to call you The Butcher. I didn't understand. Not until I followed you through the wooded area behind our house. On the weekends, you would often disappear back there for hours." She stopped to take a breath. "You were thirteen when I followed you to a spot where you had made a lean-to out of thick branches. I stayed far enough back so that you didn't see me. It was hours before you finally headed home. I had hardly moved. I was tired and sore, but I couldn't go back until I saw what you had been up to all that time." A tear ran down the side of her face.

"What did you see?"

"I can still see it in my mind. Rows and rows of dead things: squirrels, rats, mice, gophers, and birds—all sorted in nice, neat rows. I don't know how many altogether. I didn't count. More than two dozen would be my guess." Nancy was no longer looking at him. Instead, she focused on her hands folded in her lap. "Outside of the lean-to, I could see where you had dug a hole and then covered it with fresh dirt. I found a stick and used it as a shovel to dig up the soft soil. A few inches down I found bones, bigger bones that looked as if they had been scraped clean and bleached. The hole was so deep I never reached the bottom." When she met his gaze again, she looked deathly pale.

"And that's why you believe I could have had something to do with the murder of Aly Scheer?"

"That's part of it. A few days before they found her body buried in the backyard, I was in the car with Mom heading for the market when I saw you pass us in your truck. Aly was in the passenger seat. I waved, but I don't think you saw me. Two days later, her body was found buried behind our house."

"I've read the court proceedings," Ben said. "You were called as a witness. You told the court that you never saw Aly Scheer in the days leading up to her murder. Why didn't you tell anyone what you just told me?"

She visibly stiffened. "Because I came from a family of psychopaths. Of that, there's no doubt in my mind. From the time I saw your collection of animal carcasses and bones, I kept clear of you, for the most

part. But still, you were—you are"—she choked out— "my brother."
She took a breath. "Other than the neighborhood boy, I never witnessed
you harming an animal, let alone a human being. In truth, I always
thought there was a glimpse of goodness inside of you. In some ways I
felt you cared about me and that you were my protector. Maybe it was
because you stepped in whenever I argued with Mom. You would take
a beating for it, too. I can't count the number of times you saved the
family dog from Mom's wrath, which made no sense to me after seeing
all those dead animals. But overall, despite the notion of you being my
protector, you frightened me. You still do."

More than anything, Ben wanted to go to her, put his arms around
her, and comfort her as he would his own daughter. But she was definitely scared. It showed in the slight trembling of her hands, her rapid
blinking, and in the way she licked her lips. He wasn't ready to end their
conversation, so he stayed seated. "I still don't understand why you sat
on the witness stand and said nothing about what you saw, knowing
that Lou would be the one serving time."

"Because our father scared me most of all. I wanted to be able to
sleep at night, knowing he would never enter my room again. Besides,"
she said as if to erase any lingering guilt, "all the evidence pointed to
him anyhow."

Eeny, meeny, miny, moe, Ben thought. Perhaps it was her body lan-
guage, or maybe her tone, but he wasn't confident she really cared which
psychopath had been thrown in prison.

His gaze fell to her stomach as a thought came to him. "You came
to see me because you were pregnant, didn't you?" he asked suddenly
as images of Nancy's last visit filled his head. She'd come to his house
in California and had been fully engaged with his children the entire
day. She had smiled and laughed. Not once had she resembled the sad,
scared person sitting in front of him today.

She swallowed, said nothing.

"You traveled all that way to see if Abigail and Sean were 'normal' kids," he stated. The notion caused his stomach to turn. He kept his gaze on hers. "Give me an answer, Nancy. Is that why you came to visit me? Yes or no?"

Her eyes narrowed. "Yes."

Ben inhaled.

"There's nothing more to tell you," she said, letting him know they were done talking. "Wait here," she said. "I have something for you." Nancy pushed herself to her feet, and when she returned, she handed him a piece of paper and a key.

"What's this?"

"The key and mortgage note to the house in Clarksburg."

"It was paid off?"

She shrugged. "Dad paid next to nothing for it."

"Did you ever go back?"

"No. Never. Why would I?"

Stupid question.

"Do whatever you want with the key and the note. If you visit him again, don't tell him my married name or where I live."

"I won't." Ben stood, took the paper and key, and followed her to the front entry.

She opened the door and held it there, her body stiff, her expression unyielding.

He had more questions but quickly decided one more would have to be enough. "What about Mom?" he asked as he stepped outside and turned back to face her. "Do you think I could have had something to do with her death?"

"I have no idea. I only know I never shed a tear for her. Not one."

"I'm sorry for any heartache I caused you, Nancy. I need you to know that. If I could go back in time to make things right for you, I would. I saw the way you were with Abigail and Sean. They adore you. You're a good person. You didn't deserve to be stuck with a brother—a wretch—like me."

Her gaze remained locked on his. "You won't come back?"

"No. Never."

"Goodbye, then."

Before he could thank his sister for taking the time to talk to him, she closed the door, shutting him out of her life forever. He didn't move—just stood there, his breathing shallow, shaky. When he finally walked away, back to his car, he felt an empty pit in his chest.

Something told him his sister had been right all along. Somehow she'd managed to escape the madhouse and find a better life. But not him. There was something inherently wrong with him. Born to not one but two hateful people. He was the bad seed.

And yet what he'd learned about his past so far wasn't enough.

He thought of Melony and the kids, how much he loved them, and how he would do anything to keep them safe.

For that reason alone, he needed to know more.

He needed to know the truth.

The gruesome images that had recently begun to flicker through his mind like an old black-and-white film were coming to him much more often and in full color. So far he'd been able to control the bursts of unrestrained anger that sometimes bubbled up inside of him. But if he was the person Nancy had once known, the one she'd described, how long would he be able to tamp it all down?

He was a husband and a father, a family man first and everything else last. Could he be changing, morphing into the monster his sister thought him to be? He looked at his trembling hands, then back at his sister's house where he could see her looking through the curtained window, anxiously waiting for him to leave.

He climbed behind the wheel and drove off, knowing he'd never see her again. He would go back to the hotel where he was sure he wouldn't get much sleep. And in the morning he would return home to find out once and for all if there was any chance he was the psychopath his sister had talked about.

THIRTEEN
JESSIE

Jessie sat on the couch, facing Doug Mathis, a psychologist who specialized in treating phobias. He'd already given her a long explanation about how most people have fears, like of heights or of public speaking. But when that fear became debilitating in any way, it was called a "phobia."

As Dr. Mathis rambled on, Jessie thought about all the things she had to do today. Her car had been making a weird noise, and it was due for an oil change. She wanted to check on Zee, who was handling the surveillance on Easton Scott's wife. And she needed to return Ben's call.

"Are you afraid of needles?" Dr. Mathis asked her.

"No."

"How about fainting?"

"No."

"Does the anticipation of injury cause you to panic?"

"No."

"Many people experience a fear of blood, needles, and doctors." Dr. Mathis flipped through the papers Jessie had filled out when she first arrived. "I see here that you experience a temporary loss of consciousness whenever you see blood."

"That's right."

"What you're experiencing is a dramatic decrease in blood pressure at the mere sight of it."

"It happens even if it's not my blood," Jessie told him. "Is that normal?"

"I would say so. Do you have any idea what may have triggered your aversion for blood?"

"No. I think I was born this way."

He smiled.

"So how are you going to fix me?"

"I'd like to use CBT therapy. If you agree, we'll meet once a week. I'd like to start by dealing with your confidence issues. We do that by talking about your fears and frustrations in everyday life."

"I'm very confident. I don't think that's the problem."

Dr. Mathis tapped his fingers together. "Are you saying you consider yourself to be fearless?"

She wasn't sure what he meant, exactly. She thought about the other day when she'd felt as if she were being watched. Tiny hairs on her neck had stood on end. She then remembered the time Olivia had disappeared and she'd instantly been overcome with panic. And then there was her time spent in . . . "No," she said. "I'm definitely not fearless."

"Any frustrations you feel regularly throughout the day?"

"I don't think so."

"No money or relationship issues?"

She chuckled. "Doesn't everyone have those?"

He shook his head, a pitiful look in his eyes as if he might be feeling guilty for letting that particular cat out of the bag.

"Oh well, then, I guess money—or lack thereof—can be frustrating, but that hasn't been a problem until recently. Not really. I mean, it would be nice to pay the bills without feeling sick to my stomach." She sighed. "I was gritting my teeth on the drive over here when my car started making funny noises." She smiled. "Time for a tune-up, I guess. No problem," she muttered. "We just won't eat next month."

He didn't smile. He merely waited patiently for her to go on.

"My niece will be driving soon, and the thought of her being out on the road with all those lunatic drivers makes me a little crazy." She stopped when she saw the smug look on the doctor's face.

"Okay," she said. "So what now?"

"After we talk more about fears and frustrations, we'll concentrate on the fainting aspect of your phobia."

"How do we do that?"

"I'm going to train you in a technique called applied tension, which will temporarily increase your blood pressure and reduce the likelihood of fainting when you see blood. Once you have control over whether or not you're going to faint, you'll begin to feel more comfortable when you are exposed to your phobia later in treatment and in life."

"What does that entail?"

He gave her a quick demonstration. "You'll cross your legs, clasp your hands in front of your chest, and pull as hard as you can, tensing all the muscles in your body. I'll have you practice at home."

Jessie could feel her phone buzzing in her bag next to her. As he went over other techniques they would be working on down the road, she found it ridiculously difficult to focus on what he was saying. She watched his lips move instead. She'd always had a hard time sitting still for too long. So far she'd learned that she was not only losing her confidence but also fearful and frustrated.

"If you would like, we could go ahead and give applied tension a try today?"

Determined to show the therapist that she could be downright indomitable if she put her mind to it, she lifted her chin. "Sure. Why not?"

By the time Jessie walked out of his office, she'd fainted twice. She'd crossed her legs and tensed every muscle, but as soon as he pricked his finger and a drop of blood appeared, the lights went out. How the hell was she going to overcome her blood phobia when just the thought of meeting with Dr. Mathis every week stressed her out?

Back in her car, she turned the key and listened to the engine. The rattle she'd heard earlier was hardly discernible. But once she was on the highway it was back. *Damn.*

Her cell phone buzzed, lighting up the console. "Unknown Caller." Had she left something at Dr. Mathis's office? She hit the green button and said hello.

"Is this Jessie Cole?"

"This is she."

"I thought you should know that Ben Morrison is not who you think he is."

He had a low, rough voice. Definitely male. "Who is this?"

"A concerned citizen."

Just another crackpot was more like it.

"Ben Morrison killed Aly Scheer, and my guess is that she wasn't his only victim."

Her spine stiffened. "Do you have proof?"

"You're the detective. Ben Morrison cannot be trusted. You need to watch your back."

"Why don't we meet and talk about this further?"

The caller hung up.

FOURTEEN

ZEE

As far as weather went, Zee had lucked out. A couple of rays of sun forced their way through the trees, so instead of doing surveillance from her car, she found a nice bench on the edge of the city park with a great view of the hair salon where Easton Scott's wife worked.

At times like this, Zee wondered what it would be like to be married. How do you trust someone day in and day out to be loyal?

Legs crossed, she stared straight ahead and munched on the carrots and broccoli her dad's girlfriend had packed for her. According to the papers Easton Scott had filled out and emailed the agency, Diane worked at the salon from nine to six, Monday through Friday.

Every time the door to the salon opened, whether the person was coming or going, Zee made a note in her logbook.

Like right now.

She watched a woman leave her car and head for the salon.

Zee popped the rest of the baby carrot into her mouth, picked up her notebook and pen, and wrote, *"Female. Five feet two inches. Dark hair rolled into a sloppy bun. Entered salon at 10:30 a.m."*

She wondered how many people worked at the salon on any given day. And that's when an idea bloomed. It was a hair salon. And she had hair, didn't she?

She waited for one of the voices in her head to insult her.

Nothing.

How could that be?

She tried to recall the last time she'd heard Lucy, Marion, or Francis, three irritating voices that usually had an opinion on everything. They were a symptom of her psychotic disorder.

She definitely hadn't heard any of the three musketeers yesterday . . . or the day before, she realized. The notion that they might be gone should have thrilled her, but it worried her instead.

She'd never gone a day without hearing one of the voices, let alone three. Her doctor used to tell her that sometimes symptoms of schizophrenia, like hallucinations and voices, went away—poof, just disappeared. But if anything, her symptoms had only grown worse, and it wasn't long before her doctor had stopped offering hopeful words as he wrote her a new prescription each month.

Although Zee had done enough of her own research to know there was no cure for schizophrenia, she was able to manage her condition with medication and self-help strategies, which lately included talking her dad's ear off, tarot cards, and lots of rest.

The door to the salon came open, snapping her right back to the matter at hand. *Hair,* she remembered. She had hair.

And now would be the perfect time to put it to good use.

A man she'd failed to see enter the salon had just left. He must have arrived before nine. Zee wrote, *"Five ten, give or take an inch. Older guy. At least fifty. Dark hair speckled with silver and cut short around his ears."*

The dark-haired man was quickly forgotten as her thoughts turned to today's horoscope. Again, it was all about relationships and finding that special person. Love was definitely in the air, but she sure as hell couldn't seem to take advantage of it. *"Secret attractions surface, but the one you find the most surprising takes you into a new world of intensely passionate love."*

Did she even want a boyfriend? She didn't like to be touched, and if someone talked to her for more than ten seconds, her mind usually began to wander. Overall, people bored the shit out of her. She wouldn't have given the first horoscope another thought, but every day lately her astrological chart seemed to be about love and relationships. She loved the whole idea of horoscopes and how they were shaped by the positions of the sun and moon and planets at the time of a person's birth. She liked working with crystals and tarot cards, too. It all gave her a sense of peace. But this love thing was fucking with her.

Okay, enough of that. Back to her plan. She used her cell phone to look up the number to the salon, clicked on the "Call" button, and told the person on the other line that she wanted to make an appointment with Diane Easton.

"Color and cut?" the woman asked.

"Yes. The works," Zee said, because it had a nice ring to it. If she was going to change things up, she might as well go for it.

"She has a cancellation tomorrow afternoon. Will that work?"

"Perfect." Zee left her information and disconnected the call. Then she began to hyperventilate at the idea of changing her hair. It had been long and straight for most of her life. And having her hair colored and cut would mean a complete stranger would be touching her. It couldn't be avoided. She leaned forward.

Breathe, girl, breathe.

Everything would be fine. Persistence. Passion. Creativity. Those were common traits of great private eyes.

Feeling better about her day, she sat up tall again and promptly noticed a nice-looking guy as he jogged past her. If she liked to run, or exercise for that matter, she might have followed him and tried to strike up a conversation. There was no way she was going to find love unless she put herself out there. She recalled reading something about needing to love yourself before finding true love. No problem there. Thanks to her dad, she'd grown up with a healthy dose of confidence and self-worth. She loved everything about herself.

Her body felt suddenly weightless. Maybe she was ready for love after all.

Fifteen

Jessie

Jessie had only been back in her office for a few minutes after seeing Dr. Mathis when Ben walked in the door. Although he'd been using her office for a place to sleep while he and his wife worked things out, she usually didn't see him much because of the long hours he put in at the paper.

"Fancy seeing you again," she said.

"Got a minute?"

"Of course." He was carrying a duffel bag. He looked wiped out. She still wasn't used to him with short hair. It didn't help that it was flat against one side of his head.

"I just got off the plane." He set his bag near the closet and then plopped down in the chair in front of her desk. "I saw Nancy yesterday."

"How did it go?"

He ran his fingers through his hair. She could see sadness mixed with frustration in his face.

"In a nutshell, she told me she grew up with three psychopaths. Her words, verbatim."

Jessie inwardly cringed. "Did she say why she felt that way?"

"She said I was fond of collecting animal carcasses and bones."

"But she never saw you kill any animals?"

"Apparently not." He rubbed his chin. "She also overheard kids at school referring to me as 'The Butcher,' and she saw me with Aly Scheer two days before her body was found behind the house where we grew up."

"Did she say you and Aly were friends?"

"Our mother told Nancy at the time that we were dating, but according to the court records I've been reading through, Aly's family's testimony states that Aly and I were merely acquaintances. Of course, my father says otherwise. Mom was found dead by then, and Nancy told the jury what she told me, that she met Aly twice and had no idea what our relationship entailed." Ben sighed. "From the sound of it, I was a dark, mysterious sort who kept to myself. Although Nancy sometimes thought of me as her protector, she was also afraid of me. In fact, she still is."

Jessie scratched the back of her neck. "You both grew up with abusive parents. Maybe Nancy transferred her fear onto you."

"What about the bones?" he asked.

"Lots of people are fascinated by bones. If your sister had seen you torturing or killing animals, that would be another story." She paused before adding, "And the whole 'butcher' nickname is just a case of kids being kids. They can be mean. If you were big and tall for your age, they were probably afraid of you."

"Last night in the hotel and then on the plane ride home, I had a lot of time to think. I want to hire you, officially, to find the truth."

"I'm already on it. We're going to continue to put your past together, piece by piece."

"You don't understand," Ben said. "My father and now my sister are saying I had something to do with the murder of the young woman found buried in our backyard. I have a family to worry about. I need to know the truth."

Jessie didn't like where this conversation was headed. He sounded desperate and panicked. He was talking fast, as if time were running out.

"I can afford to pay you your regular hourly fee. I have some money put away," he went on. "I only took you up on your offer to bunk in your office because it's close to my work. Besides, I thought Melony would take me back by now."

Before she could protest further, he said, "I will only accept your help if you allow me to pay you. And as a paying customer, I am asking you to change your focus to Aly Scheer. Who was she? Why was she at the house in Clarksburg? Did I have a relationship with her?"

Aly Scheer. Shit. She needed to tell him about the caller. "That name," she said. "I saw a doctor this morning about my blood phobia—"

"How did it go?"

"Let's just say it will take some time. But that's not where I was going with that. I got a call on my way back to the office. It was from an unknown caller, a male voice. He said he was calling to warn me about you."

"Warn you? About what?"

"He said you killed Aly Scheer and that she wasn't the first. I asked him if he had proof, but he said I was the detective, which I took to mean that it was my job to follow the evidence and find the truth. I then asked if we could meet and talk about it, but he disconnected the call."

"The timing is interesting, don't you think?" Ben asked. "You've only just recently begun to ask questions in my hometown."

"And you visited your dad and traveled to Florida to talk to your sister."

He rubbed his chin. "I wonder if Nancy would have put someone up to this?"

Jessie shook her head. "No. She would have warned me about you when I talked to her at the hotel."

Ben dragged his hands over his face. "What about Nikki Seymour? Have you heard anything more from her?"

"No, afraid not."

He stood and pushed his chair in close to her desk.

"Where are you going?" Jessie asked.

"I took a few days off." He reached into his coat pocket and held up a key. "Turns out good ole Dad owns the house where I grew up. Nancy gave me the key and the note proving ownership. She wants nothing to do with it, so I thought I'd head to Clarksburg to take a look around."

Jessie jumped up and grabbed her coat. "I'm coming with you."

Sixteen

Colin

Colin and Ren came to their feet when the door to the morgue opened, and a young woman followed by a couple he guessed to be in their early sixties stepped inside.

"Detective Grayson?" the man asked.

Colin offered his hand. "Mr. and Mrs. Shaw. Thanks for coming."

"Call me Gabe. This is my wife, Linda, and my daughter, Amelia." Gabe Shaw shook Colin's and Ren's hands, but his wife, Linda, wanted nothing to do with them.

"We've already identified Lavinia's body," Linda Shaw told them. "I don't see why this meeting is necessary."

Amelia put her arm around her mother. "Dad already explained everything to us in the car. We needed to make the trip here anyhow. They just want to ask a few questions."

"Now that your people have cut my daughter into pieces," Linda ground out, "will she be released today?"

"The coroner is getting the paperwork together now."

"Should we have a seat?" Ren asked.

"No," Linda said. "I'd rather stand."

"When was the last time anyone in the family talked to Lavinia?" Ren asked.

"I haven't talked to her in weeks." Linda raised her chin. "It works both ways. She could have called me at any time." Linda started to weep.

Gabe Shaw ushered his wife to the other side of the room and was talking to her a few feet away when Amelia said, "I'm sorry. She's not herself. I think she feels guilty."

Colin lifted an eyebrow. "Why would she feel guilty?"

"Lavinia blamed Mom for my brother Bryson's problems with drugs. My brother and sister were very close. When he moved to California to get away from everything, Lavinia followed soon after. A few months later, Bryson was arrested for drug dealing. It would be safe to say that our family dynamic has been in a steady decline since that time."

"I'm sorry," Colin said. "We want to catch whoever did this to Lavinia, and it would be helpful to know if she ever mentioned meeting anyone."

"The last time I talked to her was about ten days ago. She sounded excited about the way things were going. She was getting good grades, and she was hopeful that our brother would be released early for good behavior." Amelia sighed. "But she never mentioned meeting anyone."

"Did she ever talk to you about her work?"

"As a waitress? Yes. She said the tips were good." She paused. "Do you think she met her killer at work?"

Ren looked at Colin.

"Have you seen your brother since you arrived in California?" Colin asked.

"No. That won't be happening," Amelia said. "Not until he cleans up his act and moves back to New Jersey."

"Is there anything at all you can tell us about your sister that you think might help us?"

"Only that I'm surprised by the police report."

"Why is that?"

"Lavinia didn't trust anyone. In my mind she would be the last person to run off with a complete stranger. I mean, come on. I saw the crime scene pictures. I saw what she was wearing. That's not the sister I knew. She was very smart. But her killer was smarter. He must have taken his sweet time getting her to trust him enough to convince her to hang out with him at some abandoned barn." Amelia shook her head. "I just don't get it."

Colin handed her a business card. "If you think of anything at all that you believe might help us, I would appreciate a call."

"Sure." She took the card. "Have you talked to my brother about Lavinia?"

"I'll be seeing him in a few hours."

"Will you tell him hi for me and let him know I think about him all the time?"

"I will."

"I can't believe she's gone." She met Colin's gaze. "I hope you catch the bastard who killed my sister."

"I hope so, too."

———

At one o'clock that same day, Colin parked in front of Folsom Prison, which was surrounded by high walls constructed from hand-cut blue granite. He'd sent Ren back to the office to make calls and find out if they'd gotten back anything on the evidence collected at the scene.

Once inside the prison, Colin slipped his gun into a tray and emptied his pockets before signing in at the front desk. He then followed a security officer through a steel door, down a wide hallway, and into a large visitation room set up with tables and plastic chairs.

Lavinia Shaw's brother was low risk; therefore, Colin was able to meet with him in a room filled with relatives visiting their loved ones. Left to choose a table, he picked a spot at the back where it was reasonably quiet.

Five minutes later, the guard was pointing him out to a man in prison garb. Bryson Shaw was five foot ten, small boned, and had tattoos covering both arms. He sat down across from Colin and asked, "She's really dead?"

Colin nodded. "I'm sorry."

"I saw her a little over a week ago," Bryson said. "She was happy." He swallowed hard. "Where is she now? You know—her body?"

"She's at the morgue. Your family is there with her."

"*My* family?"

"Both of your parents and Amelia."

"How long have they been in California?"

"I'm not sure. A few days at least."

He shook his head. "They must really hate me if they couldn't even stop by to say hello to their only son."

"Amelia said she thinks of you often, and she asked me to say hello."

Bryson brushed both hands back and forth over his shaved head.

"Listen," Colin said, "I need your help. We don't have any suspects at this time. I need to know if Lavinia ever mentioned talking to a new male friend, or to anyone at all."

Bryson had his head down, but he began to tap the table. "Yes. Holy shit. She said she was going to meet with a photographer. I didn't like it, but she said there would be three other people there at least. God. That was a month ago when she told me that, maybe longer. I never gave it another thought. Fuck." He looked at Colin. "Do you think the photographer could be our guy?"

"He could be. But I need more than that. Did she mention a name? Do you know where she met him?"

Bryson clicked his teeth as he tried to think. Then he pointed a finger at Colin. "James Parry. That was his name. He would come to the bar to watch her dance."

"Any idea how long he'd been coming to the club where she worked?"

He rubbed his head again. "I should have asked more questions. I can't believe I didn't pay closer attention to what she was saying. I'm a selfish asshole, just like I've been told for most of my life."

"It's okay. You're doing great. Lavinia loved you, and she wouldn't want you to blame yourself for what happened."

Bryson was looking straight down again. It was obvious he was trying hard not to show any emotions. Inmates took a lot a shit for showing emotion.

"Do you recall your sister saying anything else? Long hair? Old, young?"

"Yeah, but she was just having a good laugh. She said something about the guy looking like that Boo character from her favorite book—*Mockingbird*—because the guy was big and sort of pale and dead-looking. Shit." Bryson shook his head again. "I didn't take her seriously, but God, anyone who looks dead can't be good."

Colin took notes, then waited to see if Bryson would come up with anything else. A few minutes passed before Bryson said, "That's all I've got. Sorry, man."

"You've been a big help."

"I don't know if I'll be able to go on, knowing she's not around. What's the fucking point?"

Colin instantly thought of an old college friend who had committed suicide. He'd been young and smart, and he could have done so many things with his life. "Do me a favor, Bryson."

"What's that?"

Colin stood, pulled out a card, and left it on the table in front of him. "When you get out of here, come see me, and we'll figure something out, okay?"

Bryson looked up at him and nodded. "Sure. Maybe I will."

SEVENTEEN

DEAN CRAWFORD

"I can't take much more of this. They're gonna kill me."

One of Dean Crawford's duties was to help rehabilitate the new offenders during their stay, aiding them in transitioning to prison life and then hopefully back into real life. But as he listened to poor Crazy Joe McCloskey, he realized the guy might be right. In his case it was probably only a matter of time before somebody stuck him with a shard of glass or a razor blade fastened at the end of a toothbrush. "What did you do this time, Joe?"

"Nothin', I swear." Joe used his forearm to wipe snot from his nose.

He'd been beaten up pretty badly. Both of his eyes were lined with shades of yellow, purple, and black. His nose was swollen and as purple as a plum. His eyes were so bloodshot it was a miracle he could see at all.

Crazy Joe McCloskey had pissed somebody off.

"Someone told Johnny what I was in for," he whined.

Dean opened his top drawer, grabbed two peppermints, and handed one to Crazy Joe. He watched Joe fumble with the wrapper before popping the candy into his mouth.

"We talked about that, Joe. I warned you to keep quiet or word would spread like wildfire. You might as well have stamped 'pedo' on your forehead."

"I only told Zander."

Dean shook his head.

"I'm thirty-three," Crazy Joe protested as if Dean could snap his fingers and make things right again. "I should be out there in the real world. The FBI tricked me. That's the only reason I'm doing time. It's against the law to be tricked like that."

Dean knew Crazy Joe just needed to vent, so he let him. "Somebody had to shut down the operation, Joe, and who better than the FBI?"

"But what they did wasn't fair. After the feds took control of the online forum, they kept it going, literally hosted child pornography on their servers." He stabbed a finger on Dean's desk. "That's not right. The FBI didn't just host the forum, they hacked into the computers of visitors to the site and got all those IP addresses, including mine."

Genius. Dean shrugged.

"Isn't that against the law?"

"I'm just a prison counselor. But you and I both know that the FBI's case against you and the other sixty-eight pedophiles caught in the operation was tossed by a federal judge."

"Yeah, but it still sucked. My family no longer talks to me."

"That was a sign, Joe."

"A sign?"

"That was your chance to change your ways. If you had stopped, you wouldn't be here now."

"It's not that easy."

Dean looked at his calendar. "Time's up, Joe. I've got my next appointment in five minutes."

"You can't just send me out there to die. All those agitators and dirty dogs are going to kill me."

"I'll see what I can do," Dean told him.

"Promise?"

"On my mother's grave."

Joe left, but before Dean could take a bathroom break, the guard led in Lou Wheeler, chains clanking.

"There's been a mix-up," Dean told the guard. "I'm supposed to meet with Michael Bowker in a few minutes. Sorry, Lou, but we'll have to chat next—"

"Bowker ain't feeling so well," Lou cut in, "so he told me to go ahead and take his time slot."

The guard nodded. "I confirmed it with the assistant warden before I brought him to you."

"Sure. Okay. Have a seat."

"Take the cuffs off?" the guard asked.

Dean didn't like having an inmate mess with his schedule. He stared long and hard at Lou before finally agreeing.

Lou wasn't easily intimidated. He didn't move a muscle.

Dean had seen evil in many forms, but there was something about Lou Wheeler that was disturbingly fascinating. The prisoner's dark, empty eyes looked right through him. The lines in Lou's face had multiplied since he'd seen him last. He wondered if the man ever slept. Lou Wheeler made Crazy Joe McCloskey look like a Boy Scout.

After the guard unfastened the cuffs and went to stand outside his office, Dean looked around for Lou's file before he realized he didn't have it since this meeting was unplanned. "I don't have your file with me, Lou, but if I recall, you were going to meet with your son, Ben." He folded his hands on the desk in front of him. "How did it go?"

"I wasn't impressed."

"Why not?"

"He's changed."

"In what way?"

"He talks too much. He's become a real good liar, too. Looked me right in the eyes and acted like he didn't remember a thing. He's perfectly happy to let his own father rot in prison for something he didn't do."

"Did you ask him about that?"

Lou glanced at the wall clock for the second time. "Yeah, sure I did, but I'm not here to talk about the boy."

Dean leaned back in his chair. "So what do you want to talk about, Lou?"

He looked over his shoulder at the guard, who was busy chatting it up with an inmate. Then he leaned over Dean's desk and said in a low voice, "I want out of here."

"That's not up to me."

A scar split right across one side of Lou's mouth, so when he smiled, it made him look even more demented. "After our first meeting, I asked around and heard some interesting stories about you."

Now that was a surprise. Dean lifted a brow. "About me?"

"Yeah. You."

The guard poked his head inside. "Five minutes."

Dean began stacking files.

Lou dropped a hand on top of the folders, stopping Dean from picking them up. "Five minutes is plenty of time," Lou told him. "Here's the deal. I'm going to give you two weeks to work your magic and get me the fuck out of this hellhole. If you do that, I won't tell the warden what I know."

Dean let out a ponderous sigh. Lou was losing his mind. "If I had your file here, I could read back some of Harrison's notes."

"Fuck Harrison."

"He said you were a pathological liar and often fantasized about killing prison staff."

"You think you have the warden tied around your little finger, don't you?"

"The clock is ticking, Lou. Why don't you give me a hint as to what you're talking about so I know what I'm dealing with here?"

Lou slowly traced the scar on his face as he said, "Think of the worst thing you've ever done, and then imagine the look on the warden's face when I tell him what you do in your free time."

Lou started coughing again, an ugly, rattling sound. Dean reached for a tissue before he realized Lou wasn't coughing, he was laughing.

"You're angry at the wrong person, Lou. I'm on your side."

Lou's eye twitched. "Two weeks."

Dean stared back at the man. "I think you should get some rest. I don't think it's advisable for you to be making threats."

"I've got the goods, Deanie Boy. That's all you need to know."

The guard came forward.

Dean shook his head. "You need to calm down, Lou. You need to let me help you."

Lou spat at him before he held his arms straight out and let the guard cuff him. "See you next week?"

"Sure. See you next week."

Eighteen

Ben

Ben pulled his van into the driveway of the home where he'd grown up. In his rearview mirror he saw Jessie pull up behind him. They had decided to take separate cars since she had errands to run after she left Clarksburg. Through the windshield he could see her talking on the phone. He wondered if it was the anonymous caller again.

Who would go out of their way to warn others about him? Why now? Then again, he thought, maybe somebody didn't like him stirring up the past.

Letting that go for now, he looked straight ahead and focused his attention on what was most likely the backdrop to many of Nancy's nightmares.

Set against a gloomy sky was an abandoned, run-down house half covered with overgrown bushes. The two-story structure looked beaten down by the harsh rays of the sun and neglect. The once-white wood siding was dirty and gray. Most of the windows were shattered.

He climbed out. Jessie caught up to him and walked by his side across dirt and weeds. The trees were bare, and the wind whistled through the branches as he approached the front entry.

It was strange seeing the house where he'd grown up and being unable to conjure any emotion whatsoever. If Nancy had never told him the truth about their pasts, would he be attempting to summon non-existent memories? Weren't most childhoods filled with days marked by children laughing, dogs barking, and Mom calling out to let them know dinner was ready?

Jessie quietly walked around the front of the property while he approached the door and turned the rusty knob. No key was needed, just a small push.

He left the door open and headed inside. The walls were streaked with black mold, and the corners and stair railings were laced with intricate cobwebs. Broken furniture, frayed and showing patches of mildew, piles of trash where squatters had once taken residence. Sections of the ceiling had water stains and sagged where the roof was too heavy. The air was stagnant.

The floors creaked beneath his feet. Jessie had followed him inside and moved on to the kitchen, where the refrigerator door hung limply from rusted hinges. Ben walked from room to room, the bad odor heavy and cloying. Every window in the place was framed with rotted wood. In some places the mildew patches had gotten so large they completely covered the old wallpaper still clinging to the walls.

He leaned low to better see into a dark hole where floorboards had once been. A scream caused him to nearly lose his balance. He ran to the kitchen, where he found Jessie sitting on the counter next to the sink, one hand on her chest. "I'm sorry," she said. "A rat caught me by surprise. I think there's a family of babies in that cupboard over there."

"I'm just relieved you're okay."

"Did you find anything of interest?" she asked.

"Nothing but abandoned mattresses, tattered blankets, and piles of trash." Through the window above the sink, he saw the backyard. There was no fence, and the wooded area behind a row of shrubs seemed to go on forever. To the far left was the slough, a backwater that led to the Sacramento River. "I'll be outside," he said.

He filled his lungs with fresh air as he walked across the yard, past the row of scraggly shrubs he'd seen from the kitchen window. Pines and oaks covered much of the property, leaving a soft, damp layer of leaves and pine needles on the ground.

He walked slowly, hoping something, anything, might stir an old memory, but his mind was blank, his memories a black hole.

Ten minutes passed before he saw thick branches fastened together with rope. From this distance it looked like a wooden raft leaning against the trunk of a tree. It was the lean-to that his sister had talked about. He couldn't believe it was still here after all this time.

He rushed forward. When he reached the area, he walked beneath the structure, impressed by its sturdiness. He dropped to his knees, sifted through dirt and leaves, looking for something, anything, that might trigger a memory or an emotion, but found nothing.

Fifteen minutes later he gave up and headed back toward the house.

Jessie caught up to him when she saw him approaching. "I'm afraid that house needs to be knocked down. It's infested with rats and who knows what else. Anything left inside should probably be burned."

He nodded as he turned toward the slough, where he could see a strip of blue. A breeze blew over his face. Everything smelled rich and earthy. He was about to tell Jessie about the lean-to when a searing pain struck his skull. He grasped both sides of his head, his eyes shut tight, and teeth clenched.

"Ben! What is it?"

Jessie's words were barely audible above the sizzling pop, pop, pop going off like firecrackers inside his brain. He let out a guttural roar. Someone grabbed his arm and shook him.

He opened his eyes and was shocked by what he saw. It was her.

Aly Scheer was standing right in front of him. She was alive, and she was young and beautiful, her face flushed from the sun. "I can't see you anymore," she said. "I'm sorry. I've been screwed up in the head for too long. I need to get clean."

He tilted his head, trying to decipher what she was telling him, but the words, or at least the meaning, didn't register.

"Are you listening, Ben?"

He rubbed his temple. "What are you trying to say?"

"I can't see you anymore. I'm sorry."

She couldn't leave him. She was the only person he'd ever wanted to spend time with. She understood him. She knew when he needed to be alone. She knew everything about him. "You can't do this."

"I have to."

His pulse raced. Why couldn't he stop the heavy pounding inside his head?

"Ben! Stop it!"

When his vision cleared, he was horrified to see his hands wrapped around Jessie's throat. She was slugging his arms with both fists when his hands dropped to his sides.

Jessie twisted around so that her back was to him as she caught her breath.

"I'm sorry. I'm so sorry." He looked around, confused by what he'd done. His heart was still racing. "Are you all right?"

She turned back to him. Her neck was red, and she was angry. Rightly so.

"What the hell just happened, Ben?"

"I don't know."

"Bullshit! Tell me!"

He briefly closed his eyes, and when he did, the young woman's image was right in front of him, clear as day. *Shit.* He took a breath, unable to rid himself of the lingering tension in his shoulders. "I saw her."

"Who?"

"Aly Scheer. I think Lou Wheeler was right about me. I think I killed her."

Her shoulders sank as she exhaled. "Oh, Ben."

Before either of them had a chance to say another word, a woman came around the side of the house, excitedly waving a hand above her head.

Jessie quickly zipped up her jacket to cover her throat. "It's Nikki Seymour," she told him. "The woman I told you about. She used to be your next-door neighbor."

"You should go," he told her. "You don't need to be involved in this craziness."

"Stop it," Jessie said. "I'll leave when the time is right. We'll talk about what happened later."

Nikki was slightly out of breath by the time she joined them. She looked Ben over from head to toe. "Ben Wheeler. I can't believe it." She threw herself at him and hugged him tightly around the waist. Awkward didn't begin to describe how he felt, inside and out.

When she stepped back, she must have noticed his confusion. "I heard about the accident. You don't remember me, do you?"

"No. But Jessie filled me in on your conversation, and I appreciate your willingness to help me out."

"I'm glad to." She glanced at the house. "Mom said she saw two people over here, and since your cars were in the driveway, I thought I'd come and check out what was going on. Have you already been inside?"

"Not a pretty picture," Jessie answered.

"No kidding. We had problems for years with people illegally inhabiting the place. Mom used to call the police at least once a week, and the squatters would clear out for a while. But they always came back . . . until a few years ago when the rats took over."

The way the woman kept looking at him, peering deep into his eyes as if she knew his secrets, made Ben uncomfortable.

"I was just getting ready to head off," Jessie told her. "I have a few things to do before it gets dark."

"Well, then, I'm glad I caught you before you left." Again, she looked at Ben. "Do you remember Caleb Duberry? High school English teacher?" She swiped her hand through the air as if to erase what she'd just said. "Of course you don't. Long story short, earlier today I ran into one of my teachers from high school, and I mentioned you. She told me that Caleb Duberry had taken a special interest in you back then. He's nearing seventy now. She told me he would be thrilled to know what became of you." Nikki looked at Jessie. "I thought you or Ben might want to pay him a visit and see what he has to say."

"Does he live around here?" Ben asked.

"Less than ten minutes away. Here," Nikki said, handing him a piece of paper. "I wrote the address down for Jessie, but I might as well give it to you."

Nineteen

Jessie

Jessie walked with Ben and Nikki to the front of Ben's childhood home, then said goodbye, giving Ben and Nikki a chance to talk in private.

As she drove along South River Road, she unzipped her jacket and put a hand to her neck. Her throat was sore. The entire episode had left her feeling incredibly sad. Also angry and confused. All he wanted was to know the truth. For the first time since meeting Ben, though, she realized she had no idea who he really was. Her hands were trembling.

She pulled over to the side of the road, rolled down the window, and yelled, "Fuck!" *Damn it, Ben. What the hell is going on?* She rubbed her temple and counted to five before she felt a bit calmer. Despite her sudden wariness, she wasn't sure whether she was ready to give up on him. If she decided to continue with the investigation, though, she would do it solo. There was no other way.

Hoping to get her mind off Ben, she turned on the radio. She would stick with the plan, which was to visit her good friend, Andriana, whom she hadn't seen in a while. And besides, she wanted to talk to her about Olivia babysitting Dylan on Friday night.

Forty minutes later, Jessie pulled up in front of Andriana's house just as a man she didn't recognize climbed into the driver's seat of a white Ford Escape parked in the driveway and drove off. The windows were tinted, but she'd taken note of his dark wool coat and the silver hair at his temples.

Interesting.

She had assumed Andriana needed a babysitter because she was going out with her coworkers, but now she wondered if she was mistaken. Before exiting the car, she used the rearview mirror to take a look at her neck. There were no marks, and it was only slightly tender to the touch.

Jessie headed up the walkway and knocked on the door. When Andriana opened it, her face was flushed. The excited look in her eyes disappeared the moment she realized it was Jessie.

"Sorry to disappoint."

Andriana laughed. "What's wrong? You look upset."

"I'm fine. But I could use a cup of coffee or maybe hot tea."

"You never stop, do you?"

Jessie shrugged.

"Come inside," Andriana said with a wave of her hand.

Jessie followed her through the small foyer to the kitchen, where she took a seat on a stool in front of the high granite counter. "Where's Dylan?"

"Upstairs playing video games. He's allotted one hour every day after school."

"So who was that guy who just left?" Jessie asked as Andriana filled a kettle with water and placed it on the stove to heat up.

"Vince Croal, a nice man. A doctor, in fact."

Jessie's thoughts kept diverting back to the look on Ben's face when he'd wrapped his fingers around her throat. At first he'd had a blank look as if whatever he was seeing or hearing wasn't making sense. And then his lip had curled, and his body had tensed as he'd reached for her. She'd had no idea what he was doing until it was too late to back away.

"Earth to Jessie," Andriana said with a laugh. "What's going on inside that mind of yours? Busy week, I take it."

"It's Ben."

"Is he still living in your office?"

She nodded.

"What's the problem, exactly?"

Jessie shook her head. "He's still having flashbacks, and he doesn't have any idea if what he's seeing is from his past or possibly just images from crime scenes. He's just so conflicted. Anyway, I don't want to get into it now. Tell me more about your doctor."

"There's not much to tell. We met at the ATM. He made me laugh. I was intrigued, and so was he, apparently, because he asked me to have coffee with him. We talked for nearly an hour." Andriana smiled. "He made me forget that I needed to get to work."

"Wow," Jessie said. "You hate being late for work."

"Yeah. Maybe he's the one."

Jessie smiled. "So he works at the hospital?"

"He has a private practice somewhere in Sacramento. Tomorrow night will be my first *official* date with the man. Hopefully I'll get more details then."

"I did want to talk to you about Olivia watching Dylan tomorrow night."

"That's not a problem, is it?" Her shoulders sagged. "She told me you gave her permission."

"I did, but I just want to make sure we're on the same page."

Andriana laughed. "Wow, you really are a worrywart, aren't you?"

Jessie frowned.

"I'm sorry. Babysitting is a big responsibility. I get that." Andriana opened a drawer and pulled out a list of phone numbers, along with instructions for what to do in case of fire or any other emergency. "I've had a few kids Olivia's age watch Dylan over the years. This isn't my first rodeo. She'll be fine."

"I'll be doing surveillance tomorrow night, so I won't be home," Jessie told her.

"We're going to dinner and a movie. If she needs me, I'll be a few miles away at any given time."

Jessie knew Andriana was right. She needed to chill. Olivia was fifteen. She had a good head on her shoulders. Everything would be fine.

Andriana placed a mug of hot tea in front of her. "How's everything with you and Colin?"

"Colin who?" Jessie snorted. "He's busy with another homicide."

"I heard about it on the local news. Poor girl. She came to Sacramento so she could visit her brother in prison on a regular basis. She was putting herself through school, and she had big plans. But then she makes a fatal mistake by going off with a stranger."

"Very sad."

"Yeah," Andriana said. "Enough of that. I was hoping you and Colin would be married by now with a baby on the way."

Jessie sipped her tea. "I don't know if babies are in my future. I can hardly handle one teenager, a dog, and a one-eyed cat."

"What about Gus? Did something happen?"

"The hamster is fine."

"I'm not saying it's easy," Andriana went on, "but I'd like to have more children. Sooner rather than later," she added with a wink.

Jessie smiled.

"I'm going to check on Dylan," Andriana told her. "I'll be right back."

Jessie nodded, her mind already back on work. As to Ben's past, she would focus her investigation on Aly Scheer. Who was she? Whether or not Ben and Aly were dating when she was murdered seemed to be a moot point. All evidence pointed to Ben's father being responsible for her death.

And Jessie's goal was to dig deeper into Ben's past and find out more about him, which meant she wanted to talk to members of Aly's family to see if they could shed any light on the matter of Ben Wheeler.

And what was the deal with Nikki Seymour's mother? Jessie hadn't thought it would be a good idea to visit the woman while Ben was with her. But she did plan to visit Nikki's mother sooner rather than later since she was curious to know why the woman was still so afraid of Lou and Ben Wheeler after all these years.

TWENTY

BEN

Ben wasn't ready to leave Clarksburg. He drove to Delta High School on Netherlands Road and walked around. The white building with its tile roof, flagpole, and palm trees did nothing to help trigger old memories. Back in the van, he used the navigation app on his phone to get to Caleb Duberry's house on Willow Point Road. The house was small, set far back on the property and partially hidden behind weeping willows. He parked his van and sat silently for a moment, overwhelmed by the twists and turns his life had taken recently.

He missed his wife and kids. And yet how could he make a promise to his wife that he could not keep? And Abigail's coach wasn't the only reason he wanted to keep some distance from his family. Listening to his father's hateful words and then seeing the fear in his sister's eyes had taken a toll on him. What if the hallucinations and flashbacks were from his past? As long as he had doubts about who he was, he couldn't put his family in danger by moving back home.

And now Jessie.

How could he forgive himself for what had happened less than an hour ago? She had pulled herself together quickly after Nikki Seymour had shown up. But Ben wasn't sure how he and Jessie could continue to work together. It pained him to think he might be a danger to her.

When he'd been standing in the backyard of his childhood home, the smell of the slough had awakened something within him. And then Jessie had spoken to him, and when he turned her way, Jessie had been gone, and Aly Scheer had stood in her place. When Aly announced she was leaving him, his lungs had constricted, and the heartache had felt intense. In the blink of an eye, though, the anguish had turned to rage. His vision had clouded, and his pulse had raced. Suddenly he'd been back in time, not watching the scene play out but reliving the moment from his past.

If not for the painful cries in the distance—Jessie's cries—he wasn't sure what would have happened. It frightened him beyond measure to think he might have once been the awful person Nancy had talked about.

As soon as he returned to Jessie's office, he would gather his things and leave. She didn't need to be dragged even deeper into his messy and complicated life. At the moment he needed to concentrate on why he'd come to Clarksburg in the first place. He needed answers. Mostly he needed to remember, once and for all, the person he used to be.

His knee ached as he stepped out of the van and followed a gravel path to the front entry of the teacher's home. Ben knocked on the door, his body tense as he waited. If he was even half the monster everyone made him out to be, he needed to be ready to have the door slammed in his face.

The man who greeted him was short and round. Before Ben could introduce himself, the man smiled up at him, his blue eyes twinkling. "Ben," he said. "What a wonderful surprise."

Ben instantly choked up. He came from a family of psychopaths. He was quite possibly a monster. And yet this man seemed genuinely happy to see him. He swallowed the knot lodged in his throat and managed to find his voice. "Although it's wonderful to see a friendly face, I wish I could say I remember you. I was in an accident—"

The man raised a hand. "Stop right there. I've been keeping track of you since you left Clarksburg. I know you changed your name, put yourself through college, and became a crime reporter for the *Sacramento Tribune*. I've read every one of your columns and stories. I know about the accident, too." He offered his hand, and Ben shook it. "Caleb Duberry," the man said happily. "Nice to meet you again. Do you have a moment to come in for a beer and a chat?"

"I don't drink," Ben said. "But I'd love a cup of coffee if you have any."

"Do you like it black?"

"That would be great."

The interior of the house was cluttered yet cozy. Doilies yellow with age covered nearly every tabletop, and the family pictures on the wall were tilted every which way. When they finally sat down to talk, Ben learned that Mrs. Duberry had passed away two years before Caleb retired. To keep busy, he tutored kids three nights a week and on weekends.

Mr. Duberry invited Ben to have a seat at the kitchen table. He made Ben a cup of instant coffee and opened a beer for himself. "You don't remember me," Caleb said after he took a seat across from Ben, "and yet you came out of your way to see me. Something tells me you might have questions."

"I do."

"Then go ahead and ask."

"I guess you could say I'm trying to figure out who I used to be. For instance, I've been told that I was quiet and I tended to keep to myself."

"You were both of those things," Caleb said with a laugh. "But it didn't bother me. In fact, the quieter you became, the more I talked." Another guffaw. "I don't think you minded, either, because you would spend an hour, sometimes longer, in my classroom every day after school." He paused, and some of the excitement in his voice waned. "You were lonely, Ben. You just didn't know how to express yourself." He set his beer on the table and leaned forward, his eyes boring into Ben's as if he could will him to remember. "Do you have any memories at all of your parents?"

"No. I only learned recently that Lou is still alive. I went to see him at Folsom Prison, and he didn't have any kind words for me."

"Hmm. Still the same. I tried to talk to your mother and father a few times, but it didn't go well."

Ben said nothing, but he could imagine.

"Why do you seek answers now after all this time?"

"Well, after the accident I married the nurse who took care of me. It might sound mushy, but it was love at first sight. We have two children, Abigail and Sean, and I can honestly say that I am an incredibly lucky man. My family means the world to me, which is the real reason why I've come to Clarksburg." Ben fidgeted in his seat, not really sure where to start. "Recently I've begun to have flashbacks of people and events I don't remember. The majority of images that randomly come to mind are morose if not downright gruesome."

"You were reporting on crimes years before the accident," Caleb said. "Your writing has always been very detailed. When I would read your reporting of an incident, it was brilliant the way you seemed to anticipate the questions your readers would ask next." He put his hands together. "You've always made me so proud."

"Thank you," Ben managed. "You sound like my wife."

He smiled. "I would love to meet her someday."

"Melony would enjoy that, I'm sure."

It was quiet for a moment before Caleb asked, "So why do I sense so much sadness? Because of the flashbacks and your father's harsh words, you are having doubts as to who you used to be?"

"The flashbacks, and maybe the run-in I had with the Heartless Killer, triggered something within me, a need to find out who I really am." Ben paused for a moment. "I'm sorry to be so frank. I feel like you're a stranger, but you look at me like you know me better than my sister knew me. And I just need any help I can get. That day, the day I found the murderer torturing my friends, well, it gave me an incredible rage. A rage that still bubbles inside of me. When I took his life, when he took his last breath, I felt a sense of release. But now, looking back, I have come to realize that whether that man lived or died was not my decision to make."

Caleb Duberry sipped his beer, seemingly deep in thought as if he were carefully assessing everything he'd just heard. It was easy for Ben to see why he would have gravitated to the man when he was younger.

After a long moment, Caleb set his beer on the table again and said matter-of-factly, "It sounds to me as if you are on a quest to find out whether or not you're capable of murder."

Ben's insides twisted at the idea that he could be read so easily. "It's worse than that," Ben told him. "I need to know if I *am* a cold-blooded killer and whether or not I'm a danger to my family."

"You were an odd kid, there's no doubt about it," Caleb said. "Your size alone intimidated kids *and* adults. But I'm going to tell you a story, Ben, and I want you to listen closely. It was a Wednesday evening. I was done grading papers for the night and walking across the parking lot when I saw a young boy, maybe ten or eleven, shouting and waving his arms above his head, trying to get my attention. He said Bobby Fleischman was drowning in the river. The boy and I jumped in my car, and by the time I got to the edge of the river, you were in the water, trying your best to save the boy. The problem was Bobby was as big as you. He played football, and he was dragging you down with him."

Ben felt a strange tug. He was in the water, and he was being pulled under. The agony of not being able to pull air into his lungs was real.

"Ben," Caleb asked, "are you all right?"

Ben snapped out of it, but the flashback or whatever the hell that was threw him off a bit. For a few seconds he'd gone back to that moment in time. He met Caleb's gaze. "I'm fine. What happened next?"

"The kid who found me said he saw Bobby's boat capsize, and when he realized Bobby couldn't swim, he ran to find help. By the time I jumped into the river, you had managed to get close enough for me to pry Bobby's arms from around your neck and shoulders. It took every bit of strength I had to get him off you so we could both drag him out of the water."

Ben sucked in a breath as if he'd just climbed out of the river himself.

"Guess what the headlines said the next morning?" He didn't wait for Ben to answer before he said, "'*Caleb Duberry, English Teacher, Saves Bobby Fleischman from Drowning.*' I tried to set people straight, but nobody wanted to believe that Lou Wheeler's son saved anyone, let alone their star football player." Caleb straightened. "So my advice to you is to stop worrying about your past. Whatever evil you think is lurking within is just plain bull. I saw you save that boy with my own eyes. You could have died that day. You, Ben Morrison, are not a danger to your family."

TWENTY-ONE
COLIN

Colin stood at the front of the room for the debriefing. Seven officers, including Ren, were present.

"So far we know our suspect is a tall man, over six feet," Colin began. "Caucasian, with no facial hair. Bill Matthews doesn't see well, and the barn was dark. When the intruder ran, our suspect's head was covered. The Lavinia Shaw case is getting cold fast, so anything you got, let's throw it out there."

"There were no ligature marks on her wrists or arms," a detective leaning against the wall pointed out. "How did the killer put the rope around her neck and then get back to the car? She would have had plenty of time to remove the ropes."

"Maybe she was already dead and lying on the ground when the killer got into the car and put it in reverse," another officer suggested.

Ren shook his head. "Bill Matthews saw Lavinia kicking her legs while she was in the air. She was still alive."

They all threw out ideas that mostly went nowhere.

"What about the hairs found on the rope?" Colin asked.

Tom, sitting at the front, raised his hand before saying, "Two hairs belonged to the victim. The rest were all animal hairs."

Ren stood and asked Colin if it was all right if he came to the front of the room to talk.

Colin nodded.

Ren walked to the board where Colin had made notes. He pinned two pictures of shoe prints that were found at the scene. "Size twelve," Ren told the group. "That's not out of the norm for a man over six feet, but what is unusual is the outsole. Look at the thickness on the right shoe. It's an inch thicker. I faxed these prints to more than one shoe company, and I was told the difference in outsoles from the left foot to the right means our guy most likely has a leg discrepancy. He wears custom shoes with a heel and sole lift, like for someone with one leg shorter than the other." Ren frowned. "Unfortunately, it could take a while to match this particular shoe to one of the many custom shoe stores online."

Colin added "uneven gait" to their suspect's description, then looked at Ren and said, "Good work."

After Ren took a seat, Colin talked about the fact that there were no tire tracks found at the scene and that Bill Matthews had shot at the man as he ran toward the American River, which meant he either swam or he had a boat waiting for him. "Leo," he called out. "You said you spent a couple of days on the river. Any luck?"

"Not so far. As we talked about earlier, I'm concentrating on the North Fork area of the river before the water runs into Folsom Lake. The North Fork is eighty-eight miles. We're concentrating on a five-mile stretch, lots of wooded area and places to stash a boat, if that's what our suspect did. There's also a pathway for bikes. Maybe someone saw him stash his boat. Because of the time of day, someone could have spotted him. I'll be back on the river today."

"Good work, everyone. Keep at it, and we'll reconvene tomorrow." Colin returned to his office, Ren hot on his trail. "What is it?"

"There's a murderer running around here, and we've got nothing."

Colin sat down at his desk, trying to get a handle on his day, but Ren wasn't done venting.

"How do you do this day after day?"

"Easy," Colin said. "I always remember the victim. I always think, what if it were my sister or mother?"

Ren nodded his understanding.

"I meant to ask earlier, did you find anything on James Parry, the name Lavinia gave her brother?"

"So far, no luck. The only James Parry in the area is a ninety-year-old man living in an assisted-living facility."

Colin met Ren's gaze. "Anything else you want to talk about?"

"No. I'm good."

"If we stay focused and use all of our resources," Colin told him, "I think we'll get this guy."

Ren nodded as he rubbed the back of his neck. "Thanks."

"For what?"

"For your patience, and for being my mentor."

Colin had been right about the kid. He'd just needed a little guidance along with a nudge. It was moments like this that made it all worth it. "You're welcome."

TWENTY-TWO

ZEE

Zee waited in one of three chairs lining the wall of the salon reception area until Diane Scott came looking for her. "Zee Gatley," she called out.

"That's me," Zee said, trying to hide her surprise when she noticed that Diane looked ten years older and forty pounds heavier than in the picture Easton Scott had shown her on the day he'd walked into Jessie's office and left a deposit.

Zee wasn't fond of touching people, but she shook Diane's hand when it was offered. When it came to being a detective, Zee knew it was important to not stand out in the crowd.

She followed Diane to a small space with a chair, a sink, and a big fat mirror right in front of her. As the woman pushed her fingers through Zee's hair, she took a good long look at her. In Zee's opinion, Diane was a natural beauty. Not even an extra chin could distract from flawless skin, high cheekbones, and full lips. Diane's eyes were leafy green, and they sparkled when she looked right at Zee.

"Thank you for squeezing me in," Zee told her. Niceties did not come naturally to her, but she'd been practicing. With a little more effort, especially now that the voices in her head were on sabbatical, she realized she might get good at this being-normal thing.

"How do you want your hair cut?"

Shit. Zee hadn't thought about that. She looked at her reflection in the mirror. "I don't know. You're the pro. What do you think?"

Diane looped her fingers through Zee's hair and flipped it about, examining the strands in the same way Zee studied her tarot cards.

"It's dry and too long, in my opinion. I suggest we part it right down the middle and cut it shoulder length. You could also use a good conditioning, too, which we can do before you go."

"That sounds good. And how about some blue dye on the ends?" Zee asked after she looked around and admired the blue tints on the woman across the way.

Zee didn't like being around so many strangers, so she stared into the mirror for the next fifteen minutes while Diane mixed her color in the back room. By the time Diane returned and started doing her thing with color and foils, Zee racked her brain trying to think of something to talk about. "Watch any good movies lately?"

"No. How about you?"

"No."

"Do you play a musical instrument?"

Diane smiled. "I don't. You?"

"No."

Shit. Forget about being normal. She sucked at normal. Her whole body felt stiff and uncomfortable. Just holding her head up straight and not moving felt like a huge chore. She never should have made an appointment. Again she thought of Lucy, Marion, and Francis and wondered where the hell they were. She was beginning to feel a little lost without them. Ridiculous. They were mean and troublesome. She could do this. She just needed to think a little harder. "Do you like doing hair?"

"I hate it," Diane blurted out.

"Oh."

"I'm kidding. That was a joke."

"Oh. Ha. I get it."

The next twenty minutes felt like hours before Diane led her to a low-lit room with soft music playing to give the color time to take hold. Zee pulled out her phone, checked her social media, and played sudoku, and when that began to bore the shit out of her, she picked up a magazine and flipped through a ridiculous number of glossy ads. There wasn't one article worth reading until she flipped to the next page.

Why Do People Get Married?

That's it! This would be the perfect opener to start a conversation. Maybe Diane would talk about her marriage to Easton.

Zee flattened the crease so that the magazine would stay on that particular page.

"Okay," Diane said when she reappeared. "Let's get your hair washed and cut."

After her hair was washed, Zee stared blindly at her reflection while she wriggled the magazine in her lap, hoping Diane would see what the article was about.

No such luck. She was all about the hair. Snip. Snip. Snip.

"While I was waiting for the color in my hair to set, I read this article about why people get married."

For the first time since she'd shaken Diane's hand, the woman frowned. "Why do they?"

It took Zee a few seconds to remember what she'd read. "Companionship, romance, emotional reasons, I guess."

"Are you married?" Diane asked.

"Oh, fuck no. Sorry. I had a boyfriend, but that didn't turn out well at all."

"Probably for the better."

"Definitely." She didn't bother telling Diane that the weirdo had ended up being a lunatic who'd locked her in his basement.

"A better article would be five reasons *not* to get married," Diane said.

"What would be the reasons?"

"People change. Not every woman can get pregnant at the drop of a hat. And telling someone they're fat just makes them want to eat more."

"That's three," Zee said. "What would the other two reasons be?"

"Weddings are a lot of work, and being a wife sucks."

"Hmm. I'll have to remember that next time some random dude asks me to be his wife."

Diane's smile was back. She grabbed a round brush and a blow-dryer, and when she was finished, Zee looked at her reflection and wondered when she'd gotten so beautiful.

Twenty-Three

Olivia Cole

Olivia rolled her eyes when Andriana began to go over telephone numbers and people to call for the second time.

"We've been through this," Olivia said. "I can read. What am I going to do with Dylan's health insurance records?"

"You never know," Andriana said. "I just want you to know it's here."

"You sound like Aunt Jessie."

Andriana shook a finger at her. "Watch your tongue."

They both got a laugh out of that.

A knock on the door got Andriana moving again. She grabbed her coat and purse and rushed to the front entry. When she opened the door, Olivia did her best to get a good look at the man, since Jessie had told her the relationship was all very mysterious and she wanted a full accounting when Olivia returned home.

He was about the same height as Colin. His dark hair was streaked with silver. She couldn't make out the color of his eyes, not until he stepped inside and said, "Who have we got here?"

It was instantaneous. Olivia didn't like him. The way he was looking at her made her uncomfortable, but she wasn't sure why, exactly. Just kinda creepy.

"This is Olivia Cole, my best friend's niece. And this is Dylan," she said when he snuck a peek from the other room.

A low growl caught Olivia off guard. "Higgins," she said, pointing a finger toward the living room. "Go back to your bed."

Vince got down on a knee and tried to coax Higgins to come to him, but Higgins wasn't having it. Vince straightened. "I didn't know you had a dog."

"I don't. My friend insisted Olivia bring Higgins with her. He's a great watchdog." Andriana flashed Vince a wide smile. "Ready to go?"

"In one moment," he said, his gaze back on Olivia. "So what's the going rate these days?"

Olivia lifted her chin. "I'm glad you asked. I looked up the most recent babysitter survey online, and the average hourly rate for babysitters nationally is thirteen dollars and ninety-seven cents."

Andriana's mouth dropped open.

"That's nearly double the federal minimum wage," Vince said.

Olivia nodded. "That's correct. Up twenty-six percent from the average six years ago. I can take my dog and go if you two would rather cook up something here at home?"

Andriana crossed her arms and gave Olivia one of her signature looks that was supposed to scare her but only made her want to laugh.

"You are a shrewd one, aren't you," Vince stated.

Olivia shrugged.

"We'll make it an even fourteen dollars an hour," Andriana told her. "How does that sound?"

"Great. Have a good time," Olivia said as she headed back to the main room, already calculating how much money she would have saved after tonight.

TWENTY-FOUR

JESSIE

Jessie hardly recognized Zee when she walked into the office. "Wow! Look at you."

"I got a new 'do.'"

"I can see that."

"Guess who my stylist was?"

"John Frieda," Jessie teased.

Zee made a face. "John who?"

"Never mind. It was a joke."

"Well, this is no laughing matter. Diane Easton, Scott's wife, did my hair."

"The woman I'm paying you to watch cut and colored your hair?"

"Yep."

Jessie inwardly counted to three.

"What's wrong?" Zee asked.

"Private eyes are supposed to be discreet. We do surveillance from a car blocks away using binoculars for a reason. You don't think she's going to recognize you tomorrow or the next day, sitting in the car across the street with your dark hair and blue tips?"

"Hmm. That's a very good point." Zee waved a hand through the air, dismissing Jessie's concerns. "I'll trade cars with my dad and wear a hat and sunglasses. Besides, wait until I tell you what she said."

The girl could be exasperating. Jessie shut her computer, grabbed her things, and said, "You can tell me on our way to Scott and Diane's house."

"Why so early?"

"I want to get situated before she gets home and make sure nobody is in the car with her."

"What's in the bag?" Zee wanted to know.

"Sandwiches. A chickpea salad sandwich for you and a Portobello mushroom sandwich for me."

"Are you going vegan?"

"Nope. I didn't want to go to two places to grab dinner, and I knew you would starve before you'd eat meat."

"Or anything with eggs, dairy products, and all other animal-derived ingredients," Zee said as she followed Jessie out the door.

"I thought you said you were a Seagan and you ate fish?"

"Not anymore."

"Good to know."

It was six o'clock. Before Zee had walked into the office, Jessie had called Olivia to see how the babysitting was going. Olivia did not like being checked up on and had made it clear she would call her if there were any problems. In other words, *Don't call again.*

Jessie hopped into her Jeep Grand Cherokee, started the engine, then plugged in Diane Scott's East Sacramento address while Zee got situated in the passenger seat. Five minutes into their drive, Zee cut into the blissful silence. "You're frowning," Zee said. "A little uptight because Olivia is babysitting, huh?"

"How did you know she was babysitting?"

"We're friends. It's called texting."

Jessie already regretted bringing Zee along. "Remind me why I agreed to let you come with me tonight."

"Because I need to learn the ropes in case I ever decide to start my own PI agency."

Jessie shook her head. "Ahh. Yes. I remember now. Why don't you tell me about Diane? What did you two talk about while you were having your hair done?"

"It started out awkward, but then while the color was setting, or whatever, I found an article about why people get married. The perfect conversation starter! When I showed it to her, though, she got sort of tense and said a more helpful article would have been about all the reasons *not* to get married."

"She said that?"

"Yep."

"Did she elaborate?"

"Yep."

Jessie waited. "What did she say?"

"Oh, um, something about it not being easy to get pregnant, and when someone tells you you're fat, it just makes you want to eat more; weddings are overrated; and being a wife sucks."

"Wow. She doesn't sound as if she's happily married."

"No. I could tell from the picture Easton Scott showed me in the office that she's gained some weight since the photo was taken, but who wouldn't run for the doughnuts if someone was always making comments about your weight?"

"True. Anything else? Did you happen to find an article on cheating?"

"No," Zee said, "But that would have been the clincher, don't you think?"

"Yeah. I do."

Jessie parked a few blocks away from the house on H Street, a charming two-story Tudor with lots of floor-to-ceiling windows. "Once Diane returns home"—Jessie glanced at the time—"which you said is usually around seven, we'll move the car closer and then settle in until we see any activity, if at all."

It was getting dark at seven fifteen when Zee saw Diane's Honda Civic approaching. She appeared to be alone. Jessie noted the time on her surveillance log. The garage door opened, and a few minutes later lights came on inside the house. The curtains were sheer. A plus since it made it easy to see Diane's silhouette.

The next few hours passed quietly. Zee was surprisingly professional, asking all the right questions. She was serious about her work.

At nine o'clock a dark SUV pulled to the curb half a block away. Jessie didn't think much of it until she saw the man look around before jogging across the street and maintaining a fast pace toward Diane's house.

"Get down low," Jessie told Zee, "and take pictures if you can get a clean shot."

Click. Click. Click.

Thirty minutes ago, Zee had moved to the back seat so she could stretch her legs. She had the camera, and she didn't waste a second getting the shots.

Jessie made a few quick notes in her logbook. She'd gotten good at writing blindly. Sometimes she used a recorder, but not tonight. She picked up a pair of low-light binoculars and focused on the man as he made his way up the walkway to the house. He had a short and stocky frame. He wore crisp denim pants and a dark shirt beneath a zippered jacket. His hair was thinning around a bald spot. The second he reached the door, it opened, and he disappeared inside.

Jessie looked over her shoulder when she heard the back door open. "What are you doing?"

"I'll be right back," Zee said. "I'm going to get a picture of his car and the license plate. Don't worry; I'll be stealthy. Nobody will know what I'm doing."

Zee didn't shut the door all the way. When she returned, she opened her laptop and started typing. A few minutes later, Zee said, "The car belongs to a Luke Young, a car salesman for Subaru."

Jessie's pulse raced. She wasn't sure why, since she'd been doing surveillance for more than a decade. It was the infidelity part that bothered her. Each to their own and all that, except she didn't like being a part of it. Her insides turned. She'd taken the money and run, and now she would have to live with it.

"I feel sorry for Easton," Zee said as she unwrapped her sandwich.

"Yeah, me too."

"What's next?" Zee took a bite of her sandwich.

"Now we wait to see if he spends the night or if they have plans to go out."

"We already have proof that they're hanging out."

"It's not enough. We need to catch them holding hands or kissing. If he doesn't leave until morning, that works, too."

The smell of Zee's food made her hungry. She removed the wrapper from her mushroom sandwich and took a bite, surprised by how good it tasted. She hadn't realized how hungry she was until she finished the sandwich within minutes.

It was close to ten thirty when Jessie looked in the rearview mirror and noticed Zee texting. "Have you heard from Olivia?"

"Yep."

"And?"

"She's fine. The kid she's watching fell asleep early."

"Thanks for the update."

"No problem."

Jessie looked through her own messages and saw a text from Colin. Dinner next week? Olivia texted me to let me know she's in the babysitting business. I'll bring Piper.

Jessie smiled. Olivia would be thrilled to have a chance to watch Colin's ten-year-old daughter. She was about to text back when she heard a loud crash.

Zee had her face pressed against the window facing Diane's house. "What was that?"

"You stay here. Have the camera ready in case you see anybody coming or going. I'm going to take a quick look around." She zipped up her jacket and headed out.

Zee

Zee watched Jessie disappear down the driveway to the left of the house. As she readied the camera, an ear-piercing scream came from inside Diane's house.

Zee tossed the camera to the side and jumped out of the car. She had taken off her jacket and shoes earlier since they had no plans to leave the vehicle. She stubbed her toe on the way up the path to the door. Heart racing, she looked around. No sign of Jessie.

Another loud noise sounded from within—a heavy object smashing against the floor. Something was going on, and it was enough to prompt Zee to try the door. The handle felt loose, the lock flimsy. The door jiggled but wouldn't open.

At that same moment, Jessie came running around to the front. She was out of breath. "We've got to get in there." She stepped in front of Zee and knocked on the door, then rang the bell.

Somebody inside the house shouted for help.

Zee backed up and asked Jessie to move aside. When Jessie was out of the way, Zee threw her full weight against the door. Bits of wood splintered, and the door swung inward and hit the wall.

Jessie went in first. Zee followed close behind.

A tall dark figure stepped into the hallway. For half a second he merely stood there, his face disfigured and difficult to see through the hosiery stretched over his head. Before she could examine him further, he charged right at them, pushing Jessie into Zee. They tumbled to the floor, but Jessie was quick as a cat and back on her feet before Zee could sit up, let alone think straight.

"Call for help!" Jessie shouted as she ran out the door after the guy.

Zee had hit her head on the wall before landing on the floor. Her mind was hazy. What the hell had just happened? Was that Luke Young Jessie was running after?

Zee realized she was white-knuckling her phone.

She pushed herself to her feet. Without thinking about whether to call the police or 9-1-1, she hit the button for Colin Grayson since he was on speed dial. He picked up just as she got to the end of the hallway and stepped into a bedroom to the right.

"Oh my God," Zee said.

"Who is this?" Colin asked.

There was blood everywhere. Blood on the lampshade, the walls, the bed, the rug, the hardwood floor—puddles of it. She continued on, farther inside. Between the bed and windows overlooking the backyard was a man. Luke Young was naked, face up, eyes wide open. She didn't want to do it, but she knew she had to. She leaned over and felt for a pulse. He was dead.

"What is going on?" Colin asked, his voice a cross between frantic and annoyed.

What the hell are you doing, Zee? Get out of there now!

No. Stay. You need to talk to the man on the phone!

"Colin," Zee said, more surprised by the tremor in her voice than by the fact that the voices in her head were back in full force.

"Zee?"

"Hold on. I hear something." She followed the strangled sound across the room and into the bathroom. It was Diane. She was a bloody mess. One of her legs was twisted behind her in a horrible fashion.

Jessie had gone after a madman.

"Jessie might be in trouble," she said as she stepped toward Diane. "This isn't like the last time I called you. It's bad, Colin. Really bad."

"Snap out of it, Zee, and give me an address."

She'd been watching the house and the salon for two days. She knew the address by heart and rattled it off. "We need an ambulance."

She left her phone on the bathroom counter and sat down on the ground next to Diane so she could lift her head onto her lap. Diane opened her eyes and stared blankly at the ceiling. Her pretty hair was now matted against her head. Her nose was swollen to double its size, and there were scratches all over her face. "It's me, Zee Gatley," she said. But the woman didn't move or say a word. Just stared.

One of Diane's arms was twisted awkwardly behind her back. She had so many cuts on her body that it was impossible to figure out the extent of her injuries.

The only thing Zee knew was that this wasn't good.

For the first time in quite possibly her entire life, Zee didn't know what to do. There was so much blood, so many wounds. Where should she start?

She reached for a towel, ripped it from the rack, then used it to cover as much of Diane's body as she could. She was probably cold.

"Help is on the way," Zee told her.

Diane's gaze was on Zee now, but still, she said nothing. Every so often a low, raspy wheezing sounded as she struggled to breathe.

"Do you know who did this?"

Diane continued to stare at her, unblinking. No subtle movement of her head.

"Just concentrate on my voice. Don't let your mind go anywhere else, okay?"

Her breathing is growing shallow, a voice inside her head told her. *She's dying.* Francis was back.

Minutes felt like hours before Zee heard sirens in the distance. She kept her gaze on Diane's the entire time and just kept telling her that everything would be okay, and help was on the way. As she talked, she used her hand to gently push bloody strands of hair from Diane's face.

Zee had been watching the rise and fall of her chest for the past few minutes, but her breathing became shallow, followed by a pause so long that she thought Diane was gone before she took another breath. "I can hear them coming, Diane. Hang in there. It won't be long now."

Footsteps sounded before a man peeked his head into the bathroom. "Over here," he called out.

Diane's body felt so cold as the medic checked her vital signs. She felt Diane go still moments before the medic pronounced her dead.

"No," Zee said.

"I'm sorry."

Someone took hold of Zee's arm and helped her up, then ushered her from the bathroom. Another medic was working on the man on the other side of the bed. The rest of the house was already filled with technicians and officers.

Nothing made sense. One minute she and Jessie were watching the house from inside the car, and in the next, two people were dead, lying in their own blood. She didn't know who was pulling her forward until they stopped in the living area and a man asked, "Where are your shoes?"

She looked up. It was Colin. Light-headedness took over. "Can I sit down? I don't feel well."

He brought her to a chair in the dining room.

"Zee, I need you to focus. Where is Jessie?"

"She ran after the person who did this. He was wearing black and had sheer nylon pulled over his head." She pointed out the window in the direction she'd seen Jessie go.

"Stay right here," he said. "I'll be back."

Jessie

Jessie propped her hands on her knees and tried to catch her breath as she peered out into the night past the tennis courts. A light breeze whistled through the trees dotting the park.

There was no movement whatsoever. Where had he gone?

Shit.

She'd chased the dark-clad figure more than a few blocks, across two backyards and over a fence, before losing him in McKinley Park.

She had gotten close. So close she'd noticed him limping as he ran.

After a moment, she headed back the way she'd come. She was on H Street when a police car pulled over. The driver's door opened, and Colin came around front to greet her. He held her close to his chest for a long moment before stepping back so he could look at her. "Oh, Jessie. What were you thinking?"

"I was so close, Colin. If I had been faster, just a little bit faster, I could have caught him."

"And then what?"

She didn't answer him. She didn't *have* an answer. She only knew that the intruder had gotten away.

"Come on," Colin said, ushering her into the car.

"Is Zee okay?" she asked.

"She'll be fine, although she might be suffering from shock."

"What about Diane?"

Colin frowned. "You didn't enter the house?"

"After the intruder pushed me to the ground, I told Zee to call for help, and I took off after him."

Colin was quiet for a moment. Jessie knew him well enough to know he was frustrated that she would chase after the guy. "I couldn't let him just run off without trying to ID him."

"You had no idea of the risk you were taking," Colin told her. "Two people were killed tonight, stabbed multiple times. Zee was trying to comfort the female when we arrived. I don't know if she even realized the woman was dead."

Jessie rubbed a hand over her face. "I couldn't just let him run off without giving chase." She shook her head. "The intruder was either already hiding inside before Diane returned home from work or broke in while Zee and I were watching the house." It sickened her to think that two people had been killed while she sat in the car right outside.

"What were you and Zee doing there in the first place?"

"Easton Scott hired me to watch his wife, Diane, whom he believed might be cheating on him. He didn't want to confront her until he had proof."

"How long have you been watching her?"

"Two days."

Silence.

"The man in the bedroom with Diane is not her husband." She tried to remember his name. "Zee took a picture of his license plate after he went inside the house. He's a car salesman. His vehicle is parked close by."

"Any idea where Diane's husband is tonight?"

"He's away on business." She rubbed her temples. "He said he was going to Vegas. Why would he hire me to watch his wife if he planned to commit murder?"

"Jealousy can make reasonable people behave in irrational ways." Colin turned onto the street where the Scotts lived. Police vehicles lined both sides. EMTs were unloading a stretcher from the ambulance and carrying it inside. Neighbors had gathered on the sidewalk to get a closer look.

Jessie followed Colin into the house. Zee was sitting at the dining room table. When she spotted Jessie, she held up a hand to stop her from coming any closer. "Stay where you are. I'm covered in blood. You don't want to go in the other room, either."

"Good advice," Colin said.

The thought of what Zee might have experienced while Jessie was running after the intruder caused an ache to settle in her chest. She wanted to comfort her, and yet her aversion to blood stopped her from doing so. "I'm going to run to my car and grab blankets and Zee's shoes and coat. I'm assuming you're going to need to talk to both of us."

Colin nodded. "I'll come with you."

"Half the neighborhood is out there. I'll be fine." But that wasn't quite true. Two people had died. And their killer was still at large. Her skin prickled as she walked back to the car. Someone was watching her. She stopped and looked around. Most of the neighbors had already gone back inside. Past the flickering strobe lights, farther down the tree-lined street, she thought she saw movement. After staring into the darkness for too long, she looked away and texted Olivia to see if she'd made it home safely.

Olivia texted her back immediately: I'm home and $42 richer. I'm going to bed.

Jessie texted back: I'll talk to you in the morning.

No reason to freak Olivia out, Jessie thought as she opened the back door of her Jeep and gathered what she'd come for. The bottom of her shoes slapped against asphalt as she walked back toward the house. Thinking she heard something in the neighbor's yard, she stopped to look and listen. Whoever had done this was out there, watching.

"You won't get away with this," she said under her breath. As she ducked under the crime tape that was being looped around the porch, she ignored the overwhelming desire to peer into the darkness one last time.

TWENTY-FIVE

He'd never been a patient man. As he waited for the garage door to roll open, he used all ten fingers to make galloping noises on the steering wheel. Finally he was able to pull the car inside and shut off the engine.

No sooner had he heard the click of the garage door closing behind him than a giggle escaped.

The thought of all that blood made him shake his head in wonder. *What a night!* The look on her face when he first pierced her flesh with his knife had been priceless. His chortle swiftly turned into full-blown laughter that caused tears to roll down his cheeks.

A full minute passed before he was able to collect himself.

He glanced at the door to his left. He didn't want to wake his mother or his aunt. They were old and senile. They should have died years ago. But he'd learned long ago that stubborn, awful people always seemed to live the longest. One more reason why it didn't pay to be nice.

Slowly and methodically, he maneuvered his way out of the car, careful not to let blood ooze or drip from the tarp onto his leather seats. He knew too well how easy it was to detect traces of blood using Luminol or UV light. It was too damn easy to identify these days. Bleach was ineffective. Oxy cleaners were the way to go. After he hopped into the shower and scrubbed himself clean, he would bag his soiled clothes and then sneak quietly back to the garage with a bucket of water and a special cleanser he'd concocted to make sure he didn't leave any sign of tonight's murderous escapade.

Diane Scott and her extraordinarily inept boyfriend had been easy targets. But man, it had only taken five minutes before he'd grown bored listening to their annoying banter from his hiding place in the hall closet.

The man had liked to talk about himself ad nauseam.

He'd learned everything he'd never wanted to know about the idiot in the first fifteen minutes after his arrival. He was a fucking car salesman, and yet the way he'd boasted to Diane, you'd think he'd invented the automobile. Even his voice had been annoying.

After the first thirty minutes passed, he'd already known that he would kill the car salesman first and Diane Scott second.

By the time the lovebirds had moved on to the bedroom, it had taken grit and determination on his part to take things slowly. Despite catching them completely unaware, Diane had surprised him when she'd somehow come back from the dead after being stabbed multiple times and struck him in the back of the head with a heavy glass lamp.

All his carefully thought-out plans had not prepared him for Diane Scott. Her gutless boyfriend had gone down easy, but not Diane. She'd been a fighter. He couldn't remember the last time one of his victims had come so close to getting the best of him. By the time he'd shot back to his feet, she was in the bathroom, trying to lock him out.

He was fast, but she was strong. And for a very fleeting moment in time, he'd thought she might succeed in shutting him out. He had to admit he'd enjoyed the cat-and-mouse game with the clever girl until she'd gone and opened her big mouth and screamed like a banshee. Took all the fun out of his night.

He'd known Jessie Cole would be watching, but his plan had not included her barging into the house or chasing after him. He'd never expected her to find out about the double murder until the next day or maybe even the day after that.

Jessie Cole had gumption. He would give her that.

Another close call—two in one day.

As he quietly turned the knob on the door leading into the house, he inwardly scolded himself for wasting time basking in the aftereffects of a good bloody show.

He had work to do. Reminiscing would have to wait.

The second he stepped through the door and into the kitchen, he heard his mother calling for him.

His shoulders sagged. *Fuck.*

His mother had been showing signs of Alzheimer's for a while now, but it was strange how some evenings she appeared completely lucid.

He took a couple of sniffs, smelling it before he saw it. And then he clicked on the light.

Double fuck.

She'd done it again—smeared feces all over the kitchen walls as if it were paint.

It was going to be a long night.

TWENTY-SIX

JESSIE

Jessie counted to five, struggling to keep her attention on Ren Howe, the young investigator who had been questioning Zee and her for the past five minutes. But focusing on what he was saying wasn't easy since Zee's blanket had fallen a few inches from her right shoulder, revealing a streak of dried blood on the sleeve of her shirt.

It shouldn't bother her. But it did, and her stomach wouldn't stop churning. The blood had transferred from Diane to Zee's long-sleeve T-shirt.

Her heart raced at the sight of it. All she needed to do was breathe slowly and deeply. Her therapist had told her to think of peaceful and relaxing images. Not easy to do, considering she was sitting in the middle of a crime scene while technicians looked for fingerprints and any evidence possibly left behind.

The dizziness would pass, she reminded herself.

Zee glanced her way, then quickly hiked the blanket closer around her neck and mouthed, *Sorry*.

"So is this something you do all the time?" Ren asked.

Jessie filled her lungs with air and then slowly exhaled. "Do what all the time?"

"Barge into the homes of people you're being paid to watch?"

Jessie stiffened. *He can't be a day older than twenty-five,* she thought. And yet he was trying to intimidate her.

"We heard screaming, and then someone shouted for help," Zee told him.

"Most people would reach for their phones and call the police."

"My only thought was to help Diane," Jessie said. Her stomach turned at the thought that she was dead. "You would have done the same thing."

"Because it's my job," he said.

"If I called you every time I heard a scream," Zee said, "we'd practically be living together."

Ren Howe appeared befuddled by Zee's comment.

"I hear voices every once in a while," Zee explained to the young investigator.

Jessie raised an eyebrow at Zee. "I thought you said the medication you were prescribed took care of that."

"Yeah, well, I guess all the craziness brought the voices back."

Ren shifted his weight from one foot to the other. "When you first broke into the house," he went on, "did you notice anything unusual?"

"I did," Zee said. "The big man with the nylon pulled over his head was the first sign that something wasn't right."

Touché, Jessie thought.

"There was something else," Zee added. "When I first tried to open the front door, it jiggled as if the lock might be broken. That's why when I heard Diane scream again, I threw my weight into the door."

Ren made notes.

"Thinking back on it now," Zee went on, "I wonder if the intruder could have been the one who tinkered with the lock. You know, maybe that's how he got in originally and then waited for Diane to return from work."

"Good observation," Jessie said. "If that's what happened, that would mean the killer waited inside before he made his move."

"Which tells me that he's probably done this before," Zee said.

Jessie nodded. Zee was on top of her game tonight.

Ren cleared his throat.

Zee lifted a finger and held it in midair, basically telling him to hold off on messing with her train of thought. "Who would want her dead?" she asked.

Ren sighed.

Zee answered her own question. "It had to be Easton Scott, right?"

"The thought did cross my mind," Jessie said. "But why would Easton hire the agency to watch his wife if his plan all along was to kill her?"

"I don't know, but whether he hired us or not," Zee said, "Easton Scott would have been the number one suspect. It's usually the husband, right?" Zee was staring at Ren Howe.

Ren said nothing.

They all looked toward the entryway as an EMT maneuvered a stretcher covered with a white sheet down the hallway and out the door.

A wave of nausea swooshed through Jessie. And it had nothing to do with blood.

Diane Scott was dead.

From all she'd gathered so far, the poor woman had fought hard for her life while Jessie sat in her car staring into the night, worrying about all the bills that needed to be paid. Her next thought was about Easton. How was she going to break the news that his wife was dead?

A commotion coming from outside pulled her back to the matter at hand.

Jessie, Zee, and Ren all jumped to their feet at once and looked out the front window, where they could see two police officers pulling a man away from the back of the ambulance. His cries of anguish attracted the attention of the neighbors who had gone inside and who were now hurrying to put on coats and woolen caps as they made their way back to the street.

When the streetlight hit his face, Jessie realized it was Diane's husband.

"What is he doing here?" Zee asked.

Ren frowned. "Who is he?"

"That's Easton Scott," Jessie said. "Diane's husband."

"Interesting," he said under his breath.

Colin appeared from down the hall. He looked at Ren. "What's going on?"

"Apparently Diane Scott's husband has arrived."

Colin peeled off his gloves and headed outside.

Zee looked at Ren and asked, "Can I go outside and listen in?"

"Absolutely not. Stay right where you are, and don't move."

Zee did the moonwalk.

Jessie shook her head at her.

Ren stared at Zee. "What are you doing?"

"I'm moving. You can't arrest me for moving."

"Are you always this exasperating?"

"Is that what I am?"

"Annoying, exasperating, and flippant. And I've only known you for thirty minutes."

"Thirty-three," Zee said with a smirk.

A sheen of sweat covered Ren's forehead. Easton and Colin entered the house before Jessie could help him out.

Easton looked from Zee to Jessie. "Were you watching Diane tonight?"

Jessie nodded.

He swept a hand through his hair. "How could you let this happen?" He pointed to the street. "You were sitting in your car when

147

Diane—Di—" He broke down and cried; his head tilted forward and his shoulders shook.

Jessie wanted to go to him, but the expression on Colin's face stopped her. Easton Scott was a suspect. She knew the drill. Evidence needed to be collected. Photographs needed to be taken.

As Colin moved Easton aside to make room for the gurney, Easton reached out and grabbed a corner of the sheet covering the body, pulling it off the dead man's face. He looked at the man for a few seconds. "I don't recognize him. Who is he?"

Nobody said a word. One of the EMTs covered the man's face again and continued on.

Easton turned toward Jessie. "Diane was having an affair with that man?"

"Come on," Colin said. "I'll need you to come to the station with me to make a complete statement."

Easton's face reddened, and his long, pale fingers curled into fists. "My wife is dead, and yet not one of you can tell me what's happening here?"

"I'll tell you the truth," Zee said matter-of-factly. "Your wife was a great hairstylist, but she was not a happily married woman. And she was definitely sleeping with Luke Young, a married car salesman with three children who lives on C Street not too far from here. Search his name on YouTube if you want to watch him play dueling banjos on his ukulele."

Jessie tilted her head as she looked at Easton. He was too thin and small-boned to be the man she'd just chased into the night. And yet, exhaustion was setting in, and it had been a long day. "I have a question for you," she said to Easton. "Why aren't you in Vegas?"

"You can answer that later," Colin said. "Let's go."

Ren shut his notebook and slipped it into his pocket. "Am I done here?"

Colin shook his head. "No. I need you to watch over things until I return."

"I need to grab a few things," Easton protested as Colin ushered him toward the door.

"I'll have one of my people get whatever you need and bring it to the station."

"How long will this take?" Easton asked.

"That depends on your cooperation."

"Cooperation?" Easton's voice quivered. "You think I had something to do with this?"

"We just want to sit down with you for a bit and have a chat." Colin ushered him toward the door.

"I want to call my lawyer."

"You can do that on the way."

TWENTY-SEVEN

JESSIE

Jessie woke to the smell of eggs, bacon, and burned toast. She sat up and rubbed her hands over her face. Cecil was sitting at the edge of the bed, staring at her with his one good eye. Two years ago he'd lost his other eye in a catfight. The owners at the time, a young couple who lived two houses down the road, were told how much surgery would cost and decided to have him euthanized. Cecil had a habit of coming to their house regularly, and when Olivia caught wind of what was going on, she broke down in tears. She cried all day until Jessie finally drove to the animal hospital, handed over her credit card, and told them to do whatever they must to save the animal.

"Good morning, Cecil."

Cecil merely stared at her like some sort of creepy, one-eyed stalker.

She flipped the covers off and headed for the bathroom. Cecil followed her and circled her legs while she splashed water over her face and finger-combed her tangled hair. She had a splitting headache centered above her brow, and her mouth was dry. She cupped water from the faucet and drank it down. When she was done, Cecil followed her to the kitchen.

Olivia was at the stove when she heard her approach. "What happened to you? You look like you had a night on the town and brought the house down."

That's exactly how she felt. "No alcohol involved. I'm just a little behind on sleep."

Olivia placed two plates of eggs and bacon on the table. "So give me the details."

Jessie thanked her for breakfast as she pulled out a chair and took a seat. "Details?"

Olivia sat across from her. "Zee said there was a double murder in the house you guys were watching. That must have been a horrible sight."

"Zee really shouldn't tell you these things."

Olivia chewed and swallowed as she pointed her fork at Jessie. "You shouldn't try so hard to keep everything from me. There's evil in the world. I get it. It's part of your job. It's what you do. I'm old enough for you to tell me these things. It won't be long before I'm out in the world without you around to protect me."

Jessie was too tired for this conversation, so she took another bite of eggs and chewed very slowly.

"There are hurricanes and tsunamis," Olivia continued passionately. "Terrorists, hunger, pollution, threats of nuclear war, mass shootings, and just a whole lot of craziness out there! There's murder in our own backyard. I get it. It's everywhere. So please stop treating me like a child."

"I'll try."

Olivia glanced at the clock.

"Are you going somewhere?"

She nodded. "I'm walking Paula Swihart's dog this morning."

"Who is that?" Jessie asked. "And how and when did you get that job?"

"I put up a few flyers, and Paula called yesterday. She wants to try me out first. See if the dog and I have a connection."

"A connection?"

Olivia got up and took her plate to the sink. "Yep. Her words. Not mine."

"And if the dog likes you?"

"Then I'll be walking him every Saturday at nine."

"How much do you charge?"

"Fifteen dollars an hour."

Jessie nearly spit up her food. "Fifteen dollars?"

"That's cheap. Experienced dog walkers charge twenty-five dollars an hour. I figured since I'm new at this, I'd start low and work my way up."

Clearly Jessie was in the wrong business. "So how did Andriana's date go last night?"

"Not so good."

"Why? What happened?"

"That Vince guy is a doctor, and he was called away in the middle of dinner. Andriana had to call a cab." Olivia shrugged. "At least he gave her cash for the ride home and for me, the babysitter. He even paid for an extra hour."

"So I guess you didn't get to actually meet him."

"I met him before they left on their date. I didn't tell Andriana since I didn't want to hurt her feelings, but I didn't like him."

"How come?"

Olivia shrugged. "I just didn't like the vibe I got when he spoke to me. There was something insincere about him." She wagged her fork in the air again. "He seemed fake. Higgins didn't like him, either."

"It's usually females Higgins tends to be wary of."

"I know. Strange, huh?" Olivia looked at the wall clock again. "I better go." She took her dishes to the sink, then hurried off.

"I'll be in the office today if you need me," Jessie called out as Olivia rushed down the stairs and out the door.

Higgins whimpered.

"Did she abandon you?" Jessie petted the dog on the head. "Let me clean up these dishes, and then we'll take a run around the block. Sound good?"

His tail thumped against the floor in approval.

———

Sweat dripped down Jessie's back as she entered her office with Higgins at her side. They had just finished a good run through Midtown. She needed to get in shape. If she could have run faster, she might have caught up to the intruder who'd broken into Diane's house.

Her phone buzzed. It was Colin. She picked up the call and said, "Good morning."

"Good morning. I wanted to see how you were holding up."

"I'm doing okay. Higgins and I just took a run. I am worried about Easton Scott, though. Was he released last night?"

"Yes, for now. Why do you ask?"

"I don't think he's your guy. I mentioned it to Ren, but I wanted to make sure you heard it from me. Easton Scott is much thinner than the man who bolted from Diane and Easton's house."

"It was dark out," Colin reminded her. "And he could have been wearing multiple layers of clothing. The report Ren took stated that neither you nor Zee saw the man's face."

"That is true, but the man I chased after had a limp."

"At this time," Colin told her, "Easton Scott is merely a person of interest. I appreciate the information you've given us, but now you need to let me do my job. Easton Scott was depressed, and he had motive—"

"And most homicides are domestic in nature, I get it."

"I need you to trust me."

"I do."

"Okay. I should go." There was a short pause before he added, "I miss you."

"I miss you, too. Thanks for calling."

After the conversation ended, Jessie stood in place for a moment and took a breath. Higgins had gone straight to his water bowl when they entered the office. Now he was resting in his bed in the corner of the room.

She walked to the closet and opened the door. Most of Ben's things were gone.

After what had happened between them at his childhood home in Clarksburg, she'd had an inkling he might move out. Jessie didn't want him to leave like this, with any sort of tension between them. He was going through a lot right now.

She went to sit at her desk and rang his number just as Ben walked through the door. He pointed to the closet and started walking that way. "I left a few things in the closet."

"I understand if it's time to get your own place, but I'm not going to stop looking into your past," she told him.

He stopped in his tracks. "It's too dangerous, Jessie. I'm too dangerous."

Ben's recent conversations with his father and sister were making him doubt himself. He was a good man. "I know you didn't mean to hurt me."

He came forward and took a seat in the chair facing her desk. "You're right. I didn't mean to hurt you, but the fact is that I did, plain and simple." He raked a hand through his hair. "I put a deposit down on an apartment closer to work. I got a good deal, and it's not too far from here. I'll be right around the corner if you need me."

"I don't think it's good for you to be away from your family."

"I appreciate your confidence in me. I do. But here's the thing I don't think you truly understand," Ben said. "When I suddenly find myself in another place, as I did yesterday, it's time for me to take a step back and reevaluate things." He rubbed his chin. "To put it more succinctly, when I had my hands wrapped around your neck, I was looking at Aly Scheer. It was her face, not yours. When she told me she couldn't see me again, my muscles tensed, and I felt a wave of heat sweep through my body. The anger was real, Jessie. Everything around me was real. I could smell the river, just as I could smell Aly's fear when my grasp tightened around her throat." He peered deeply into Jessie's eyes. "If we continued to work together, I'm afraid that I couldn't promise you it wouldn't happen again."

Her throat constricted, and she had to make a concerted effort not to brush her fingers over the area of her neck where his hands had been. He could have easily strangled her. But he hadn't.

"I get it, okay? Just let me continue to help you finish what we started."

He started to say something, but she stopped him. "I'm just asking you not to push me away. It's too soon. If you continue to experience these out-of-body events, if things ever get to the point where I feel as if you've lost control, I'll quit working on your case." Her gaze was on his as she reached across the desk and offered her hand. "Deal?"

He was a stubborn man, and judging by the uncertainty in his eyes, he wanted to turn her down. But he didn't. His big hand wrapped around hers, and they shook on it.

For the next fifteen minutes they talked about the double murder that had occurred last night. She told him about Olivia's big plan to make enough money to buy her own car. That conversation led to Andriana's date with the doctor, the price of babysitting and dog walking, and finally back to his past. "Did you meet with the teacher Nikki told you about?"

He nodded. "Caleb Duberry. Frankly, he was the first person I've met from my past who had kind things to say about me. Nothing that will help us along with the investigation, though."

"If you agree, I'd like to talk to Aly Scheer's family and see if they'll be willing to talk to me about their daughter. I also plan to pay Nikki Seymour's mother a visit in the next couple of days. And I'd also like to talk to Lou Wheeler."

Ben frowned. "I don't want you going near him."

"Why not?"

"There's nothing for you to gain by doing so."

"Maybe he'll open up to me. It's you he's angry with. Not me."

He shook his head. "I'd prefer that you stay away."

Jessie decided to let it go for now. She tapped her pen against her chin. "If our investigation of Aly Scheer's death leads us down a road that comes to a dead end, my advice at that point will be to let your past stay in the past as your sister first suggested."

Ben tilted his head. "It took you ten years to find out what happened to your sister. What happened to perseverance and never giving up?"

"The Aly Scheer case is much different. Your father went to trial, and a jury found him guilty."

"You're forgetting about DJ Stumm, the man I envisioned killing and whose blood was on my ax."

"DJ Stumm murdered his family, and you only remembered it all because you reported on the case," Jessie stated flatly. Deep down, though, the thought that Ben had been right all along about his connection to Stumm did niggle at her mind.

"And the Heartless Killer was responsible for dozens of murders," Ben said. "Are you saying it's okay if I killed these men in acts of vigilantism?"

"I don't know the details of what happened with DJ Stumm, but I do know he needed to be put away," Jessie said. "And you were protecting me and others when you took the Heartless Killer's life. I know what I saw. So yes, if you want to call that an act of vigilantism, go right ahead. I'm good with it."

"And do you think your friend Colin Grayson would feel the same?"

"No. Because guilt isn't clean-cut or absolute. Being a vigilante should not be romanticized, but that's not what we're talking about here."

"It's exactly what we're talking about."

"No!" She thumped her fist on the top of her desk. "I saw you save my life and Zee's. End of story. As far as DJ Stumm goes, there is no proof. It's all in your mind, Ben."

Ben closed his eyes and took a breath.

"You need to get some sleep," Jessie told him. "You look as if you're running on empty. I suggest we take this one step at a time. Let's continue our investigation and find out what we can. After that, we'll discuss it all again, and you can tell me where you want to go from there."

There was a long pause before he agreed.

Jessie straightened the papers on her desk while Ben collected the items he'd left behind. When he got to the door, she said, "I'll miss seeing your mug around here."

"You'll see plenty of me, I'm sure." He opened the door and then turned to face her once more. "Thank you for letting me stay here."

"You're welcome."

He pointed a finger at her. "Keep away from Lou Wheeler."

And then he walked out the door.

Twenty-Eight

He usually preferred to let the dust settle before he sought another victim so quickly, but his time with Lavinia Shaw had left him feeling unsatisfied and wanting. He needed to get it right this time.

He flapped the blanket in the air, making the young woman laugh when her hair flew every which way. Once the blanket was situated, he told her to simply relax while he set everything up.

Her name was Sunny. She was a prostitute—one of Frankie's girls. "Are you sure Frankie agreed to this?"

"I paid him thousands of dollars to have you all to myself. What do you think?"

She smiled. "It's a little cold up here in the middle of the woods," she said, rubbing her arms.

He looked up through the trees, where a few rays of sunlight fought to make their way to the ground. He searched through his bag and found an old sweater that had once belonged to another young woman, God rest her soul. "Well, look at this! It's your lucky day."

As he helped her put on the sweater, he said, "So tell me something about yourself. What did you do before you met Frankie?"

"I was a nanny for three well-behaved children. The parents treated me well. I never should have . . ." She stopped midsentence and left it at that.

"You can talk to me, darling. My lips are sealed." He made a zipping motion over his mouth and tossed the invisible key.

She smiled again, but it was tentative. He wanted her to relax and feel comfortable around him. It always made the whole process much more enjoyable.

"Tell me what you would do all day with three children?" He shook his head in wonder. "I've never been around children. I can't imagine."

"Three girls," she said with pride. "The eldest child was sixteen. She did a lot of the work. I think it was just ingrained in her to do what she could to help her little sisters. After breakfast, I would take the two older girls to school. When they returned for the day, we would work on homework. Then I would show them how to braid their hair, and we would polish our toes and bake cookies." Her brow furrowed. "It was nothing at all like my upbringing."

"Tell me about your childhood." He set up a folding chair for her on the blanket, helped her into it, then lay a small blanket over her lap and handed her a glass of Zinfandel. She took a sip, and her head fell back slightly as she enjoyed the taste.

"That's very good," she said.

"Only the best for you, my dear."

"My childhood was okay, I guess. My parents worked hard, and so they weren't around much."

Sounded to him like she was a spoiled bitch, which would explain the flawless skin and smooth hands. She'd come to the United States from one of those Nordic countries. Frankie had been quick to get her away from the family she'd helped by showering her with gifts, ridding her of all forms of ID, and then making sure she was addicted to drugs, most likely heroin.

He pulled a fork and a piece of cheesecake from the picnic basket and fed her a bite.

"Delicious," she said.

Next he fed her a fresh strawberry and a bite of frosted chocolate brownie. He watched her chew, taste, and swallow. She had a lovely mouth.

"What about you?" she asked. "Aren't you going to eat?"

"I will. Soon." He sat down and stretched his legs as if he didn't have a care in the world.

Her shoulders relaxed somewhat as she took another gulp of wine.

"Did you ever hope to have a family of your own someday?" he asked her.

"I still do."

"But what about Frankie? I don't think he'll ever let you go," he reminded her.

"I'll find a way," she said before guzzling the rest of the wine.

He fed her at least half of the cheesecake before she said, "No more, please. I'll burst if I eat even one more bit. And if I gain another pound, Frankie will—"

"Will what?"

"Never mind. I'd rather not talk about it."

"Frankie. Frankie. Frankie. How do you girls get yourself into these predicaments in the first place?"

"That's easy," she said. "It all starts just like this. A picnic in a beautiful glade surrounded by a perfectly blue sky and tall trees." She licked a crumb from her upper lip. "A little cheesecake and delicious wine goes a long way, too."

"And that's all it takes to get you to leave a job you love for a man you can't escape from?"

She was quiet for a moment as she thought about it. He could see the wheels turning. Something clicked and she stiffened. "I'm happy," she said without conviction. "Frankie treats me well."

He knelt down beside her, reached for her wrist, then pulled back the sleeve of the sweater far enough so that they could both see the red welts where she'd cut herself, most likely with a razor. "So why did you try to kill yourself?"

She tried to brush his hand away, but she was already feeling the effects of the Rohypnol he'd put in her wine and cheesecake.

"You know why," she said, each word sticking to her tongue.

"I want you to tell me." He went back to his bag of tricks and pulled out a ball of twine. Back at her side, he unraveled it and began to fasten her forearm to the arm of the chair, making sure her scars were clearly visible.

"Please don't."

"I paid good money for you. And you're happy with your job, remember?"

She frowned.

"You wouldn't want me to ask Frankie for my money back because you didn't do as I asked, would you?"

She shook her head, clearly panicked by the thought.

Once both of her arms were well secured, the ugly red welts facing the sky, he played with her hair, twisting the ends between his thumb and forefinger.

Her eyes were squeezed shut.

"Open your eyes," he told her.

She did as he said.

Frankie sure knew how to get into a person's head and fuck with it until they couldn't think for themselves. Even without the drugs, she wouldn't have fought him. But he liked it better this way since she wouldn't have the strength to scream, let alone fight him off. They were far away from the people and trails, so even if she did scream, nobody would hear her.

"I'm not comfortable." Her head lolled to one side.

He pulled a razor from his pocket and put the sharp edge next to one of the many scars on her small wrist. "Should I start right here?"

She tried to straighten, gave it her all, but she just couldn't manage it.

He made a slow, straight cut. The blood came easily, dripping onto the chair and blanket.

"Why?" she asked.

"I'm trying to help you," he said. "You can't fool me, darling. You're not happy at all. And Frankie won't be happy when he finds out you didn't tell him where you were going or who you were spending the day with." He made a tsking noise. "I'm pretty sure he'd beat you to a pulp, and don't you think a slow, peaceful death is the better way to go?"

"You know Frankie. You said that you do."

He shook his head. "I lied." And then he made another cut across her other wrist. It was like slicing fresh butter. She tried to wriggle away, but it was a useless attempt. "There is another reason why I picked you. Do you want to know why?"

"Let me go," she begged.

"Do you remember Chance Johnson?"

He could see panic in her eyes.

"He talks about you all the time." He pulled out his phone and played a beautiful love song he'd uploaded earlier, the same song Chance had told him he used to play for her on his guitar.

He then untied the ropes from her wrists, leaned over, and pulled her into his arms, snug against his chest. As they danced, her feet dragged over the blanket. She was growing weak, dying in his arms. "Chance loved slow-dancing with you," he whispered close to her ear. "It was all he lived for."

Her body tensed.

"Chance was looking forward to seeing you again, but you fucked him over good, didn't you?"

"Don't do this," she said, her voice a whisper.

"I must. Someone has to punish you for your betrayal."

When he finally stopped swaying, he made sure she was dead before he stripped her clothes off and propped her upright in a sitting position against the trunk of the closest tree. With gloved hands, he set her purse with all its belongings intact next to her. He then folded her bloodied hands in her lap and tilted her head just a bit so that it looked as if she were watching him as he tossed anything that would burn into a pile, including the clothes he was wearing. Using greased cotton balls, he lit the mound of clothes and whatnot on fire.

After he took a few pictures, he sat next to her, his back against the tree and his head tilted against hers, and watched the flames. Although he didn't practice necrophilia, he considered it, but only for a moment before he stretched and then pulled out his knife and found the perfect spot on the side of her face to leave his mark.

"Time to say goodbye," he said moments later as he scooped her into his arms and carried her to the river. He placed her face down in the cold water, took his time washing the blood from her body, then gave her a little push. Her body dipped, then floated a few feet away, stopped, then moved with the current once more, until one of her arms appeared to get caught up in the rocks about twenty feet away. He scrubbed the blood from his own body, careful not to miss a spot or leave any prints behind, and then he hurried back to put on some clothes and warm himself by the fire.

He'd been killing for a while now. He searched through his bag for a paper clip, then pushed his left sleeve up so he could scratch a line next to the others. He could have used the tip of his blade, but it was sharp and wouldn't leave the desired effect. He put the paper clip away and counted the number of lines on his arm.

Sunny was number seventeen.

Twenty-Nine

Colin

Colin rubbed his eyes. They felt gritty. "Come in," he said when there was a knock on the door.

It was Ren. The clean-cut rookie always looked as if three nannies had helped put him together before pushing him out the door with a bag lunch.

"Have you been here all weekend?" Ren asked.

Colin watched Ren glance around the office, his gaze holding steady on the couch as he asked, "You didn't sleep here, did you?"

Colin said nothing.

"I don't get it," Ren said. "You work all these crazy hours, and for what?"

"Really?"

"Yeah. We weren't even close to figuring out who killed Lavinia Shaw before Diane and her lover were killed. How do you keep going?"

Colin sat up and stretched until his bones cracked. "Sometimes I don't. Anything else?"

"Yeah. I've been thinking—"

He didn't have time for chitchat, but the rookie was starting to grow on him. Colin was running on empty, and when that happened, he tended to get easily irritated. But his mother always told him that if he had nothing nice to say, he should say nothing at all. He sat quietly and watched the kid reach into his leather briefcase. He didn't realize anyone other than a banker used those things. "So you were thinking about . . . ?"

"A lot of things, but mostly that you need to see what I found."

Colin recognized the sketchbook Ren had in his hands as he came forward. Ren stood at Colin's side and showed him one of the pictures he'd drawn of Lavinia Shaw as she'd hung from the rafters.

"You're talented," Colin said. "I'll give you that, but what am I supposed to be looking at?"

"Right there." Ren pointed at the girl's ankle. "I didn't think much of it until it woke me in the middle of the night. Now fast-forward to the double murder," he said. "I don't think the husband had anything to do with the murder of his wife."

"Why not?"

"While forensics took photographs and fingerprints, I made a sketch of Diane Scott. Did you know she was stabbed at least twenty-three times?"

"That could point to a revenge killing acted out by an angry spouse. This was an explosive act, Ren. One filled with rage. There was no robbery or sexual element between killer and victim."

"Just hear me out."

"Go on."

"The point I was trying to make is that there were so many stab wounds that there was no way I could get an accurate drawing of the wounds, so I focused on Diane Scott's face, neck, and shoulders. There was some blood and bruising there, too, but I kept going back to the wound on the left side of her neck. It looked as if it could have been made with the tip of a knife. It wasn't a full-on stab like the other wounds. The one on her neck was more of a precise cut, not too deep, and in the shape of a crescent moon." Again, Ren pointed to the marking on his sketch, this time of Diane Scott.

Colin had no idea what Ren was getting at, but he took a closer look at the drawing.

"Are you thinking what I'm thinking?" Ren asked Colin when he looked up at him.

"Probably not." Colin looked at Ren and saw that there was genuine interest. "You don't happen to have a photograph from forensics, do you?"

Ren brightened. "I do." He went to his briefcase and brought back more than one eight-by-ten glossy of Diane Scott on the bathroom floor. "Right there," he said, pointing at her neck.

The marking did look fresh, and it looked as if some care might have been taken with it.

"I woke up in the middle of the night when it came to me," Ren told him. "This crescent moon, or whatever it is, on Diane's face looks similar to the marking on Lavinia Shaw's ankle."

He had Colin's interest. "Okay, slow down. You think these markings somehow connect the double murder to Lavinia Shaw?"

"Yes."

"One was hung," Colin reminded him. "The others were stabbed multiple times."

"I know." He pulled out another photograph. Ren had circled the marking on her ankle in red pen. "If we just focus on the markings . . ."

Colin wished he'd shown him all the photographs from the start, but there was no point in saying anything since he could see that Ren was enjoying himself.

"The markings do look very similar," Colin said as adrenaline coursed through his veins. "It could be a branding of sorts."

Ren nodded. "That's what I thought."

"This is really good work. I'm impressed."

"Thank you, sir."

"What about Luke Young, the man found murdered in Diane's bedroom. Any markings?"

"I looked at the photographs in the lab, but I didn't see anything that looked close enough."

"With regard to the crescent shape on both victims, I want you to have someone on the team input the data in our records management system and see what they come up with. Let's also run this information through CopLink."

"Will do."

"And then talk to the ME on the case and see if she has anything on Luke."

Ren nodded. He looked pumped up as he placed his sketchbook and the photos back into his briefcase.

Colin stopped him at the door, and the kid turned to face him. "I know you were sort of pushed into this job by your father, and I could be wrong, but I think you were fighting it at first. I just want you to know that you're doing a great job. You have a knack for this line of work."

"Thanks, but I'm still not sure I'm willing to dedicate as much time as you do to this investigating business."

"I appreciate your honesty, but I have my reasons for spending so much time here."

"I'd love to hear them," Ren said.

"Are you sure about that?"

"Absolutely."

"When I first started out," Colin began, "me and the guys were making ten to twenty arrests a night. I nearly got hit by a train while running after a suspect, and I found more decaying corpses than I care to remember. Everything happened so fast I never had time to stop and think."

"Inspiring," Ren interjected.

Colin chuckled. "Once I became a homicide detective, everything seemed to slow to a standstill. At least that's how detective work felt in comparison with what I'd been doing up to that point. I realized how important it was to not only examine everything before me but also follow my gut. Unfortunately, even though everything had slowed down, 'nine to five' just didn't cut it when it came to solving cases. There wasn't enough time in the day to use my instincts. So after work, I would do things my way. Call it a hunch or instinct or a sixth sense—it doesn't matter. But if you're passionate about this job, you need to follow that *thing*, whatever it is. Sometimes it doesn't lead anywhere, but sometimes it does."

"Are you saying if I really want to follow my hunch, do it on my own time?"

"No," Colin said with a smile. "In a very roundabout way, I guess I'm telling you that *you* have that thing, whatever it is, and don't stop using it."

THIRTY

BEN

Ben arrived at Abigail's elementary school at 9:25 a.m. His assigned start time was ten o'clock. It was more important to Melony than to Abigail that he get to the school early. He wore the suit Melony had suggested for the occasion. It was ill-fitting and scratchy around the collar, but that was a small price to pay if it would make Melony happy.

He'd been to Abigail's classroom before, past the library and up a small flight of stairs. Her room was midway down the hall to the right.

A bearded man waited by the door.

Ben peeked through the window and smiled when he saw Abigail sitting front and center. She'd always loved to learn. She was smart, like her mother.

"Are you here for Career Day, too?" the bearded man asked.

"Yes."

"My name's Wayne Brennan," he said as he straightened and offered his hand.

"Ben Morrison."

They shook hands. A bit of chaos at the end of the hallway caused Ben to look over Wayne's shoulder, where he saw Abigail's soccer coach,

Roger Willis, surrounded by kids. Willis popped a piece of gum into his mouth and then waved another stick of gum over his head and asked the students who wanted a piece. They all jumped up and down, making a game of it as they tried to reach the gum.

Willis pretended to try to silence them, but it was obvious he wanted everyone in the vicinity to see how much the kids adored him. He took his sweet time picking who would get the coveted stick of gum. Right before Ben turned away, Willis looked right at him and smirked.

"I can't believe I'm nervous. It's just a bunch of kids in there."

"Kids are scary," Ben said with a smile.

Mr. Brennan held up his hands, palms down. His fingernails were black with grime. "Guess what I do for a living?"

"A mechanic?" Ben guessed.

"You got it!" Brennan said, frowning.

A squeal of laughter made Ben look toward Willis again.

Ben's jaw clenched as he watched Willis try to impress the young girls. It sickened him. Willis was arrogant yet also childlike in the way he chewed his gum, and he seemed so desperate to fit in. Ben thought of Melony and Abigail. Refusing to make a scene, he turned the other way so he didn't have to look at the creep.

"Looks like I'm up," Mr. Brennan said.

"Good luck," Ben told him as the door swung open.

The parent who had just finished made a quick exit, and the door closed behind him.

"What are you doing here?"

Ben turned around and found himself face-to-face with Willis. "I didn't come here to see you." Willis was a little man with big round eyes and a fake tan. He puffed out his chest like a rooster in a henhouse.

"You're welcome," Willis said.

"Excuse me?"

"I didn't press charges after you attacked me on the field. You're welcome."

"Now isn't the time or place to talk about this," Ben said.

The man couldn't seem to stay in his own personal space. He kept inching closer until Ben could feel his warm breath against his neck as Willis said, "Keep away from me and my family."

Ben stiffened as he looked through the window, hoping Mr. Brennan would finish up before Coach Willis left Ben with no choice but to knock out some of his pretty white teeth.

"Abigail is looking good."

Ben's jaw hardened.

"On the field I mean, of course."

Ben looked down his nose at him. "I've been making some inquiries, and I noticed that you have had a lot of gaps in your employment over the years. Why is that?"

Willis's cocky expression was replaced with a quick, false smile.

"Was it because of loss of employment?" Ben asked. "Or incarceration?"

Willis's eyes narrowed.

"Stay away from my daughter."

"You don't scare me, Morrison."

Abigail exited the classroom and grabbed his arm. "Come on, Dad," she said excitedly, oblivious to the tension between him and Willis. "It's your turn."

Ben followed Abigail inside, his heart racing and his mind swirling with speculation, wondering why no one else could see through Willis's facade. The only thing Ben knew for certain was that the man had to be stopped before he did something that might destroy all their lives.

Thirty-One

Jessie

Aly Scheer's family hadn't been easy to track. The address Jessie had found in Clarksburg brought her to a two-story house sitting on fifty acres in the wine grape–growing region. The woman who answered the door said she'd been renting the property from the Scheers for ten years. Jessie made up a story about being an old friend of the daughter they'd lost more than twenty years ago and that she had photographs she wanted to share with them. The woman didn't think twice about handing over their address in Elk Grove, twenty-five minutes away.

On her way there, Jessie called the Folsom Prison to make an appointment to see Lou Wheeler. Although Ben was against it, she figured he was speaking from emotion rather than logic. Her hope was to get some leads from Lou that Ben hadn't been able to. The woman on the phone sounded distracted. She asked for Jessie's number and told her she would have to get back to her.

Immediately after ending the conversation, Jessie heard the rattle in her engine again.

She made a left onto Elk Grove Boulevard.

Her phone buzzed. It was an anonymous caller. She considered ignoring the call, thinking it might be the same man who had warned her about Ben. And then, exactly for that reason, she picked up the call.

"I see that you heeded my warning and kicked Ben Morrison out of your office."

She had been all set to let the guy have a piece of her mind, but her anger turned to dread when she realized he might be stalking her. She took a quiet breath in the hopes of collecting herself. She didn't want him to think he frightened or worried her. "Who am I talking to?"

"Your worst nightmare."

Her hands shook as she pulled to the side of the road. Gravel ricocheted off the chassis and hit her windshield. She thought of the Heartless Killer. "I'm afraid my worst nightmare is dead. Try again."

"Let's see. Hmm. Let's just say he is someone who knows you better than you know yourself."

"That would be unsettling," she agreed. The guy was a nutjob.

"Your worst nightmare knows things about you."

She considered hanging up on him, but before she did, she thought it might be to her benefit to see how far he would take this craziness if she called him on his bluff. She didn't like the idea of the prankster causing her to look over her shoulder every time she left the house. "Okay," she said, "why don't you go ahead and tell me what you know about me?"

"I know you're good at reading lips, that you have been raising your niece since she was four, and that you have an aversion to blood."

Silence. Who was this guy, and what did he want?

"Do you want to know more?"

She wanted to throw up. Instead, she said, "Yes." Mostly because the three things he'd just told her about herself were things that had been reported at one time or another when she was all over the media after the Heartless Killer incident.

"I think that's enough for now. I want to hold you in suspense for a bit longer."

"What you need to do is fucking grow up."

"One more thing," he blurted out, obviously sensing she was about to disconnect their call. "You might want to check the wires under your hood."

"Fuck off."

"I'm serious. Your engine doesn't sound right. My guess is that a rodent has been chewing on your wiring. It's pretty common. Trust me. Just open the hood and you'll see what I mean." Three beeps indicated that the call had ended.

She sat there for a moment before shutting off the engine. She looked around and waited for traffic to pass before climbing out and walking to the front of the car. She opened the hood. "Eww!"

Not only were there rat droppings scattered about, but there was also a dead rat. Turning away, she took a deep breath to collect herself. She then walked to the back of the car and opened the trunk. She grabbed the umbrella and used it to scoop the rodent from her engine and place it at the side of the road. *Gross.*

She shut the hood, climbed back behind the wheel, and closed her eyes as she calmed herself. There had been no blood visible on the rat, so that wasn't the problem. It was the realization that the caller was watching her every move.

Since she was less than a mile from the Scheers' house, she decided to continue on. She believed it was important to her investigation that she talk to Aly's family and see what they had to say about Ben and Aly's relationship, if anything. But first she would call the Jeep dealer in Sacramento and make an appointment.

A few minutes later, she turned the key and hoped the wires would hold together for a bit longer. The Scheer house was located on Walnut Drive at the end of a cul-de-sac. A cat ran from the porch to the high shrubs separating the front yard from its neighbor.

Jessie got out of the car and headed for the door. She refused to let the caller get to her. He didn't know more about her than anyone else in Sacramento. And yet he'd known about the rattle in her engine.

Was he the one who'd placed the rat there to begin with?

She anchored her hair behind her ear as she took a breath. She would give Colin a call later on and see what he thought.

Before she could knock, the door opened. The man standing directly in front of her had lots of thick, curly hair and the sort of stubbly jaw reserved for male models. His eyes were dark and bright, his smile genuine. "I don't want any," he said.

"Oh," she said, "I'm not selling anything."

He chuckled, and it took her a moment to realize he'd been teasing. "I'm sorry," she said. "I'm not quite with it. Prank callers and dead rats will do that to a person."

His smile left him. "Dead rats?"

She nodded and pointed to her car. "In the engine. It's still working, though. I made an appointment to take the car in, but since I was so close, I decided to see if anyone was home." When she looked at him, he was smiling again. "Maybe I should start over."

"I think that's a lovely idea," he said.

"My name is Jessie Cole. I'm a private investigator, and I was hoping to speak to Mr. and Mrs. Scheer about their daughter, Aly."

He sighed. "You are a buzzkill, aren't you?"

Olivia had accused her of being Debbie Downer, which she guessed was probably pretty much the same thing. "I'm afraid so," she said.

"Well, I hate to disappoint, especially a beautiful woman such as yourself, but my aunt and uncle are off enjoying the world now that their six children have grown up and had kids of their own. I'm just a nephew they can't seem to escape. The guy who hates the idea of having a nine-to-five job and would much rather bring in the mail and take care of my aunt and uncle's pets while they're cruising the Bahamas."

The man flustered her, and she wasn't sure why. He was handsome. There was that. But it was everything put together. The good looks, the humor, and calling her beautiful. That didn't happen often, if ever. He'd completely stripped her of the ability to think straight.

"Sorry, did I say the wrong thing?"

"No. No. It's me. It's been a weird day, that's all."

"Yes. Pranksters and rats. I get it."

It was her turn to smile.

He offered his hand. "My name is Casey. Casey Scheer, Aly's cousin. Aly and I were very close back then." He kept nodding his head as if he were thinking back to that time. "What happened to her . . . Well, it was a very sad time for us all." He gestured behind him. "You're welcome to come inside and grill me if you'd like."

"That's very kind of you to offer. I would appreciate that."

He led her inside and shut the door behind him. They passed by the living area, a nicely decorated room done in shades of gray and white. A large canvas painting of a meadow hung above the sofa. As they continued on toward the center of the house, the distinct and pungent smell of cannabis clung to the air. The family room consisted of a leather sofa and two cushioned armchairs surrounding a table made of pine.

He made a quick detour into the kitchen to grab a couple of beers. "Glass, or right from the can?"

"I better stick with water since I'll be driving."

"Have it your way."

He grabbed a water bottle from the fridge and brought it to her. She didn't hesitate to take a long gulp, quenching her thirst as he gestured for her to have a seat on the sofa facing the backyard.

He sat in one of the armchairs and exchanged the beer for a joint. "Want a hit?"

"No, thanks." She held up her water. "This is perfect." She set the bottle on the table and searched through her purse for a notebook and pen.

"Fire away," he said after she'd settled in.

"I was hoping you could tell me what you know about Aly. What was she like? Did she have any hobbies . . . things like that?"

"I guess my first question to you should have been, why do you want to know?"

"The truth is . . ." She grasped for the right words since she didn't want him to kick her out of the house for not being more forthcoming from the beginning. "I am working with Ben Morrison."

He rubbed the end of his joint between his fingers and set it in the ashtray in front of him, then took a swallow of his beer. "Ben Morrison," he said. "The name sounds familiar."

"He used to go by Ben Wheeler."

Casey exhaled as he raked a hand through his curls. "The son of Aly's killer."

"Yes. After the incident, Ben moved to Sacramento and became a crime reporter."

"Fitting."

She could see he was uncomfortable, but she continued on. "Ten years ago, Ben was in a car accident that left him with retrograde amnesia, which means he doesn't recall anything prior to the accident. He's just trying to piece his past together."

"I don't think my aunt and uncle would be pleased to know I was talking to you."

"I was afraid of that," Jessie admitted. "I wasn't sure how they would react."

"But you came anyhow."

She nodded. "Should I leave?"

"No, but you might want to after I tell you what I remember about Ben Wheeler."

"Fair enough."

"I'll start with Aly," he said. "She was a year younger than me growing up. I'm not going to get into it, but my parents had problems and therefore tended to leave me with my aunt and uncle." He paused to sip his beer. "Aly and I were like sister and brother. She was one of the kindest, most compassionate people I've ever known."

Jessie made notes.

"Right after high school she started hanging with the wrong crowd, and things got out of control. Once her parents realized she was doing drugs—heroin, I believe—they spent a lot of money on rehabilitation centers and whatnot, but nothing worked. Every once in a while, Aly would hang out with the old gang, which included *moi*." He lightly tapped the can of beer to his chest. "The last time I hung out with Aly happened to be the first and last time I met Ben Wheeler. Every once in a while, a bunch of us would hang out in a marshy area over the bridge and through the woods. It was the same place where we'd hung out since the sixth grade. There weren't a lot of places to party in Clarksburg."

He chuckled as his mind seemed to wander down memory lane, then he chugged his beer, and said, "We would make a bonfire, drink beer, smoke a joint, and talk about the good ole days as if we'd already lived a lifetime. On this particular evening, though, Aly brought along a guy named Ben Wheeler. To put it bluntly, I thought the guy was a freak. He sat quietly away from the rest of the group and observed. At least that's what it looked like to me. He was watching us. Taking it all in and contributing nothing in the way of conversation. It was strange, and I didn't understand why Aly would be hanging out with a guy like that. He wasn't even her dealer." He raised his hands. "At least that would have made sense. But the one thing this character Ben made clear was that he liked Aly a lot. He liked her so much he almost killed a guy."

Jessie stopped writing. "What happened?"

"Like I said, we were all partying and having a good time. This other guy in the group, I forget his name, had a few drinks too many and kissed Aly. That's all it took. One kiss and Ben was on top of him. He had the guy in a choke hold before any of us could blink an eye. I thought the guy was a goner. We all did. It was as if Ben had Herculean strength, because it took four of us to pull him off."

"That's awful."

"Yeah. It was like a bomb going off. One minute he's sitting quietly in the dark, and the next he's choking this guy to death." He shook his head.

Jessie stiffened as she recalled the sensation of having his hands wrapped around her throat. She'd been scared. Was she in denial when it came to Ben Morrison? Ever since she'd met him, he'd been telling her he didn't feel the same, that he was changing all the time, seeing and feeling things he wasn't comfortable with. Who was the real Ben?

Casey leaned forward, grabbed a lighter and his joint, and took another hit. "Any further questions?"

She nodded. "Were Aly and Ben dating?"

He shrugged. "That was the big question back then, but not one of us had the answer to that. We were in the courtroom every day when Lou Wheeler was on trial. I just kept thinking that the apple doesn't fall far from the tree. Lou said that he overheard Aly breaking up with his son before Ben choked her to death. I can't say I wasn't surprised when the father was the one locked up. To this day I wonder if they both killed Aly. Because nothing else seems logical, considering it was Lou's DNA all over my cousin. Lou said his son killed Aly and then drove off. Why would Ben have driven off without her unless she was dead?"

"I read that Ben was put on the witness stand, and he said he and Aly were just friends and that he didn't see her on the day in question."

"I guess we'll never know the truth, will we?" Casey asked.

Jessie said nothing because she didn't have the answers.

"Bottom line," Casey said, "is that Aly is gone, and nothing will bring her back. I do have a bit of advice for you, though. The same advice I gave Aly. Stay away from Ben Wheeler. He's bad news."

THIRTY-TWO

BEN

Ben sat in a rental car outside of the Willis house, which was located in Citrus Heights only a few miles from Melony and the kids. No matter how hard he tried, he couldn't get Willis's words out of his head. "Your daughter is looking good . . ."

Willis had been taunting him. His motives were clear. It was just a matter of time before he would strike. Although Ben had yet to find definitive proof, he'd interviewed enough pedophiles to know that Willis had many of the characteristics: male over thirty, time gaps in employment, a master manipulator fascinated by children, and employed in a position that allows daily contact with them.

At dinner the other night, Melony had told Ben that she had it on good authority that he had spent an entire Saturday parked outside Willis's house. For that reason, after he'd left Abigail's school today, he'd left his van parked outside the apartment building in Sacramento where he was now staying and called Lyft to take him to Enterprise to rent a car. He'd gotten a good deal on a silver Honda Civic. It was a tight squeeze for his large frame and long legs, but it would have to do.

He tapped a finger against the steering wheel as he watched the Willises' house. Most of the shades were open, and lights brightened nearly every room.

Every once in a while, he'd see somebody walk past the kitchen window. It irritated him to think that Willis was most likely eating a nice dinner in a warm house, enjoying his family and sharing stories about their day, while Ben sat in a cramped car in the cold.

More than once over the past few days he'd considered letting his concerns about Willis go. Maybe he was being paranoid and Willis wasn't the man he thought he was, but after what had happened today at the school, he knew he was doing the right thing. Protecting his daughter came first. His comfort and well-being and everything else came second.

By ten o'clock most of the lights inside the house were shut off. Ben waited another thirty minutes before he turned the key to crank the engine and drove off.

He was heading down Old Auburn, thinking about how quickly his life had turned to shit, when a deer shot out of the brush and darted into his path.

Ben tried to swerve around the animal, but it was too late. The impact caused him to jolt forward and hit his head against the windshield. He sat still for a second, dazed, before finally driving to the side of the road. His fingers gripped the steering wheel as he sat quietly, trying to catch his breath. The engine coughed and died. In the rearview mirror he saw the animal in the middle of the road.

His heart sank when he saw that it was a young deer. The animal wasn't moving. Was he dead? Injured? Writhing in agony?

He needed to get the deer out of the road before the next unsuspecting driver came upon it. He climbed out. As he drew closer, he saw that the animal was still breathing. Ben knelt down and stroked his neck. The animal's eye was open, but it didn't move. He scooped it into his arms and moved it to the side of the road beyond the pavement, where he found a stretch of grass. He heard a rustle of leaves and brush. In the darkness standing near a tree, he saw another deer, probably the mother.

He stroked the young deer's broad neck. "Come on," he said softly. "Get up. Your mother is worried."

He exhaled, then stood and headed back for the car. It wouldn't start. He got out to take a look at the damage. The front of the car was in bad shape. Pulling out his cell, he called the rental company and told them what had happened. After being put on hold for a few minutes, he was told to wait there. They were sending a tow truck.

As he walked back to where he'd left the deer, headlights lit up his path. The front of his new button-down shirt was smeared with blood. Great. When he got to the spot on the side of the road where he'd placed the deer, he was surprised to see nothing there.

He looked around, peering deep into the trees.

The animals were gone.

Jessie

Jessie had gone straight from the Scheer home to the mechanic after he'd called to tell her his next appointment had canceled and he had an opening. While she waited for her car to be fixed, she called Olivia to let her know she wouldn't be home until late.

Exhaustion was beginning to set in by the time her car was ready. She walked with the mechanic to the cash register and handed him her credit card.

As he rang her up, he said, "You might want to set traps under your car or block any openings leading to the engine with a wire screen."

"Thanks. I appreciate you getting me in on such short notice."

"No problem."

She climbed into the car and saw that she had a message from Folsom Prison. She wasn't sure how she'd missed it, but after playing it back, a weighted feeling washed over her.

She needed to talk to Ben right away.

She dialed his number. Her call was directed to voice mail. The apartment where he was staying was five minutes from her house. Ben never got to sleep before midnight. She would stop by on the way home.

Jessie parked at the side of the building. Years of foot traffic and tenant use had left the building looking drab. The roof needed to be replaced, and the lawn area was dead. As she rounded the corner, she saw a man heading up the stairs leading to the second floor. "Ben," she called. "Is that you?"

He stopped and looked over his shoulder. "Jessie. What are you doing here?"

"I tried calling you, but my call went straight to voice mail."

"What's going on?"

Upon closer view, she noticed the welt on his forehead and the stain on his shirt. "Is that blood?"

He sighed. "It's been a rough day. I hit a deer."

She felt woozy and held on to the railing for support.

"Why don't you come inside and have a seat while I get changed."

She plopped down on the stair. "You go on ahead. I'll be right there."

"You're sure?"

She nodded. She just needed to follow Dr. Mathis's instructions. Focus on how she was feeling dizzy, knowing it would quickly pass. In seconds she would be calm and clearheaded again. She started to stand. Her legs wobbled. *Nope. Not ready yet. Shit.* She plopped back down and waited for the nausea to pass.

It was important that she talk to Ben about his father. Before she attempted to push herself to her feet again, she noticed Ben's van from

183

where she sat. Even from here she could see that nothing appeared to be wrong with his vehicle.

Images of Ben's hands around her neck and then Ben covered in blood flashed through her mind, making her suddenly alert. She pushed herself to her feet and walked down the stairs and across the parking lot to Ben's van. Her heart raced as she examined the vehicle up close. There were no signs of a dented front bumper.

No blood. Nothing.

A sick feeling settled within. Was she being naive in trusting Ben?

She shook it off. She needed to talk to Ben and find out what he had to say before she jumped to any wild conclusions. And then she needed to tell him about his father.

By the time Jessie found Ben's apartment, he'd changed into sweatpants and a T-shirt. He invited her to take a seat on a threadbare couch and then went to the kitchen to fetch her a glass of water.

"That's a pretty massive knot on your head," she said loud enough for him to hear.

No response.

"What happened?"

She heard a cupboard open.

"I told you. I hit a deer on my way here. It was dark."

"I'm sorry."

He reappeared and handed her the water. "It was a fawn. I could see its mother off to the side of the road hidden within the trees."

"So why all the blood on your shirt?"

"The animal was still alive, so I carried it to a safe spot on the side of the road."

"I didn't see anything wrong with your van out front."

"I was driving a rental. Long story."

Her stomach knotted. "What were you doing out so late?"

He rubbed the back of his head. "Why all the questions? What's going on?"

She shook her head. "Never mind. I'm sorry. None of my business. I had a rough day myself."

He crossed his arms. "Why are you here, Jessie? Did you get another warning?"

"Yes." She didn't bother telling him that she'd gotten two warnings—one from the anonymous caller and one from Casey Scheer. "Someone is definitely keeping an eye on me. My car engine has been sounding out of sorts lately, and the caller knew it. He also knew what the problem was."

Ben raised his eyebrows in question.

"Rodents. A rat chewed through the wires. I think this stalker of mine put the rat there. Anyhow, I took the car in, and it's all been taken care of."

"You didn't recognize his voice?"

"No." She exhaled. "I tried my best to pretend like I wasn't completely freaked out by the call by asking him questions and keeping him talking. He said he was 'my worst nightmare' and that he knew more about me than I knew about myself."

"Have you talked to Colin about all this?"

"He's been busy."

"You need to report it."

"I will in the morning." Something stopped her from telling Ben about her conversation with Casey Scheer. Ben hadn't been himself lately. Besides, she had more important things to tell him. "There is something you need to know."

He sat down. "What is it?"

"I called the prison to set up an appointment to talk to Lou Wheeler."

The lines in his forehead deepened. "I asked you not to."

"I figured that was your protective nature talking. I'm an investigator. It's what I do. But I didn't come here to argue with you, so if you could just let that go for now, I would appreciate it."

"Fine." He exhaled. "So when are you going to talk to him?"

"Never. Your father is dead. He was killed this morning by another inmate."

Thirty-Three

Ben

The buzz of the fluorescent lighting above became more noticeable as Ben followed a prison guard through the wide hallways to Dean Crawford's office. Although Ben had wanted nothing to do with his father after his first and last visit, the timing of Lou Wheeler's death boggled the mind.

He needed to know what had happened. He needed closure. And while he was here, he figured he would ask Dean Crawford if Lou Wheeler had ever talked about his life before the arrest.

Because at the rate he and Jessie were hitting brick walls as far as gathering information, she might have been right when she suggested that at some point soon it might be best to just let it all go.

His childhood . . . his past . . . was beginning to look like an endless black hole that led nowhere. The guard stopped to knock on a door.

"Come in," a voice answered from within.

Ben stepped inside, and the officer shut the door behind him.

The office was small and dimly lit. The desk before him took up most of the room. Dean Crawford stood and offered his hand as Ben came forward. The man was as tall and broad shouldered as Ben himself. His hair was dark, his skin pale.

"Mr. Morrison? Or are you going by Wheeler these days?"

Ben didn't like the idea of anyone referring to him as Wheeler. "I go by the name Morrison. And please, call me Ben."

"Sorry for your loss," Crawford said.

"Thanks. I only came to see him once," Ben said, "and I won't pretend that my visit with Lou Wheeler left me with any warm feelings."

The counselor gave him a knowing smile as he sat back down. "Truth be told, I hadn't known your father for very long before the unfortunate event occurred. Jacob Harrison was his counselor until recently."

"Where is Jacob Harrison now?"

"Retired." Crawford reached into a desk drawer. "Peppermint?" he asked as he placed the candy in front of Ben.

"No, thank you. I appreciate you seeing me on such short notice. I just wanted to talk to someone about Lou Wheeler's death and find out what happened."

Crawford spun around in his chair, opened a cabinet drawer behind him, and pulled out a file. He laid it on his desk and opened it up. He picked up the paper on top and handed it to Ben. "Your father—I mean, Lou Wheeler—hasn't even been dead for twenty-four hours. All I have at this point is one inmate's account of what happened."

Ben read it through. According to the witness, Lou Wheeler had been tortured for hours before his death. "How could something like this occur without anyone hearing or seeing anything in time to stop it from happening?"

"I can assure you it's being looked into. Once everyone involved has had their say, we hope to have a better understanding of the hows and whys. I'll be happy to give you a call at that time so you can come back and talk to me or the warden."

"I was wondering if you could tell me why I wasn't notified of Lou Wheeler's passing?"

Crawford's jaw hardened. "Like I said, it only just happened. But either way, I'm sure it was just a glitch. Maybe it's the fact that you have a different last name." He skimmed through the file. "As you mentioned, you've only visited the man once since he was locked up."

Ben thought the counselor was coming across as defensive. He wondered if the higher-ups were worried about liability. Or maybe Dean Crawford was simply a bit of an asshole. Ben slipped the piece of paper back across the desk. "Can I look through Lou's file?"

"No, I'm afraid not. I don't normally talk about my counseling sessions with family members; however, under the circumstances— Lou Wheeler's death and your amnesia—I fail to see why I can't try to answer a few questions."

"That would be helpful," Ben said. "Did Lou ever mention my mother or sister?"

"Only negatively and using descriptive words I don't think you would appreciate me repeating."

"In your opinion, was Lou Wheeler a psychopath?"

Crawford visibly stiffened. "Most definitely not."

"Did he ever talk to you about his own childhood?"

"Not to me personally, but I believe Jacob Harrison made notes about the extreme physical and emotional abuse Lou Wheeler endured as a child."

It was quiet while Ben pondered Lou Wheeler's early life and his own life as a crime reporter. After meeting his English teacher, he'd assumed Caleb Duberry had inspired him to acquire a degree in journalism. But what had motivated him to delve into the world of crime as his life's work? Had his father's abuse motivated him to be a crime reporter?

"I know about your accident and the amnesia," Crawford said. "Is that why you're really here?"

"Yes. That's part of it. I didn't know Lou Wheeler was alive until recently. When I visited, I had hoped we would have a conversation about the past, but he said many of the same things he'd said in the courtroom, which I only recall from what I've read." Ben sighed. "I guess I was hoping Lou Wheeler would shed some light on other aspects of his past and ultimately mine, too."

"I don't know much, but your father did claim to be a simple man who spent his days fishing in order to provide for what he considered to be an ungrateful family. More than anything, Lou Wheeler appeared to be obsessed over the injustice of serving time for a murder he said he witnessed from his bedroom window."

Ben said nothing.

"Lou Wheeler felt betrayed," Crawford added.

Ben already knew Lou Wheeler had been a bitter man who'd felt betrayed by his only son. No need to ask for clarification. "Do you believe Lou Wheeler was innocent?"

Crawford folded his hands on the desk in front of him. "Aren't we all?" He sighed. "There is innocence in all mankind, no matter how deeply buried."

Ben sat quietly, waiting to see if Crawford had more to share, but the man surprised him when he abruptly stood. "Well, there really isn't much more I can say. It was a pleasure to meet you, Ben Wheeler. I am sorry I could not be of more help."

Ben met Crawford's gaze as he pushed himself to his feet, wondering if the man had purposely used Wheeler instead of Morrison. But he saw no animosity in Crawford's expression, so he let it go. "I'll let myself out."

"I'm sure your father is in a better place," Crawford said as Ben made his exit.

Ben didn't bother responding. He just kept walking.

THIRTY-FOUR

JESSIE

Jessie was finishing up with some paperwork before she headed off to Clarksburg to see Nikki Seymour's mom when she realized Zee had been unusually quiet all morning. "I received two more workers' comp cases this morning."

Zee looked over her shoulder. "Okay. I'll get right on it."

Jessie thought about Ben, the blood, and the deer. She didn't have time to call every local car rental business at the moment. "Would you mind doing me a favor?" she asked Zee.

"What is it?"

"Ben hit a deer, but I didn't see any damage to his van. Apparently he rented a car—"

"You don't believe him?"

Jessie scratched the side of her face, started to say something, then stopped. Finally, she lifted her hands and let them flop back to her desk. "I just need to know for sure."

"I'll look into it."

"Thanks."

Zee's stooped posture and monotone voice concerned Jessie. "Is something wrong?" she asked Zee.

"I can't get Diane Scott out of my mind." Zee turned to face Jessie straight on. "I've got Marion, Lucy, and Francis flinging words inside my head, tormenting me since the day I was born. I've been through some fucked-up shit even before I started working for you, but seeing Diane Scott like that just wasn't right. Nobody deserves to die that way. What is wrong with this world? Every day my dad reads about another real-life murder, and he warns me to be careful. It's happening in every city, county, and state across the country." Zee exhaled. "It's becoming white noise, and that scares me most of all."

"Maybe you should talk to someone about what you've been dealing with."

Zee laughed. "I've been seeing a therapist since I could walk. I'm good, thanks." She muttered something under her breath.

Jessie ignored it.

"I wish we could have saved her," Zee said. "That's all."

A knock on the door put a stop to any further talk about Diane.

"Come in," Jessie called out.

A young man came inside. Jessie recognized him instantly from the coffee shop upstairs. His name was Tobey. His hair was light brown with streaks of blond, and his bangs swept over one eye. The other side of his head was shaved.

Jessie usually only saw Tobey standing on the other side of a counter when she bought her morning coffee. She'd always thought he was a skinny kid, but the short-sleeve T-shirt revealed sturdy biceps. He stood a few inches taller than Zee, and he couldn't seem to keep his eyes off her.

Jessie was fascinated. Zee had an admirer and didn't seem to notice.

He was carrying two Styrofoam cups and a white paper bag. "I brought you a vegan chai latte and some scones," he told Zee.

She took the tea and the bag and headed back to the file cabinet.

"I brought you a black coffee," he told Jessie as he set the other cup in front of her.

"Thank you, Tobey. That's very kind of you. What do I owe you?"

"Oh no. This is on me. I felt bad for scaring Zee the other day and making her spill her tea."

"You didn't scare me," Zee said as if that was the stupidest thing anyone had ever said.

"So how long have you been working at the coffee shop?" Jessie asked.

"It will be a year next week. The owner is talking about making me manager."

"That's wonderful."

"Yeah, I guess. My real passion is cycling. I love riding my bike around the city, enjoying the sights and smells."

"You two should go riding sometime," Jessie said. "I have a bike Zee could use."

He shoved a hand in his pocket. "That would be great."

Zee looked at Jessie as if she were crazy. "I've never ridden a bike. What if I fell and broke my wrist. Then what?"

Jessie smiled. "I have wrist guards you can use."

Before Zee could answer, Easton Scott walked through the door. His face was red, his posture rigid. She wasn't sure if he was angry or just out of breath. She also had no idea if he was a danger to them.

"I'll come back later," Tobey said.

"Okay," Jessie told him, doing her best to stay calm and act natural. "Thanks again for the coffee."

The moment the door shut, Easton looked from Zee to Jessie and said, "My lawyer just informed me I might be a suspect in the murder of my wife."

Jessie stood and gestured toward the chair in front of her desk. "Why don't you have a seat?"

He ignored her request and began to pace the room.

Just as Jessie had noted the night of the murders, Easton Scott was lanky, and he walked with a stiff spine, no sign of a hobble.

"I need to know what the two of you learned about my wife while you were watching her." His face sort of crumpled. "Was Diane truly not happy? Do you have pictures? Anything?"

Zee looked at Jessie, giving her one of her signature wide-eyed looks that said, *What do we do?*

"We only have pictures of Luke Young when he was arriving," Jessie said. "There aren't very many."

"I want to see them."

"Show him the pictures you took," Jessie told Zee.

Zee grabbed the camera from inside the closet where they kept most of their equipment. She then walked over to Easton and began clicking through the images. He stared at the last photo the longest. His wife had leaned in for a kiss before pulling Young inside.

"I can print them for you if you'd like," Zee said.

"That won't be necessary." He looked pale. "I loved her. I can't believe she's gone."

"Why weren't you in Vegas?" Jessie asked. "Was that a lie?"

"It was the truth," he said as he raked his fingers through his hair. "But as I sat at the airport, thinking about everything, I realized I couldn't go through with it. I decided I didn't care if she was having an affair as long as she never left me. I canceled my flight and left for home. My plan at the time was to call you the next day and tell you not to follow her." His bottom lip trembled, and for a moment she thought he might lose it again.

Zee took the camera back to the closet, leaving Jessie to walk to his side and try to comfort the man. As she patted him on the back, she examined him closely and saw no sign that he might be carrying a weapon.

"I'm sorry," Jessie told him.

"I'm sorry, too," Zee said. "I really liked Diane."

"I don't think they will have enough evidence to arrest you, Mr. Scott, but please know that Zee and I will do whatever we can to help you."

He nodded. After a quiet moment, he straightened and tried to get control of himself. "I need to go."

"Please, wait," Jessie said. "I need to write you a check and return your retainer."

"Keep it," he said with a subtle wave of his hand. He walked to the door and left without another word.

Thirty-Five

Colin

Colin was on the phone when Ren walked into his office without knocking. He told the person on the other end of the line that he needed to go and he'd get back to him.

Ren was grinning as he came forward. "You're not going to—"

"Stop right there." Colin frowned. "I've been lenient with you, kid, not because your dad works for the FBI but because you impressed me as someone who could use a break and a little understanding. But never, and I mean never, walk into this office without knocking. Do we understand each other?"

"We do," he said, but Colin wasn't convinced.

Ren placed two black-and-white photos on the desk in front of Colin. "I did as you asked and put the information on the markings through the system, and I found these. Two more victims with the exact same marking."

Colin picked up a photo. The victim was male. He was wearing a bathing suit and was stretched out on a lounge chair. His arms dangled off the sides, his hands slumped against the grass near the pool. A crescent moon, much like the others, had been "tattooed" on his shoulder.

The other photo was of an elderly woman. She lay in a crumpled heap on the kitchen floor near the sink. The marking was easy to find—on the side of her face—and it looked just like the others. His heart began to race. "Who are these people?"

"Both are cold cases. Both occurred in Reno, Nevada."

"Did you talk to the detective there?"

"No, but I have his name and number. I thought it best if I talk to you first."

"Have a seat and let's give him a call."

"Before you make the call, there's one more thing," Ren said.

Colin waited.

Ren pulled another photo from his briefcase and slipped it on top of the others. "Luke Young, the guy found in Diane Scott's bedroom. I talked to the ME, and she had pictures, too. She let me take copies. I've been examining that particular picture for hours, and I almost missed it."

Colin examined the photo, but like all the photos, there was a lot of blood, and he couldn't find the marking.

Ren pointed it out. "Right here, above his belly button. It looked like the scar I have from my emergency appendectomy, so my gaze kept skimming over it. It's not as deep of a cut as the others. I called Luke's wife and asked her if he'd had an appendectomy or any other kind of surgery. She said he hadn't."

Colin nodded. "This is good. Anything else?"

"That's it," Ren said, clearly pleased with himself.

The detective's name in Nevada was Brian DeMoss. Colin punched in his number and then was put on hold after he said he needed to talk to Detective DeMoss.

"Detective DeMoss here."

"Hello," Colin said. "You're on speakerphone. I'm Colin Grayson, homicide detective in Sacramento. And I'm here with Detective Ren

Howe. We have three victims in the area who have similar markings that we believe were left by the same killer."

"A killer with a signature," Detective DeMoss said. "Interesting."

"Even more interesting is that when Detective Howe ran the marking through the system, two murders in your jurisdiction came up."

"What are their names?"

"Andrea Fuentes and Pete Flynn."

"No shit?"

"That's right," Colin said. "I take it the names are familiar to you."

"Yes, indeed. Andrea Fuentes was seventy-one when she was killed nearly twenty years ago. She'd never been in trouble with the law. She was very involved in helping families in her community." Detective DeMoss took a breath. "That would be quite a feather in my cap if I could put her murder to rest before I retire in six months."

"What about Pete Flynn? Did you work that case?"

"Hold on one minute while I pull his file."

Thirty seconds passed before he was back on the phone. "I don't need the file. I remember that case, too. Pete Flynn wasn't the model citizen like Andrea. He was a troubled teen and carried some baggage forward into adulthood. He'd made a habit of overstaying his welcome at the homes of family and friends. I believe he was watching a relative's house, sunbathing at the time of his death."

"That's right," Colin said. "I have a grisly picture in front of me as we speak."

"Flynn was murdered six months after Andrea Fuentes," Detective DeMoss added. "Although Fuentes and Flynn were both stabbed, no connection was ever made between those two."

"At this point," Colin said, "we have a total of five victims with the same marking: Andrea Fuentes, Pete Flynn, Luke Young, Diane Scott, and Lavinia Shaw."

"What about a suspect?"

"Not yet, but we thought you would want to know what's going on."

"I sure do appreciate the call. Any information you can share with me about the other victims might help me as I dig a little deeper."

"Not a problem," Colin said. "I'll have copies made and files sent to your office."

"I'll look forward to talking to you soon."

Colin stood as he ended the call.

"Time to call everyone together for a debriefing?" Ren asked.

"You bet. Let's show the guys what we've got, and then I'll hand out new assignments." Colin rubbed his hands together. "You, kid, have put new life into a case that was growing cold quick."

"I'm beginning to see the appeal of being a detective. Gathering evidence, piecing it all together—it's sort of a rush." Ren frowned. "But we still don't have a suspect."

"Not yet," Colin said. "But we're close. We'll find him."

Thirty-Six

Abigail Morrison

Abigail didn't like to admit it, but her dad's constant nagging about her coach had sort of gotten to her. After her father had made a scene on the soccer field and gone after Coach Willis, she'd been embarrassed. To make up for it, she'd made a point of doing the opposite of what Dad had told her to do. Instead of staying away from Coach Willis, she'd gone out of her way to become friends with his daughter, Paige.

Now, though, she regretted it. Paige was spoiled and sort of snobby. The last time Abigail had gone to her house after school, Paige had yelled at her mom. She cursed a lot and talked badly about both her parents. She also acted as if she had Abigail wrapped around her little finger, which was sort of true.

She heard footsteps right before Mom walked into her bedroom. "Are you ready to go?"

Abigail groaned. "Do I really have to?"

"What? I thought you were excited about going to the movies with your teammates."

Abigail sighed.

"What's wrong?"

"I don't know, really. It's just that sometimes I wonder if Dad might be right about Coach Willis."

Mom's eyes widened. "Why would you say that? Did something happen?"

"No, but it is a little strange how he tries to be best friends with all of us, and—"

"And what?"

"I miss Dad, and I wish he would move back home."

Her mom sat on the edge of the bed and put her arm around her. "This isn't your fault, you know."

"I know."

Her mom lifted her chin so that Abigail had no choice but to look her in the eyes. "Your father has seen a lot of bad things over the years, and for that reason he can be overprotective. It might take a little time, but I don't think it will be long before your dad sees for himself that Coach Willis is one of the good guys."

"And then he'll move back home, and we can all be a normal family again?"

"Absolutely." She kissed Abigail's forehead. "I want you to stop worrying. Everything is going to be fine. I promise."

———

Shortly after Abigail's mom dropped her off at Paige's house, she waited with Jane and Emma in the living room for Coach Willis to bring his SUV to the front of the house. The rest of the team, it turned out, would be meeting them at the movie theater. If she'd known that, she would have had her mom take her there instead.

Coach Willis had left the car running, and he came rushing into the house with his usual boundless energy. When she'd first met him, she thought he was funny and super nice. But now he seemed annoying, almost fake. Before she could head out with the other girls, he said,

"Abigail, could you come to the kitchen with me and help me carry the popcorn and snacks to the car? No reason to spend all that money at the theater when we can bring it with us, right?"

She hesitated as she watched Jane and Emma run off toward the car. "Where's Paige?" Abigail asked, wondering why his daughter wouldn't have gotten a ride with her dad.

"Paige got impatient and had her mom drop her off earlier. Come on. Help me with this, pretty please?"

Her stomach turned, and her feet felt like giant blocks of cement as she followed him into the kitchen. Dad had told her to be careful and never get stuck alone with Coach Willis, but here they were, just the two of them. She didn't like the way he was staring at her; his lingering gazes were making her feel yucky inside. She wanted to run off and find the other girls, but then she told herself that was silly. She was being paranoid like her dad. Jane and Emma were right outside. She would just grab the popcorn and leave.

"I'm sorry about your dad," Coach Willis said out of the blue.

Abigail frowned. "What do you mean?"

"I heard that your mom kicked him out of the house because of the way he attacked me after the soccer game."

"He didn't really attack you," she said.

He lifted the sleeve of his shirt and showed her a long red scar. "Your dad did this. But I wanted you to know that I'm not going to talk to my lawyers or have him put in jail. I think he's just overprotective." His usually friendly smile looked creepy and gave her chills. "You're a beautiful girl, Abigail. That's why it makes sense that your dad might not like anyone from the opposite sex talking to you. Do you have a boyfriend?"

She didn't want to talk to him about boys. She grabbed one of the bags from the kitchen table. "I'll take this to the car."

He called her back, but she ignored him. She was already outside walking down the path when she heard him locking the front door behind her. "Come on, Abigail. Hurry," Jane said from the car. "We're going to be late."

"Get in the passenger seat," Coach Willis told her, but she pretended not to hear him and jumped into the back with Emma and Jane. On the drive to the theater, Coach Willis kept talking about weird things like how the first movie he ever saw showed a young couple having sex and he ran from the theater screaming. The other girls laughed. Abigail just wanted the whole day to be over with.

"Anyone want some candy?" Coach Willis asked. "You three lucky girls get first pick." He tossed a bag filled with licorice, Milk Duds, and Dots over his shoulder. Emma caught the bag. While Emma and Jane sifted through the candy, Abigail looked up and caught Coach Willis watching Jane through the rearview mirror.

He must have noticed that Abigail was no longer laughing at his jokes or playing along with his games that she once thought were silly but now seemed creepy, like tagging her or the other girls and saying, *You're it*, for no reason other than to have an excuse to touch them.

She wanted to call her mom and ask her to pick her up, but she didn't have her own cell phone. She had brought some money, and she knew she could borrow one of the other girl's phones to call home if she needed to, though.

It seemed like forever before they arrived at the theater. As soon as Coach Willis parked the car and turned off the engine, Abigail and Emma jumped out and ran to the front entrance of the theater. Emma ran ahead inside, but Abigail decided to wait for Jane when she noticed that Coach Willis had pulled Jane to the side and was talking to her about something.

By the time she and Jane got their tickets and made their way inside the theater where the movie was playing, there weren't enough seats in a row for everyone to sit together. All the girls had to break up into sections. Abigail made a point of sitting behind Coach Willis since he'd taken the seat next to Jane. He was sitting on an end seat closest to the aisle. Jane was to his right. Paige was sitting in the row in front of her dad but far enough away that she didn't have to deal with him. At soccer practice, whenever he made a joke, Paige usually rolled her eyes at her father.

About thirty minutes into the movie, Coach Willis passed around the popcorn. He turned about, his eyes peering into Abigail's as he asked her if she wanted some.

"No, thanks," she said. Abigail knew something wasn't right when she smelled his breath. Thinking fast, she leaned over the seats between Coach Willis and Jane and asked him for a sip of his Coca-Cola. He quickly covered his drink with his hand. "Share with the other girls," he told her.

A few minutes later he offered popcorn to the girl sitting on the other side of Jane. She saw his arm rub across Jane's chest as he reached over her. He then unfolded a paper towel and took his time laying it over Jane's lap before pouring popcorn there. Every few minutes Coach Willis would reach over and take his popcorn from Jane's lap. His movements seemed slow and strange.

Abigail told him she was going to the bathroom, but instead she went straight to a pay phone and called her dad. The moment she heard his voice, she started to cry. She couldn't help herself.

"Abigail," he said, "what's wrong?"

"I'm at the movie theater with Coach Willis and the rest of the team. I need you to pick me up right away."

"What did he do?"

"I think you were right about him, Dad, but I don't want my friends to know why I'm leaving. I don't have any proof, but I think he's got alcohol in his soft drink. And he won't stay away from Jane."

"Who is Jane?"

"One of the girls on my soccer team. He keeps leaning into her and sliding his arm over her body. He's been acting strange all day. Please come get me."

She gave him the name of the theater. He told her to stay in the lobby and he'd be there in thirty minutes. Abigail didn't like the idea of leaving Jane for too long, so she went back to her seat. It wasn't until the girl next to Jane left to go to the bathroom that things went from bad to horrible.

As hard as Abigail tried to watch the movie, she couldn't keep her eyes off Coach Willis's hands, which she could see through the space between his chair and Jane's. He kept finding reasons to lean toward Jane, and this time when he leaned that way, Abigail saw Jane struggling to move his hand away. Her shoulders shook, and Abigail realized she was crying.

Abigail jumped to her feet and leaned forward over the chair to see what was going on. Coach Willis's hand had disappeared beneath the napkin.

The look on Jane's face when she looked up at Abigail caused a cold chill to sweep through her. "Stop it!" Abigail shouted at the top of her lungs. "Stop it! Stop it! Stop it!" She didn't stop yelling until movie-theater staff rushed through the side door and headed her way. She pointed at Coach Willis. "He keeps touching Jane, and he won't stop!"

The coach lifted his hands to show that he wasn't doing anything wrong.

The theater attendant pointed her flashlight at Jane. "Is he bothering you?"

She nodded her head, but she couldn't speak because she was crying so hard, her lips trembling and tears streaming down her face as the woman helped her out of the seat and pulled her behind her, away from the coach.

Abigail felt sick to her stomach. The zipper on Jane's pants was halfway down, and her shirt was twisted upward. She went to Jane, wrapped her arms around her, and cried with her.

"Sir, have you been drinking?" the attendant asked Coach Willis.

He took his soft drink and threw it toward the woman, barely missing her before the plastic cup hit the wall and splattered everywhere.

"Dad!" Paige said. "What are you doing?"

"Sir," a male attendant said as he approached Coach Willis, "I need you to come with me."

Coach Willis didn't like it when the man took hold of his forearm. He struggled for his freedom, even tried to punch the guy, but the attendant was bigger and stronger and seemed to have everything under control as he ushered Coach Willis away.

People in the audience clapped as he was removed from the theater. Most of the audience had no idea what was going on. Abigail helped Jane straighten her clothes and then wiped some of the tears from her face.

"How many of you are in this group?" the female attendant asked.

"There are ten of us altogether," Paige told her.

"Let's move right outside the exit door and let these people finish watching their movie."

The woman was friendly yet stern about keeping their group together. Once they were gathered in the hallway, she said, "I want all of you to call home and have a parent come get you. If you don't have a phone, please borrow someone else's and make the call. Nobody can leave our little group until the police arrive. But don't worry. I won't leave you until you're safe with one of your parents or a guardian."

Paige was on her phone, speaking in a hushed voice to her mom. Abigail overheard her saying that "Dad had done it again." When Paige finished her call, she turned and handed her phone to Abigail.

Abigail shook her head. Heat flushed through her body. "My dad is on his way. You knew this could happen, didn't you?"

"I'm sorry."

Abigail truly didn't understand. "I thought we were friends. Why would you leave us at your house and in the car alone with him if you knew?"

"He promised us he would stop." Paige was crying now, her hands covering her face.

By the time Abigail saw her dad rushing down the carpeted hallway, most of the girls were crying. Emma and Jane were holding each other tight.

"What's going on?" Ben asked the woman in charge.

She pulled him away from the group, and they talked for a few minutes. Abigail had no idea what they were saying, but she could see the pain on her dad's face as the woman explained what had happened.

Ben pointed at Abigail, gesturing for her to come with him. The woman nodded before she approached Abigail and told her she could sit with her father until the police arrived.

Abigail ran to her dad and hugged him tight. She'd been trying to be strong for Jane and all the girls, but she couldn't stop the tears. Her dad stroked the back of her head and said, "It's okay. Everything is going to be okay."

She broke away just enough so that she could look up at her dad. "You were right about Coach Willis." Tears streamed down her face. "I didn't want to come. I had a yucky feeling. I'm sorry."

"You did nothing wrong."·

"I should have listened to you, Dad."

"You didn't know." He pulled her close and hugged her tight.

Her chest ached for her friend and what she'd been through. "I feel so bad for Jane." She sniffed and wiped her nose. "It was awful, Dad."

———

Ben

Ben stood next to Melony, his heart twisting as he watched Abigail, a few feet away, tell her story to the police. She was the last of the girls to give her statement.

Jane had been the first to be released. Both her parents had been distraught, but they did their best to stay strong for their daughter.

Paige's mother had been unable to make eye contact with the other parents. She never questioned where her husband was, which was inside a police car on his way to the Sacramento Police Department.

Melony had arrived thirty minutes ago. She and Ben stood out of earshot of Abigail as they talked. Melony rarely cried. Not even when they watched a heartwarming story on television. It was usually Ben and Sean who got sniffly and watery-eyed.

Melony did her best to wipe the tears away, but it wasn't working. "You were right," she said.

"I'm not happy about it," Ben assured her.

"I know you're not. But I didn't listen to you. He seemed so normal, so damn nice." She wiped her eyes again, then gulped air as she tried to regain her power of speech. "Abigail told me that Paige knew he had problems," she said. "If Paige knew, then so did the rest of his family. Why would his wife allow him to be alone with young girls if she knew?"

"I wish I had the answer."

"I need to ask you for your forgiveness, Ben. I know it's not fair, especially knowing I might not ever be able to forgive myself." Melony grabbed hold of his coat and tugged. "I made Abigail go today. She didn't want to. She was having second thoughts. I think she's like you, Ben. She has good instincts, and they were telling her something wasn't right. But I made her go."

"What that man did today is not your fault, Melony. If Abigail hadn't been here, who knows how far this might have gone and what would have happened to Jane? Our little girl is strong, and she stood up for what was right. She wasn't afraid to make a scene. That's not an easy thing to do. I have never been so proud."

He wrapped his arms around Melony and held her tight. "We're both doing our best. That's all we can do."

She pulled away. A tear ran down the side of her face as she looked at him. "I've treated you wrong, and yet you held strong. You're a good man, Ben Morrison, and a wonderful father."

He sighed.

She gave him a quivery smile. "You'll come home?"

He thought about everything that had happened recently and knew it was too soon. He needed to be sure he wasn't a danger to his family before he moved home. "Let's get Abigail and take her home. We'll talk later."

Thirty-Seven

Jessie

Jessie had been trying to get ahold of Nikki Seymour since they'd last met at the Old Sugar Mill, but Nikki hadn't been returning her calls. Jessie had additional questions. Mostly she wanted to ask Nikki about her mom.

Jessie looked at her calendar and decided now was as good a time as any to pay Nikki's mother a visit. She gathered her purse and coat and headed out the door.

She climbed behind the wheel, set the navigation for Clarksburg, and drove off. Her stomach had been churning all morning. Ever since Easton Scott had barged into her office and blamed her for his wife's death, Jessie had felt unsettled. The tightness in her chest wouldn't go away. And deep down she knew Easton Scott wasn't the only problem.

It was Ben.

She hadn't been sleeping well. The thought of his strong hands wrapped around her neck wouldn't leave her. And then seeing Ben the other night with blood smeared across his shirt and a knot on his forehead had merely added to her confusion when it came to everything she thought she knew about him. His own sister considered him to be a psychopath, and his father had blamed him for Aly Scheer's death. Casey Scheer had warned her to keep her distance.

Waking up in a cold sweat was becoming the norm.

She hoped that her talk with Nikki's mom would bring some sort of closure. For years the woman had lived directly across the street from the Wheelers. And yet even now, long after the Wheelers had been gone from the neighborhood, she was too frightened to talk about the family. There had to be more to the story.

An accident on the highway added fifteen minutes to her drive. It was past noon when she pulled her car into the driveway of Ben's childhood home and then crossed the street to Nikki's house. The air was brisk. Gray clouds gathered overhead. The neighborhood had an eerie feel to it.

She knocked on the door. As she waited, she glanced over her shoulder at Ben's home. Shivers coursed over her, and she quickly looked away.

She thought she heard someone walking around inside.

"Mrs. Seymour? It's me, Jessie Cole. I talked with your daughter recently, and I was hoping I could have a word with you."

She heard movement and then a loud crash. *Shit.*

Jessie rushed to the kitchen window and looked through it. Nikki's mom was on the floor. She ran back to the door. It was locked. She picked up the mat, hoping to find a key, but nothing was there. When she lifted a potted plant, she found what she was looking for. She used the key to get inside, dropped her purse, and rushed to the woman's side.

"Nikki," the woman said, "where have you been?"

Thank God she was alive. Jessie helped her to the couch and then grabbed her crutches and leaned them against an armchair nearby.

The room reeked of alcohol.

A half-empty bottle of bourbon sat on the table next to a stained-glass lamp.

"Mrs. Seymour, do you want me to call Nikki?"

The woman's eyes narrowed as she attempted to push tousled gray hair out of her face. "What are you doing in my house? Who are you?"

The woman didn't sound scared, just confused. "My name is Jessie Cole. I met with your daughter recently. Are you okay? Did you hurt yourself in the fall?"

"What fall?" She pulled a blanket over one bony shoulder. "Why is it so cold?"

In her hurry to get inside, Jessie had left the door open. She went to the front entry and shut the door, then returned to the living room. "Is there anything I can get you?"

Mrs. Seymour squinted up at her. "You're the girl who wanted to know about the family next door, aren't you?"

"Yes. That's right. I left one of my business cards here about a month ago."

"Nikki called you and told you everything, didn't she?"

Jessie swallowed. "Yes, she told me everything." But that wasn't exactly true. Jessie had no idea if there was more to the story than what Nikki had told her.

"She loved that stupid boy. Did she tell you that?"

Jessie nodded. "She told me she had a crush on Ben Wheeler."

Mrs. Seymour chuckled at that. "A crush." She shook her head. "She was obsessed with that boy. I never understood it. The whole family was strange. I tried to keep Nikki away, but it was impossible. I think she fell in love with Ben Wheeler the moment she first set eyes on him."

The woman was drunk and her words were slurred, but that didn't stop her from pouring bourbon into the empty glass on the coffee table in front of her. Liquid sloshed over the rim as she brought the glass to her lips.

Jessie watched her and waited, hoping Mrs. Seymour would tell her more of what she thought Jessie already knew. The woman held the glass in her lap and stared at it. For a second or two, Jessie thought maybe she had fallen asleep until she said, "I saw Ben pull up in his van with a young girl. I thought it was Nikki. I was angry that she had gone off with that boy without telling me."

She looked at Jessie then with a mischievous gleam in her eyes. "I decided to spy on them. I ran across the street and made my way to the back of the Wheelers' house, and that's when I saw the two of them. But it wasn't Nikki. Ben and another girl I didn't recognize were arguing."

A chill raced up Jessie's spine.

"Next thing I knew he had his hands wrapped around the girl's throat. He didn't let go until her legs crumpled, and she fell to the ground."

No, no, no. Jessie's chest tightened. "What did you do?"

"I ran back to my house, shut all the curtains, and kept my mouth shut. When Nikki came home an hour later, I told her to do the same thing."

"Did you tell her what you saw?"

"Yes."

"You never called the police?"

"No. We spent the rest of the day baking cupcakes for a church event."

"Why do you think your daughter called me?"

"She thought it was strange that a private detective would be coming around asking questions after all this time. She wanted to find out how much you knew." She sighed as she dipped her finger into her glass and stirred.

"Are you sure about what you saw?"

She took another swallow of her drink. "I remember it like it happened yesterday."

Jessie sat in a chair across from Mrs. Seymour and leaned forward. "Isn't it possible the girl was still alive, and Lou Wheeler finished her off after Ben drove away?" Jessie hated the sound of her own hopelessness, as if she were desperate to prove Ben's innocence but knew the ship was sinking fast. She'd been sticking to the refrain that Ben was a good man, a family man. But did she know Ben at all?

"It's possible," Mrs. Seymour said as she met her gaze, her eyelids heavy-looking.

Jessie sat unmoving, saying nothing. She felt disoriented, completely lost.

A few minutes later, the phone in the kitchen rang.

Mrs. Seymour had dozed off.

Jessie stood and walked that way. Caller ID told her it was Nikki, so she picked up the receiver and said, "Hello."

"Who is this?"

"It's Jessie Cole."

"What's going on? Is Mom okay?" Nikki didn't ask her how she'd gotten inside, and Jessie didn't offer the information.

"Your mom had too much to drink, and in her attempt to get to the door, she fell on her crutches. She dozed off a few minutes ago. I'm going to make her something to eat." Jessie could see Mrs. Seymour from where she stood. Seeing the woman passed out reminded her of long days spent with her dad, trying to take care of him and make sure he was okay. "If you don't mind, I think I'll stay with her for a bit before I leave."

"You don't have to watch her," Nikki said.

"I'd feel better if I did. I've been through this before with my dad. I just want to make sure she's okay."

"She told you what she saw that day, didn't she?"

"Yes."

"What are you going to do?"

"I don't know."

"When you and Ben visited recently," Nikki said, "I was shocked to see that he still drove the same van. It was so strange seeing him again after all this time. Even with the scars, he still looks the same. But—"

"But what?"

"But it took me all of fifteen seconds to see that he wasn't the same person I once knew. His face looked expressive, and when he looked at me, it was as if he really saw me. He seemed genuinely interested in what I had to say about the neighborhood." She chuckled. "The Ben I used to know wasn't interested in small talk and couldn't fake it if his life depended on it."

Jessie couldn't help but think how strange it was that Nikki didn't seem worried that she'd kept such a big secret for all these years. "Does it ever bother you that Lou Wheeler might have spent years in prison for a crime he didn't commit?"

There was a short pause before Nikki said, "I guess I don't see it that way. The man was convicted by a jury. And in my mind, no matter what the verdict, he was guilty as sin. Lou and Dannie Wheeler were horrible, awful people, and they deserved what they got. Nancy was lucky to get out of there with her head on straight. Ben was the way he was because of them."

Jessie sighed.

"In a way, Lou Wheeler killed them all . . . the whole damn family, and I'm just glad Ben got another chance at life."

THIRTY-EIGHT

COLIN

It was 7:00 p.m. by the time Colin walked across the parking lot toward his car. He planned to pick up some Chinese food on his way home, take a long hot shower, and then hopefully get some shut-eye before delirium set in. He heard footfalls behind him and picked up his pace, afraid it might be—yep—too late.

"I found it," Ren called after him.

Colin kept walking. "Found what?"

"The connection between the victims."

Colin stopped and turned his way. "Okay. I'm listening."

"Andrea Fuentes's father was convicted of manslaughter and sent to Folsom Prison. Lavinia Shaw's brother was convicted of selling heroin and is doing time in . . ."

"Folsom Prison," Colin said.

"That's right."

"Shit." Colin turned and headed back toward the building he'd just left.

Ren was on his heels. "And that's not all."

"Talk as we walk," Colin said.

"They just found another body here in Sacramento, less than a mile from where Lavinia Shaw was found. I heard it on the scanner."

Colin's phone buzzed. He picked up the call. It was friend and first responder Malcolm Jones, letting him know that a female in her thirties had just been located in a wooded area between Mormon Ravine and the American River.

"Was she stabbed?" Colin asked Malcolm.

"No."

Colin had his eyes on Ren as he talked. "She doesn't happen to have a cut in the shape of a crescent moon on her neck or face or anyplace on her body, does she?"

"How did you know?"

"Where is it?"

"On her face."

Colin picked up his pace, his spine stiff, every step pronounced. "What's her name?" he asked Malcolm. "It's imperative that I have a name."

"It's dark out here. I don't think—hold on."

Colin swept through the main door, then worked his way back to his office. Ren jogged ahead and held open his office door for him before following him inside.

"We're in luck," Malcolm said. "She's not wearing a stitch of clothing, but her purse was located at the base of a tree not too far from where she was found. According to the ID, her name is Ashley Coons."

Colin told him he'd be there soon, then finished the call. "Ren, get on my computer and see what you can find for Ashley Coons."

Ren sat in Colin's seat and waited for the computer to boot. "I need your password."

Colin leaned over the kid and typed it in, then left the rest to Ren while he made a phone call to Folsom Prison. It took a while, but he got through to the warden and explained what was going on. He then read from the list of names Ren had put together, along with the names of the relatives who were doing time. "We're in the process of researching one more name to see if—"

"I got it!" Ren said. "Chance Johnson. Ashley Coons was engaged to Chance before he went to Folsom Prison for sex crimes against a minor. She was a witness at his trial."

"I have another name to add to the list," Colin said into the receiver. "Chance Johnson. Are you still there?" he asked after a stretch of silence.

"I'm here," the warden said. "Give me some time, and I'll call you back if I find anything."

Ren sat tensely while Colin paced the room. He pointed at Ren. "You said Ashley was a witness at Chance Johnson's trial."

"That's right."

"What about the other victims with the same crescent-moon marking? See if you can find out if any of them had someone close to them go to prison. Better yet," Colin added, "see if you can find out if they were witnesses for the prosecution. While you work on that, I'll give Detective DeMoss a call and let him know what's going on."

Ren clacked away on the keyboard while Colin paced the room with his phone to his ear. Detective DeMoss was at home, but he promised to see what he could find and call him back as soon as possible.

Colin dialed the prison again. When the warden picked up, Colin said, "Hate to pester you already, but I was wondering if it would be possible for you to gather the inmates' files for the names I gave you so I can come have a look?"

"Not a problem. I was about to call you. I input the names into our system, and it seems all three of the inmates you mentioned have the same prison counselor."

"Is that odd?" Colin asked. "I mean, is every inmate assigned a counselor?"

"Every inmate is evaluated, yes. Many of the hard-core criminals talk with their counselor on a regular basis. Others need to see someone before they're released so they know what to expect. Every case is different."

"What is the counselor's name?"

Colin heard papers rustling in the background before the warden said, "Dean Crawford. He signed in for work earlier today. I already put a call out, but I haven't been able to locate him."

"It's imperative that we talk to him right away. Do you have a home address?"

The warden was quiet, and for a second Colin thought he might have to throw his weight around to get the information. But that wasn't the case.

"If I remember correctly, he takes care of his mother, but ah, here it is. I have two addresses for him. Scratch that. One is in Nevada, so you won't need that one. The other is in Foresthill."

He used to live in Nevada. Coincidence? Colin wrote down the address in Foresthill and shoved it in his coat pocket. "I appreciate your help," Colin said.

"Certainly."

Colin hung up, then looked around the office. There wasn't anything he needed. He was wearing his coat, and he had his gun and his phone.

"You think the counselor at the prison might know something?" Ren asked.

"I think the counselor knows a lot. At this point, though, he's simply a person of interest since he counseled all three inmates."

Colin put a hand on Ren's shoulder. "Since we can't be two places at once, I need you to see what you can find out about the other victims being witnesses at trials. Call me if you discover anything, and then go meet up with Malcolm Jones." He scribbled down the address he'd been given earlier—the spot where they'd found Ashley Coon's body—and handed the piece of paper to Ren.

"You're putting me in charge of a crime scene?"

"Yeah, I guess I am."

"You're going to talk to this guy alone?"

"I'll hook up with dispatch on my way."

THIRTY-NINE

OLIVIA

Tonight Olivia was babysitting for Ben and Melony Morrison at their home in Citrus Heights. It had taken a lot of finagling, but Jessie had finally agreed after Zee had let Ben know that if he ever needed a sitter, Olivia was available.

Olivia, Abigail, and Sean watched the Morrisons' car pull out of the driveway and disappear down the street. "I'm glad you brought your dog," Sean said. "Our dog is being neutered." His eyes widened. "And I think it's going to hurt."

"I hope he's okay," Olivia said.

"Mom and Dad said he'll be fine," Abigail chimed in. "We pick him up tomorrow."

"So what do you guys want to do first?" Olivia asked.

Sean stopped petting Higgins and looked at Olivia with big round eyes. "You're going to play with us?"

"Of course. That's what I'm here for."

"Usually our babysitters put on a movie and talk on their phone," Abigail said.

"Well, that's ridiculous." Olivia pulled her phone from her pants pocket and held the button down until the screen went black. She even set it on the marble table near the front door. "There. It's off. I'll leave it right there until it's time to go so you know I'm not using it."

"What if your boyfriend calls you?" Sean asked with a snicker.

"I don't have a boyfriend."

"Really?" Abigail asked. "You're so nice, though, and so pretty."

"Aww, thanks." Olivia held up a piece of paper. "Look at this. I brought a list of things we can do." Olivia had been researching how to be a good babysitter so she would always be asked to come back again.

In just a short amount of time, she'd already saved $250. She knew Jessie wasn't thrilled with the idea of her driving, but she would feel differently when she realized how much help she could be with her own car. She could pick up milk, go to the post office, and get to and from school.

Abigail took the list from her and read it aloud. "Watch a Movie."

"Cross that one out," Sean said, arms crossed tightly over his small chest.

"Play Music," Abigail continued.

Sean snorted. "Nope."

"Draw Pictures."

"Lame."

"Let me finish," Abigail scolded. "Do Not Laugh, Hide-and-Seek, Make Noodle and Popcorn Necklaces, Paper Airplanes, Sock Puppets, Make Pet Rocks, and Play Board Games."

"Hide-and-seek," Sean said. "I want to play hide-and-seek."

"No," Abigail said. "Maybe later. If you're good."

"You're not the babysitter," Sean told her.

Abigail rolled her eyes. "How do you play Do Not Laugh?"

"Come on," Olivia said. "I'll show you." Once they were in the family room, Olivia plopped down on the carpeted floor and sat with her legs crossed. Jessie used to play this game with her when she was small. It was one of her favorites. "Sit down," she told them when they stood unmoving, staring down at her. "Crisscross applesauce."

Abigail did as she said, but Sean looked wary. Finally he joined them.

"Okay," Olivia said, "the object of this game is not to laugh. If you laugh, you lose."

"This is easy," Abigail said before clamping her lips together.

"It's a dumb game," Sean said.

Olivia crossed her eyes and stuck out her tongue.

Sean laughed.

"You lost!" Abigail said, laughing.

"You lost, too!" Sean said, pointing a finger at her.

It didn't take long for Sean to get into the game. Every time he made a face, Abigail laughed, which was more like a high-pitched squeal that prompted Higgins to bark. For the next twenty minutes, they all rolled around on the ground laughing until Olivia had a bellyache.

Hours later, after making paper airplanes and popcorn necklaces, they all sat in the family room and ate pizza and ice cream while they played Mario Kart. Olivia had a new appreciation for Aunt Jessie and how tough it must have been for her to raise Olivia on her own. Exhausted, she was about to suggest a movie when Sean begged her to play hide-and-seek. "You promised," he said when Olivia failed to move from the couch.

"Give her a break," Abigail told her brother. "She's tired."

Abigail was right, but Olivia looked at Sean and said, "Let's take Higgins outside to do his thing, and then I'll play hide-and-seek, okay?"

Sean jumped up and down, pumping his hands in the air. The kid had way too much energy.

All the excitement caused Higgins to jump to his feet and bark.

"Everyone grab a coat," Olivia said. "It's cold out there."

As they stood on the covered porch waiting for Higgins to find just the right spot, Sean looked at Olivia and asked, "Are Mom and Dad going to get divorced?"

The question took Olivia by surprise. She knew Ben and his wife were having problems, but Jessie had seemed confident everything would work out in the end. Olivia knelt down so she could look Sean in the eyes. "Your parents love each other very much. They're just working out a few kinks, that's all. It happens to most married couples."

He scrunched his freckled nose. "What's a kink?"

She smiled. "It's a problem, sort of like when you have a math problem to solve. Some equations are a little more difficult to figure out than others, and you just have to think extra long about the problem, and maybe talk to the teacher. But in the end you figure it all out and move on."

"So is that what they're doing right now? Math homework?"

Abigail laughed. "You're such a dork."

"I am not."

Olivia straightened when she heard Higgins growling near the fence surrounding the pool. She stepped onto the grass, trying to see better, but it was a cloudy and starless night, and she couldn't see a thing.

"Come on, Higgins," she said as she caught up to him. A rustling of leaves caught her attention. She froze. Listened. A low growl from Higgins made her shiver.

"Is something wrong?" Abigail called out.

It was probably a neighbor's cat. Besides, she didn't want to scare Abigail and Sean. "Just a cat," she told them. It took some muscle, but she pulled Higgins away from the fence and back toward the kids. "Let's get inside," she said. "I'm freezing."

Olivia shut and locked the sliding glass door, then peered into the night one more time before pulling the curtains tight.

"Here are the rules," she explained. "No hiding outside, in the garage, or your parents' bedroom, okay?"

Abigail nodded.

Sean moaned.

"I'm going to count to one hundred, and then Higgins and I are coming to look for you."

Sean ran. Abigail took her time walking off, trying to be cool about it. Olivia held on to Higgins's collar while she counted so he wouldn't follow the kids and give them away.

"Okay. That's one hundred. I'm coming." Olivia walked through the kitchen and around the dining room table. She opened the door in the hallway, but there wasn't enough space for Abigail or Sean to hide. Next, she opened the closet door in the front entry. It was filled with long coats and shoes and rain boots.

She heard what sounded like someone jiggling a door handle. She closed the closet door and stared at the knob on the front door. The hairs on the back of her neck stood on end.

Nothing happened.

What was wrong with her? She didn't scare easily. But first Higgins was acting funny outside, and now this. Higgins ran up the stairs ahead of her as she peeked out the tiny peephole in the entry door.

The porch light was on, and she could see the branches of the tree in the front yard dancing in the wind. Rain dotted the path leading to the door. Nobody was there. As soon as she turned away, she thought she heard footsteps outside.

Stop it, she inwardly scolded.

She'd never been to this house before and therefore wasn't used to the creaks and rattles. She never should have agreed to play hide-and-seek. At the top of the landing, she stopped and listened.

Not one little sound. Nobody was whispering or giggling. Clearly Abigail and Sean were good at this game.

She checked out a hall closet and Sean's bedroom before she finally stepped into the bathroom, where she heard noises in the bathtub. She yanked open the plastic curtain and saw Abigail and Sean.

She tagged Sean because he was closest. "You're *it!*"

Higgins wagged his stumpy tail, and it thumped against the porcelain tub.

"Not fair. Higgins gave us away."

Olivia laughed. "Sean, you stay here with Higgins and count to fifty while Abigail and I show you how it's done."

It only took thirty seconds for Olivia to lead Abigail to the hall closet, where they removed their shoes and slid their feet into the oversize rain boots already there. Their bodies were hidden behind all the coats. When Sean opened the closet door, he wouldn't see anything out of the ordinary.

It took about fifteen minutes before the game became too much for Sean. "Come out. I don't like this game anymore."

"We're in the closet," Olivia said.

He opened the door. "Where?"

"Boo!" Abigail said, scaring her brother.

Olivia quickly stepped out of her hiding place, put on her shoes, and ushered Sean into the kitchen for a snack, anything to distract him from being scared. "Your parents should be home in less than an hour. Your mom said you could stay up until then. Ready for a movie now?"

Higgins was at the sliding door ready to go out again. She slid back the curtain, opened the door, and watched him run to the grass, where he circled a tree.

"*Batman Returns!*"

Abigail groaned. "No way. It's my turn to pick the movie."

She turned to see Abigail tossing Sean's DVD on the couch. And that's when she heard a loud squeal. Higgins was no longer near the tree. She stepped outside and called his name.

"What was that noise?" Abigail asked from the door.

"Stay inside," Olivia said as she clapped her hands. "Come on, Higgins! Let's go!" Although it was pitch black outside, she saw a lumpy silhouette near the shrubs surrounding the fence. She heard the dog whine. "What's wrong, Higgins?" As she drew closer, she saw Higgins lying on his side. There was blood on his belly and his neck.

"Higgins!" she cried. As she tried to examine the dog more closely, she heard leaves crunch and branches snap. Her muscles tensed. Before she could get to her feet, a dark figure bolted from the brush and grabbed hold of her.

"Let me go! What did you do to my dog?"

She kicked and screamed as he dragged her a few feet across the lawn toward the side yard. He squeezed her around the middle, making it hard to breathe. Anger turned to panic. She gasped for air.

She needed to get away! She thought of all the lessons Jessie had given her. *Bite. Kick. Scream. Do not let anyone get you into their car.*

Pressing her chin into her chest made it possible for her to reach his hand. She bit down hard and ground her teeth into his flesh and refused to let go.

He cursed and shook her off.

She fell to her hands and knees and scrambled across the yard back toward the house, screaming all the way. The grass was damp and slippery. When she tried to get to her feet, she immediately fell back down. Before she could set off again, he grabbed her foot and yanked her backward.

Olivia lifted her head, looked toward the house, and saw Abigail's anguished expression. "Lock the door!" she shouted at the girl.

Abigail didn't move.

"*Now!* Hide! Don't come out until I say it's okay!"

Abigail was crying, but she managed to shut the door and run off.

The man kicked Olivia in the gut and then ran to the door, rattling the handle, trying to get inside.

Knowing this might be her only chance to get away and alert the neighbors, Abigail ignored the pain in her ribs as she pushed herself to her feet. She got as far as the side of the house before he caught up to her.

His fist made contact with the back of her head.

Her knees buckled.

Numb with pain, she couldn't see or think clearly. By the time the dizziness passed, she realized he'd dragged her back to the sliding door.

What did he want?

Abigail and Sean.

Nothing else made any sense. The Morrisons were not rich people. There was nothing inside that was worth any monetary value that she could tell. He wanted the kids. This had to have something to do with Ben or Melony. This was personal.

With the light from the house shining on him, she could see dark hair with flecks of silver peeking out beneath a black-knit head covering. Claw marks ran down the side of his neck, the only visible skin. In his grasp was a good-size rock. He slammed it into the door.

Olivia squeezed her eyes shut as glass shattered around her.

He reached a gloved hand inside the hole he'd made and unlocked the sliding door before opening it wide.

The moment he turned, Olivia scrambled away.

"Come out, come out, wherever you are," he called calmly. "I won't hurt you." He then came back for Olivia, grabbed her arm, and pulled her to the door. Glass cut into her as he dragged her inside.

"Do not come out!" Olivia shouted.

He kicked her in the ribs. She cried out. He pulled her into the kitchen and opened cupboards and tossed pans out of his way before bending over to have a look inside.

Every time Olivia struggled, he yanked her arm or kicked her. She felt nauseated and prayed Mr. and Mrs. Morrison would come home before it was too late. She wanted to slow him down, but she was in too much pain to try to get away.

He dragged her through the dining room toward the stairway by the front entry. His shoes, she noticed, were sturdy and brown. When he walked, his body wobbled from side to side as if he had an injury. The front door was still locked. She'd hoped that maybe Abigail and

Sean had run to the neighbors. Her heart sank at the thought that they were still inside the house.

Olivia glanced up at his face in the hopes of remembering everything about him. The knit cap had risen an inch or two, and she could see his chin. He had a dimpled chin.

Her mind flickered.

He looked familiar.

Dark hair speckled with silver. Dimpled chin. And that voice.

It hit her like being doused with a bucket of cold water. It was him. Andriana's date. "You're the doctor," Olivia said, her voice almost a whisper.

"Well, someone just sealed their fate." He laughed.

Her head bumped against the stairs as he pulled her that way. From this vantage point, she could see her phone on the entry table. If only she had it on her. Using her free hand, she felt her pockets for the pepper spray Jessie had given her before she realized she'd left the small canister at home. *Stupid. Stupid. Stupid.*

Alarm bells went off in her head when she realized he was dragging her into the bathroom where Abigail and Sean had hidden earlier.

His hand curled around the edge of the shower curtain.

Olivia couldn't breathe. *Please don't be there.*

He yanked the curtain clear off the pole. Plastic rings flung around the room, bouncing around on the floor and inside the tub.

Nobody was there.

Thank God.

Back in the hallway, he shouted, "Your father is a bad seed. He's a killer. He let his own father go to prison. Come out of hiding now, and I won't hurt you."

He stood quietly for a moment before saying in a sweet voice, "I have peppermints for you. Candy for whoever comes out of hiding first."

Silence followed.

"You fucking brats. Get your asses out here now if you don't want me to cut you!"

He continued to drag Olivia from room to room as if she were a rag doll. He knocked objects over and kicked furniture to the side as he went. He opened closets and cupboards, tossing clothing and objects at his feet. He looked under every bed and grew angrier with every passing moment.

As they descended the stairs, she struggled to free herself, but he didn't seem to care. "Ben Morrison," he shouted, "and everybody your daddy knows must be punished!"

Olivia heard a noise—a muffled voice.

He must have heard it, too, because he stopped on the second-to-last stair. He yanked open the door to the entryway closet.

Olivia was readying to bite his ankle, anything to give the kids a chance to run and get away.

He stuck his arm inside the closet and swung it hard to the right and left. Hangers rattled. One fell and clattered across the tile floor. A set of headlights lit up the living room, causing him to stop his search and stand perfectly still.

Olivia heard the faint rumble of a car pulling into the driveway.

Mr. and Mrs. Morrison were home.

FORTY

COLIN

Colin clenched his teeth as he got out of his car and walked toward what looked like an abandoned cabin in the woods. **TROUT CLUB** was burned into the wood sign hanging over the entry door. The door wasn't locked, and Colin stepped inside. The floor creaked beneath his feet as he walked to the middle of the room. It was small, and he could see that the place was empty. There was no furniture. No appliances. Nothing at all.

Until this moment he'd only planned to chat with Dean Crawford to find out if he knew of a bitter staff member. Or maybe an inmate who had served his sentence and might be looking for revenge. But now, standing inside an old deserted cabin, it all started to make sense.

If Dean Crawford was their guy, he wouldn't want to make things easy on anyone. He might even list a false address as his permanent residence.

Unfortunately, there was no way Colin would be able to get a search warrant at this very moment. Number one, because he didn't have an address, and number two, because he didn't have probable cause, let alone anything from the crime scenes that could be specifically connected to Crawford.

He walked back to his car, climbed in behind the wheel, and picked up his cell phone. He called Ren in the hopes of talking things out with him. "How's it going?" Colin asked when Ren picked up his call.

"I've got a command post set up. We've established the perimeter, and the area has been secured. This place is lit up like Christmas. Hey!" Ren shouted to someone at the scene. "Booties and gloves, or you aren't entering the crime scene."

Colin heard muffled voices before Ren was back on the phone. "The body has been bagged, but I was able to see the marking. It's the same. Any luck with the counselor?"

"I'm beginning to think I'm being led on a wild-goose chase."

"What's that?" Ren asked, obviously preoccupied.

"Nothing. Before we get off," Colin said, "any chance the crescent moon on the victims could be the letter *C* in a fancy font?"

"Definitely," Ren said. "Henry, I need a tape recorder. And watch out where you're stepping."

"I've got to go," Colin said. "Just wanted to check in and make sure you had a handle on things over there."

"I'm good. Talk to you later. And hey—" Ren said.

Colin waited.

"Never mind. It's nothing."

Colin hung up. If the marking was a letter *C*, he wondered, did it stand for Crawford?

His adrenaline spiked.

He needed to find the man.

But where?

The warden had mentioned that Crawford was taking care of his mother.

Colin needed an address before he could call dispatch. It was late, and the staff in the department was overworked. According to Jessie,

Zee had subscribed to databases most people, including cops, couldn't get their hands on because of the high cost. There were some things his own department just didn't have access to because they couldn't afford it. He dialed Zee's number.

"Hey, Colin, I'm about to eat dinner," Zee said when she picked up. "Can I call you back?"

"This is important," he explained. "I need help locating someone."

He could hear her walking to another room. "Okay," she said. "What do you need?"

"Dean Crawford works as a counselor at Folsom Prison. I need his mother's name and address."

He heard her fingers tapping the keyboard. "Let's see. You're right. He is a prison counselor. I don't see anything about a mother. Oh, wow. His father received death by lethal injection in Nevada."

"I need you to keep looking," he said.

"You're going to owe me big-time."

"I realize that."

Colin turned on the engine and was headed back the way he came when Zee said, "Still no mention of a mother, but it looks like he has an aunt Jillian who lives in Folsom."

He typed the address into his system, then thanked her again as he drove toward the main road. Adrenaline was the only thing keeping him awake as he merged onto I-80 West, into a thick line of Friday-night traffic.

FORTY-ONE

BEN

As Ben and Melony walked side by side up the stone pathway leading to the front door, Ben laughed at a story Melony had just told him about something Sean had said to his teacher. When asked what he wanted to be when he grew up, Sean had said a bird.

Eager to check on the kids, Melony inserted the key into the lock when he stopped her. She turned toward him, and he cupped his hands around her face and said, "I love you."

"I miss you," she said. "The kids miss you, too. Come back home where you belong. Please?"

The kiss they shared was long and memorable. Melony meant the world to him. She was everything good in his life, and yet he needed more time to sort through his past and figure things out. Before he could respond, the door flew open.

Abigail stood just inside the house, her body shaking, her face red and blotchy, her eyes swollen from crying. "He took her," she said before lunging forward and burying her face in Melony's chest.

The hairs lifted at the back of Ben's neck as he stepped inside the house. Tables were overturned, and dining room chairs had been flipped on their sides. The kitchen floor was littered with broken glass and pans and utensils. What the hell had happened here?

His heart pounded against his rib cage. He turned back to where Melony stood with Abigail. "Where is Sean?"

About to rush upstairs, Ben abruptly stopped when a soft whimpering in the entry closet caught his attention. The door was ajar. He opened it wide and dug through coats. Sean's legs were buried deep inside Ben's old rain boots, and a long coat covered his body and face.

Thank God! Ben reached for his son, who was sucking his thumb, something he hadn't done in years. He held Sean close and whispered soothing words to him.

His first thought was that Roger Willis had come to his house seeking revenge. But Willis was in jail. He knew that for a fact and had even asked a friend to let him know if the coach was released on bail.

His second thought was that he had to find Olivia.

Ben carried Sean close to his chest as he ushered Melony and Abigail to the couch in the living room. He positioned Melony in the center of the sofa, then settled a child on both sides so they could huddle close to their mother.

He shut the front door, then turned away and headed for the kitchen. The slider leading to the pool had been broken. It was wide open, and shards of glass covered the floor inside and out. He called 9-1-1, gave them his address, and hung up the phone before stepping outside, where he called Olivia's name.

He scanned the yard for any sign of her.

Instead of Olivia, he found Higgins unmoving and half-hidden beneath thick shrubs at the far end of the yard. He grabbed a beach towel hanging on the pool railing and wrapped it around the dog before carrying him into the house.

The animal's breathing was shallow, and he didn't have the strength to lift his head when Ben set him down.

Ben was desperate to find Olivia. After checking the rest of the house, he bent down in front of Melony and the kids. "I need you to tell me what happened."

"They're too upset," Melony told him.

"I know," Ben said. "I'm sorry. But we must find Olivia."

Melony nodded. "Abigail," she said softly, stroking her daughter's head, "tell us what happened."

"He took her," Abigail said.

"Who took her?" Ben asked, trying to keep his voice calm.

"A doctor," Sean said, the clarity of his voice obstructed by the thumb.

"A doctor?" Ben asked. "Your doctor?"

He shook his head.

"Did you see his face?"

Another shake of his head.

"Tell me, Sean. It's very important so that we can find Olivia. Tell me what happened before we came home."

Sean removed his thumb from his mouth. His hands were shaking, and it broke Ben's heart.

"We were hiding in the closet," Sean said. "Olivia was outside with Higgins when someone grabbed her. She screamed and told us to hide and not come out no matter what. And then I heard someone crash through the door."

Abigail inhaled. "He said our daddy was a bad man and that you made your own dad go to jail for something you did."

Ben rubbed the area above his brow. Nothing made sense. He straightened and pulled out his cell and called Jessie.

"Hello?"

"Jessie, it's me, Ben." She had him on a speakerphone. "Where are you?"

"In the car on my way home from Clarksburg."

"I need you to come to my house in Citrus Heights."

"Why?"

"It's about Olivia."

"God. I forgot Olivia was babysitting for you and Melony tonight." There was a short pause before Jessie asked, "Did something happen? What's going on, Ben?"

He closed his eyes. "Someone broke into the house and took Olivia."

A long pause. "I don't understand."

Heat flushed through his body. He exhaled. He had to keep it together for all their sakes. "Olivia was outside with Higgins when she told Abigail and Sean to run and hide," Ben explained. "Higgins is hurt. It's bad." Every muscle in Ben's body quivered. "Sean said the man was a doctor. Does that mean anything to you?"

"Hold on a minute. I need to pull over for a minute. My hands are trembling. Did you call the police?"

"The police are on their way," Ben told her. "Listen," he said as steadily as he could manage, "we both need to keep it together. You need to take a breath."

"Okay. Okay." He heard her exhale. He did the same.

"What do you need to know?" Jessie asked.

"Sean said the man who took Olivia was a doctor."

"My friend Andriana is dating a doctor. God, Ben. I can't think straight. I don't know any doctors. Not personally."

"He walks funny, too," Abigail said from the couch.

"What did she say?" Jessie asked.

"Abigail said that the man who took Olivia walked funny." Ben looked at his daughter. "Did you see him walk funny, or did you hear him?"

"I saw him outside, and I heard him walking by the door and on the stairs when we were hiding in the closet. It sounded like he had a hurt leg, like our dog, Jake, when he had a bad leg."

"Diane Scott's killer had a limp," Jessie said. "I'm coming straight to your place."

Ben disconnected the call.

"He said he'd give us peppermints," Sean said, "if we stopped hiding."

Abigail's body was shaking. Melony pulled her close. "It's okay. We're here now. You're safe."

Ben thought about what Sean had said about the man who took Olivia blaming Ben for his father's incarceration. That narrowed down the list drastically.

An inmate, he thought.

Peppermints.

A prison counselor.

Dean Crawford.

He hit "Speed Dial" and began to pace the room. Zee answered on the first ring. "I need your help."

"What is it?"

"I need you to search the internet and find a photo of Dean Crawford. He's a counselor at the Folsom Prison."

"Yeah, I know."

"Then I need you to get a hold of Jessie's lawyer friend, Andriana, and find a way to send her the photo via text. And I want you to ask her if Crawford is the doctor she is dating. Got that?"

"This has been a busy night."

"Do you need to repeat any of that back to me?" Ben asked, ignoring her random thoughts.

"Nope. Got it."

"If it is the same man," Ben told her, "I'll need Crawford's home address."

"The only address I have for Crawford is his aunt's in Folsom."

She rattled off the address, and Ben didn't bother asking how the hell she'd managed that so quickly.

"I'll call you back when I have more," she said before hanging up.

Ben shoved his phone into his coat pocket. "Melony, I can't leave you and the kids here. It's not safe." He helped her and the kids up. "I'm going to take all three of you across the street to the neighbors'. The police should be here soon. I'll call Jessie back in a minute and tell her where you and the kids are. Okay?"

Melony nodded.

After Ben felt sure his family was safe, he climbed inside Melony's car and took a breath. Before he could get his seat belt fastened, his cell phone rang. It was Zee. She'd been quick.

"The doctor known as Vince Croal," Zee said, "is also Dean Crawford. Andriana is upset, and she wants to know what's going on."

"Call her back and tell her not to make contact with the man unless I ask her to. Tell her it's a life-and-death situation."

"Anything else?"

It was too soon to mention anything about Olivia. He'd leave that up to Jessie. "Thanks, Zee. I'll fill you in later."

"Ten four."

He plugged Crawford's aunt's address on Crestview Drive in Folsom into the navigation system. It was less than eight miles away.

Forty-Two

Dean Crawford

Dean wasn't worried about getting caught. He'd been watching Ben's wife and kids long enough to know the layout of the property and the neighborhood. There was no security system in the vicinity, which he found odd considering Ben was a crime reporter.

He tapped his finger on the steering wheel. Unfortunately, Ben's children would live to see another day. How many days, exactly, was a mystery.

Ben would pay the ultimate price for being at his father's trial and doing nothing to stop him from being incarcerated. He'd betrayed the man who had given him life.

He squeezed his eyes shut for half a second, trying to block out the pain. But it was always there. Every single day for forty years, he'd relived his daddy's death.

It had been raining that day. His mom had gotten dressed up all pretty the day she'd brought him to see his dad in prison. He'd loved his daddy. Every single decent and good memory he had was from time spent with him.

Instead of taking him to the room where he got to talk to Dad on the phone and look at him through the glass, his mom ushered him to a bench inside a dimly lit room. It reminded him of a movie house with a curtain and everything. He and his mom sat and waited for a long time. There were metal risers, too, like you see at a baseball game. There weren't a lot of people inside the room. His main thought that day had been how excited he was to see his dad.

When the curtains finally divided and he saw his daddy strapped to a table, needles in his arms, he didn't know what to think. "There now. Aren't you happy?" his mom asked. "You've been nagging me to bring you to see your daddy. So here we are." She patted his knee. "You're not supposed to be in here, so keep quiet. You get to see your daddy's execution."

He'd only been seven at the time, and he wasn't really sure what she'd meant. He could see lots of tubes running from a machine to his daddy's body, though, and it didn't look good.

"Those men are going to shoot your daddy up with some medicine that will help him sleep. And then they're going to give him something to paralyze his muscles." Mom smiled at him then and patted his leg as if everything was going to be okay. Never mind that he wished *she* were the one strapped to the table behind the window.

"Once he can't move," she went on, "they're going to give him something that will stop his heart, and it will all be over, and you'll never ever have to think of your daddy again."

"I don't want him to die."

"That's too bad now, isn't it?"

On the other side of the glass, a man stood by his dad's side and was reading from a book. And then came a loud whirring sound of monitors as they began to blink. His daddy started thrashing his head from left to right, left to right. His mouth opened wide, and his whole body started shaking and jerking. Dean thought he was going to be sick. Two people sitting on the other bench jumped up. The lady walked quickly to the back of the room with her hand over her mouth.

Dean had visited his daddy twice in prison. Daddy had told him how awful it was being there and how the other inmates tortured him and did things to him that were so horrible he couldn't repeat them to his only son. He'd said how much he loved Dean and how he wished he could get out and they could go fishing and to the movies.

Dean wanted that more than anything.

As he watched his daddy on the table, he could still remember how his heart started beating real fast, and his hands got clammy.

He needed to save him. He ran to the front right as Dad's body lurched upward. The straps around his body strained to keep him in place as his daddy gasped for breath.

Dean screamed as he pounded his fists against the glass. An officer grabbed him, said kids weren't allowed, and steered him toward the exit.

Dean looked at his mom as he passed her by. Her eyes were bright, and that smile was still plastered over her face. She looked the happiest he'd ever seen her.

Dean's life had been mostly shit since he was born, but the time spent in that room had changed something inside of him, filling him with such deep hatred that it had become a part of him, like the blood flowing through his veins.

Months later, he and his mom moved from Nevada to California to live with his aunt. And every single day his dark thoughts became darker. All he could think about after viewing the execution was, *Daddy's not coming home. Nobody's coming home.*

Dean's breathing was erratic as he tamped down thoughts of Daddy.

It was late. His plan was to drive down a familiar dirt track off Auburn-Folsom Road, across the street from the outlets. He would park his car within the trees and take care of the girl inside his trunk.

His cell phone buzzed. He pulled it from his pocket. It was his mother, so he didn't answer.

Thirty seconds later it buzzed again.

Fuck. "What is it?"

"Aunt Jillian is dead."

"She's probably in a deep sleep," he told his mom. "Leave her alone and go back to bed."

"I think I killed her."

"You didn't kill her. Please go back to bed, and I'll be home soon."

"I'm going to call 9-1-1."

"Don't call the police!"

"I have to."

"Okay. Okay. I'm going to turn around and come right home."

No response.

"Do you hear me?" There were hardly any other cars on the road, but he couldn't risk making an illegal U-turn with an unconscious child in the trunk. He'd kicked her a few times and thumped her on the head pretty good before shoving her in the trunk. Maybe she was already dead. That would make things easier.

"I think I should call the police," Mom said. "Jillian is dead."

He exhaled. "Where is she right now?"

"On the sofa."

He tried to think of a list of questions he could ask Mom to keep her on the phone. It would take him another three or four minutes to get home. As soon as she hung up, she might call the police. He couldn't let that happen. They would try to contact him at his work, which was tonight's alibi.

Fuck. Fuck. Fuck. "Did you take Aunt Jillian's pulse?"

"I don't know how. She's dead. I need the police to take her away."

Why was she so fucking sure she was dead? His mom didn't know her own name most of the time. And since when did she have enough clarity to even know to call the police? He'd never bought her an emergency home alert for just this reason—he didn't want her contacting the authorities . . . ever. He'd gone to great lengths to keep from being found out. He wasn't going to let two old ladies fuck it all up.

"Why do you think she's dead, Mom?"

"She was choking. Her plate is on the floor." A long pause, and then a scuffling noise in the background. "Looks like she was eating chicken."

"You didn't see her choking, did you?"

"Yes."

Aunt Jillian was his mom's twin sister. There was no way she would watch her sister choke and do nothing about it. "Did you try to help her?"

"No."

Crazy old bat. "Why not?"

"I was mad at her."

"About what?"

"I don't remember." Another pause. "The police will know what to do."

He pulled into the driveway forty-five seconds after she hung up on him. He shut off the engine and ran inside the house.

He found his mother in the kitchen, dipping an Oreo cookie into a puddle of milk on the counter before taking a bite. Her other hand held a phone against her ear. He grabbed the phone from her and held it to his ear. There was no dial tone. Nothing.

"They're busy," she said. "They asked me to hold."

"Who?"

"The police."

He yanked the cord from the wall. "I asked you not to call them. I'm sick of your bullshit." It had gotten to the point lately where she was either rubbing her feces on the wall or making trouble with her sister. He tossed the phone across the room. When he turned back to face her, she had a knife pointed at him. "Stay away from me."

This wasn't the first time she'd threatened him, but her timing couldn't be worse. "What the hell is wrong with you?"

"Your father left me because of you."

Now *that* was a first! He nearly doubled over with laughter. "Daddy left because you were a nagging, dirty whore."

She wagged the knife at him, her hand trembling.

"The only reason you're still alive is because I allowed you to be." He stabbed a finger into his chest. "I'm God, do you understand?"

She set the knife down and went back to eating her cookie.

He shook his head in disgust before he went in search of Aunt Jillian. He found her on the sofa right where Mom had said she was, with a plate of food upside down on the ground by her feet. Jillian's head had fallen back on the cushion. Her skin was a grayish pasty white. Her mouth was open. He wrapped his fingers around her wrist and felt for a pulse.

Definitely dead.

Some sort of sauce dribbled off her chin and down her neck. No point in sticking his finger down her throat to see if there was a bone lodged there. He needed to put her in her room and lock the door, where Mom wouldn't see her. Deal with her later. He was bending down to lift his aunt into his arms when the front door opened with a bang.

Ben

Ben pulled up next to the curb outside the house. He jumped out and ran to the car parked in the driveway. It was a beat-up, older-model Chevy Impala. He tried to open the trunk, but it was locked. He peeked through the windows. The floor was littered with papers and fast-food wrappers.

Olivia had to be in the house. Intent on finding her, he followed the pathway leading to the house. Heat flushed through his body at the thought of the man terrorizing his children. As he approached the front door, he decided to keep the element of surprise on his side. He did not want to give Crawford a chance to hide or run out a back door. He would knock down the damn door if he had to. Consequences be damned.

Ben wrapped his fingers around the door handle, surprised to find it unlocked. He thrust the door open and stepped inside.

A powerful stench filled his nostrils. His eyes stung. Garbage and food scraps covered the floor. Every part of the house was piled high with boxes, clothes, paper, and plastic bags.

There was an elderly woman on the couch. Food covered her face and trickled down her throat. He didn't have to take her pulse to see that she was dead. His gaze moved from the woman to Dean Crawford.

The man was definitely surprised to see him.

Ben's hands curled into fists at his side. "Where is she?"

Crawford straightened. "I don't have a clue what you're talking about."

He made the mistake of glancing out the window toward the Chevy Impala parked in the driveway.

Olivia must be in the trunk.

She had to be.

Ben thought of his children at home. Finding Sean trembling inside the closet, afraid for his life. His children would never be the same. He felt edgy and twitchy as adrenaline rushed through his body. What had Crawford done with Olivia?

Ben lunged for the man, slamming into him and bringing him to the floor.

Crawford grunted as the coffee table buckled beneath them.

They rolled across the living room. Ben grabbed hold of Crawford's wrist and yanked hard and fast so that Crawford was pinned beneath him, his face pressed against the floor, his arm restrained behind his back.

Crawford bucked and kicked, then used his free arm to reach behind Ben and grab a chunk of his hair, a maneuver that allowed him to free himself from Ben's grasp.

Crawford shot to his feet.

Ben reached for his legs, yanked him back down, and dragged him toward him. Crawford jabbed an elbow into Ben's temple, sending bolts of pain through his body. It took Ben a second to find his bearings and get to his feet. The fireplace utensils caught his eye, and he grabbed the fireplace poker and caught up to Crawford before he made it out the door.

Holding both ends of the poker, Ben lifted the iron over Crawford's head, snug against his neck, and pulled the man backward against his chest, choking him.

Gasping for air, Crawford reached over his shoulders and clawed at Ben's face. He then leaned backward, putting his full weight into Ben, and they both toppled to the floor. Ben's head smashed into a corner of the brick fireplace. A sharp pain shot through his side. His chest tightened and his vision blurred.

Crawford coughed and gasped for air. Before Ben could get upright, Crawford was on top of him, using all his strength to push the iron poker against Ben's throat. Ben grasped on to both ends of the poker, grimacing as he fought to push him away.

"You can't suppress what's inside of you," Crawford said through gritted teeth, his face red. "I know firsthand. It'll make you crazy. I tried. For years I stopped killing, Ben. I stopped just like you. It doesn't work. Once the seed has been planted, the urges never go away."

The veins in Crawford's neck bulged as he pushed down hard, trying to cut off Ben's airway. Ben wasn't sure how much longer he would last. He could feel the oxygen leaving his brain, his muscles weakening as he looked into the eyes of a deranged man.

"You should have left well enough alone," Crawford ground out. "You killed that girl and let your dad rot in prison for a murder *you* committed."

Ben couldn't hold him at bay any longer.

It was over. Fatigue was setting in. He thought of Melony and the kids, and that's when an old woman appeared like an apparition. As she rushed toward them, a flash of steel glimmered in her hand. Her silver hair flew around her face. Ben saw the whites of her eyes as she stabbed the sharp blade of a knife into the back of Crawford's neck, again and again.

Blood sprayed across Ben's face.

Crawford arched upward and let out a high-pitched wail before the full weight of him slumped forward on top of Ben.

Ben turned his head to one side, wheezing and struggling for air. Trapped beneath the man, he attempted to push the deadweight off him, but it was no use. He couldn't move his arms.

FORTY-THREE

COLIN

Colin was on the highway, five minutes from his destination, when he got a call from Jessie.

"She's missing," Jessie said, her voice lined with panic. "Olivia is gone!"

He kept his eyes on the road in front of him. "What happened?"

"Olivia was babysitting for Ben and Melony when someone broke into the house and took her."

"What about the kids she was watching?"

"Olivia told them to hide, and that's what they did. He was unable to find them before Ben and Melony returned home and scared him off. I'm on my way to Ben's house in Citrus Heights right now," she said. "Ben believes a staff member at Folsom Prison is the culprit."

Colin's heart dropped to his stomach. *Dean Crawford,* he thought. If he told her what he knew about Crawford, that the man could be responsible for the recent murders in the area, she would be even more terrified. "I'm going to have to get off the phone," he said calmly. "Stay with Melony and the kids when you get there, and I'll call you back as soon as I can."

Colin disconnected the call and then hooked up with dispatch and told them to send backup as he pulled up to the curb and parked. He climbed out of his vehicle and looked around. The street was quiet.

Nobody was inside the car parked in the driveway. As he walked toward the house, he noticed that the front door had been left wide open. He readied his gun as he walked that way.

The quiet was downright deafening.

Where were Ben and Olivia?

The only sounds were his footfalls hitting the pavement as he approached the front entry. A horrible smell greeted him just outside the door. Chills swept over him. His senses were on high alert, but nothing could have prepared him for what he saw when he stepped inside the house.

Straight ahead, a wild-eyed gray-haired woman stared at him from the kitchen. Blood dripped from her hands onto her nightgown. To his left was another elderly woman sprawled out on the couch, her mouth open, her dinner plate at her feet. And in front of the fireplace was a man with a knife protruding from his back.

Stepping closer, he saw movement.

Ben Morrison was pinned beneath a dead man, struggling for air.

With one hand, Colin grabbed hold of the man slumped over Ben and pulled him to the side. Once he knew the man was dead and not a danger, he strapped his gun in its holster.

"Olivia," Ben croaked.

"Can you get up?" Colin asked.

Ben shook his head. "Olivia. I think she might be in the trunk of the car parked in the driveway. Keys," he said, gesturing with his chin toward the dead man. Ben didn't look well. He closed his eyes.

Colin reached around in the dead man's pockets until he found the keys. Pushing himself to his feet, he rushed from the house and to the driveway, where he used the key to pop open the trunk.

Olivia was on her side, curled in a fetal position. When Colin reached for her, she came alive, legs kicking and one skinny arm flailing as she used her fingernails to claw at his face. The guttural sound coming out of her broke his heart.

He pulled back a few inches. "It's okay, Olivia," he said. "It's me, Colin."

She didn't stop fighting, only screamed louder, determined to pluck out his eyeballs. Her small fist connected with his chin before she realized nobody was fighting her.

All movement stopped.

Her breathing was ragged as she blinked. "Colin?"

"It's me. You're safe now."

Her body began to shake, her bottom lip trembling. Reaching for him, she squeezed his arm and looked at him through badly swollen eyes. Her face was almost unrecognizable. "Abigail and Sean? Are they okay?"

Her voice was hoarse. "The kids you were babysitting are okay," Colin said. "Their mother and Jessie are with them now." He couldn't bear to see her like this. There was a deep laceration on her arm and cuts and bruises everywhere. "Everything is going to be okay."

Olivia was as tough as they came. He'd never seen her cry before, but she was crying now.

He scooped her into his arms and carried her to his car. She clung to him tightly, and there was no way he would leave her alone. Her sobs were broken up by short pauses as she tried to recover her breath. "It's okay," he said again as he rocked her like he used to rock Piper when she was small.

Forty-Four

Jessie

On the drive to Citrus Heights, Jessie tried her best not to panic, but it was no use. Her heart raced, and she couldn't stop horrible thoughts from running through her mind. Was Olivia really gone? Gone from her life forever, like Sophie?

Stay calm, she told herself. She couldn't possibly be of any help to Olivia in her current state of mind.

When she finally arrived at Ben's house, she had to park at the end of a long line of police vehicles. She sat there for a moment, her fingers curled tightly around the steering wheel. "Olivia," she whispered, "where are you?"

A few minutes later, Jessie watched as a woman approached her car. She recognized her from a picture she'd once seen on Ben's desk at his work. Jessie climbed out of the car. "Melony?"

Melony nodded as she wrapped her arms around Jessie. "Ben's going to find her," Melony said when they stepped apart.

The tears came then, and Jessie wiped her eyes as she nodded, hoping it was true. "You haven't heard from him, have you?"

Melony shook her head. "Higgins is in bad shape. My neighbor," she said as she gestured across the street, "took him to the vet. I'm afraid he's lost a lot of blood."

Jessie's stomach turned. Lost in her fears of Olivia being alone with a madman, Jessie rubbed her arms as she watched the crime scene technicians searching the front of Ben and Melony's property for evidence. Crime tape secured the property. "Did you or Ben see anyone leaving the premises when you arrived?" Jessie asked Melony.

"No."

"How did he get inside?" Jessie asked.

"It looked as if he used a large rock to shatter the glass door leading to the backyard."

"Why would he go after the kids?" Jessie asked. "It makes no sense." She was shivering. Not from the cold but from fright.

Melony shook her head. "I've been wondering the same thing, but I'm at a loss."

Jessie's phone rang. A million thoughts swept through her at once. "It's Colin," she said in a shaky voice as she picked up the call.

"Olivia is okay," Colin said. "She's with me."

"Thank God." Jessie's knees buckled, and she sat on the curb, held the phone to her ear, and wept.

"Are you there?"

"Yes. Yes, I'm here." All the tension had left her shoulders. Jessie looked up at Melony, whose palm was pressed to her chest. "Olivia is okay," Jessie told her. Her heart filled with gratitude.

Melony brightened before rushing off to the neighbors' house to share the news.

"Colin," Jessie asked, "where is Olivia now?"

"I'm in the ambulance with her. Meet us at Mercy Hospital in Folsom."

"Okay," she said as she pushed herself to her feet. "I'll be there soon. Thank you, Colin." Jessie rushed to her car, jumped in behind the wheel, and started the engine just as Melony stepped outside again. Jessie rolled down the window. "Olivia is being taken to Mercy Hospital," she said before she drove off.

Her phone rang again. It was Andriana. She hit the green button on the console. Andriana's sobs made it difficult to understand what she was saying. "Is she okay?" Andriana asked again. "Is Olivia going to be all right?"

"Colin said she is okay. I'm on my way to the hospital now. I'll call you when I know more."

"I should have known something was going on with that man."

"What man?" Jessie asked.

"You haven't heard? Vince Croal, the man you saw leaving my house, was actually Dean Crawford, a counselor at Folsom Prison."

Why? Jessie thought. *Why would this person go after Andriana?*

"After he left me at the movies to catch a cab home, I knew he wasn't the man for me, but he kept calling and saying all the right things. And I fell for it again."

Jessie had no idea where Andriana was going with this. "What happened?"

"He was going to come over tonight for dinner, but I had to work late, so I canceled."

She was crying again. "If I hadn't turned him down tonight, maybe he never would have taken Olivia."

Jessie knew where this was going. "Olivia and Ben's kids are okay," she said. "If you hadn't canceled, we might not be talking right now." Jessie pulled into the hospital parking lot and began searching for a parking space. "I'm here now and I have to go. Will you be all right?"

"We'll talk later," Andriana said. "Let me know how Olivia is doing, and let me know if you need anything."

"I will." Jessie disconnected the call, jumped out of the car, and ran across the parking lot to the hospital entrance. The glass sliders opened automatically, and Colin greeted her in the lobby. "Where is she?" she asked, out of breath.

"They're taking her to a room. They want to keep her overnight so they can keep a close eye on her."

Her heart rate plummeted. "Why?"

Colin reached for her hand. "She's going to be fine, but she doesn't look like herself. You need to prepare yourself, Jessie. If Olivia sees you looking upset, she's going to get upset, too, and that's not going to help matters."

"What did that monster do to her?"

"She took multiple blows to the head and body. Her face is badly bruised and swollen. The doctor wants to make sure there's no internal bleeding. Her shoulder was dislocated, which surprised me because she put up a good fight when I found her, and she showed no signs of giving up."

Jessie had a difficult time swallowing. The thought of some lunatic beating up Olivia made her sick. "How could this happen?"

Colin shook his head.

Jessie couldn't think straight. "I need to see her."

Colin took her hand and led her to the elevators. They waited in silence until the doors opened, and they stepped inside. They got off on the second floor. Jessie took a couple of deep breaths to prepare herself for what lay ahead.

Colin showed his badge and explained to the nurse at the front desk that Jessie was Olivia's aunt and legal guardian, and they were given the okay to go on. "The next door on the right," Colin told her.

Jessie walked right in and rushed to Olivia's side. Her head was wrapped in gauze, her eyes tiny slits encircled by black and blue. She had myriad nicks and cuts over both arms. She took Olivia's hand in hers. "It's me, Jessie," she said. "I'm here."

Olivia's fingers twitched.

A nurse fiddling with the machines close by said, "She was given some pain medication. In another ten minutes she'll be out."

"Higgins," Olivia said, her voice raspy.

"He's at the vet," Jessie said, closing her eyes, hoping Olivia didn't see the pained expression on her face.

Jessie squeezed Olivia's hand. "Get some rest."

She glanced at Colin.

He came to her side and kissed her forehead before letting her know he needed to head out but would be back later to check on both of them.

Olivia was already asleep, so Jessie followed him just out the door and into the hallway. "I need to know what happened to the man who did this to Olivia."

"He's dead."

She rubbed her temple. She had many more questions, but now wasn't the time or place. Colin had work to do, and Jessie needed to be with Olivia. "Thank you for finding her and keeping her safe."

"I hate to think of how this might have turned out if Ben Morrison hadn't gotten to Dean Crawford first and kept him from leaving before I arrived."

Jessie had had no idea. "Ben was already there?"

Colin nodded. "He and Crawford had a run-in. Ben is messed up pretty bad. He was in the emergency room downstairs when they brought Olivia to her room." Colin tipped her chin upward so she had no choice but to look in his eyes. "Are you okay?" he asked.

"I'll be fine. Go," she said with a tight smile. "I'll see you later."

As Colin walked away, she thought about Ben. She'd been looking into his past for a while now, and yet she wasn't any closer to knowing the truth about who he really was. Nikki's mother had said Ben had killed Aly Scheer, but she wasn't a credible witness. Lou Wheeler had served time for the murder, and now he was dead.

Jessie hadn't had time to process the information. Like it or not, for now she planned to keep what she knew to herself. Maybe she would never know who Ben Morrison really was. Good? Bad? Satan or saint?

Ben had saved her and Zee from a monster. And now Olivia.

He was a complex person, and she'd never met anyone like him. Ben hadn't chosen to lose all memory of his past.

A machine beeped in Olivia's room. She turned and stepped inside. Her sweet Olivia was a fighter, and she was alive.

She stood silently watching over her niece. Ben Morrison had saved her life.

Fuck it, she thought. She was done inwardly tormenting herself as to whether Ben was good or bad. It was her decision to make, and her cross to bear.

Team Ben all the way.

Ben

Ben opened his eyes, struggling to figure out where he was and how he'd gotten there.

A woman with a familiar face pushed open the curtain.

"You're awake," she said, her eyes bright.

The moment he laid eyes on her, the tension left his shoulders, and his body relaxed. It wasn't until she brushed her lips across his and took hold of his hand that he remembered that she was his wife, Melony.

"The doctor said you've suffered a mini stroke, also known as a TIA."

He knew it was true. His vision was cloudy. He'd lost coordination, and until a few minutes ago he'd been unable to understand what the people around him were saying. "I'm fine," he said, although he wasn't sure.

"You have a broken arm and a bruised hip," she told him. "And you could be suffering from a concussion on top of everything else. They will only let you go if you sign a document saying that you have someone to take care of you."

Ben wasn't sure what she was getting at until she asked, "Will you come home now and let me take care of you, please? I won't leave you here alone. I'll sleep here in the room if I must."

Enough of his senses had returned for him to recall that he'd been steering clear of Melony and the kids because he hadn't been sure if he was a danger to them. But that was ridiculous.

His family needed him.

And he knew deep down that he would never cause Melony or his children harm. He looked at her and said, "Where are those papers? I'm ready to come home."

EPILOGUE

JESSIE

Thanksgiving Day had come and gone, but Jessie and Olivia had a lot to be thankful for and decided to celebrate anyway. Better late than never.

"Come in," Jessie called when she heard the doorbell. She greeted Ben and Melony with a hug. "Olivia is in her room," she told Abigail and Sean, then watched them run in the direction she pointed.

"I'll be right back," Melony said. "I want to say hello to Olivia and see how she's doing."

She headed off, and Jessie took a moment to look Ben over. He'd suffered a TIA, concussion, broken arm, and cuts and bruises. Like Olivia, he wore a sling on his left arm. "I'm glad you could make it," she told him.

She peered deep into his eyes, thinking about all they had been through. Jessie had recently decided she would tell Ben everything she knew and let him figure out what to do with the information. "You look happier than I've seen you in a very long time," she told him.

"I feel good." He smiled. "I'm almost back to my old self. I haven't had a flashback or seen images of any sort since leaving the hospital."

"That's great," she said. "And it looks like you and Melony are back together."

He nodded. "Our family is whole again. We're doing well. How's Olivia been?"

"She's bruised, physically and emotionally, but we'll get through this like we get through everything else."

"And you?"

"I'll be fine. I always am."

"You're a rock," he said.

"Will you be returning to work soon?"

"Next week."

"Wonderful."

He nodded. "I was hoping you and I could get together and talk about what Nikki Seymour's mom had to say when you visited."

"Sounds good," Jessie said, and she meant it. "You know where to find me."

The doorbell rang again, and Jessie excused herself. Zee had brought Tobey. A few days ago, Zee told Jessie she couldn't fight the recent influx of intuitive messages. Her crystals, tarot cards, and daily horoscope readings all pointed to Tobey being the "one." They were growing into fast friends.

"Where's your Dad?" Jessie asked.

Zee rolled her eyes. "He and his girlfriend are in Sonora, visiting with her family."

"I came in Mr. Gatley's place," Tobey said. "I hope you don't mind."

"Not at all. We're glad to have you."

"Can I talk to you for a second?" Zee asked Jessie.

They stepped a few feet away. "I found the car Ben rented," Zee said quietly. "The front of the car was badly damaged. There was fur and blood stuck to the bumper. He definitely hit an animal."

Jessie smiled.

"That makes you happy?"

"No," Jessie said. "Not at all." She knew Zee didn't like to be touched, but she didn't care. She put her arms around Zee and hugged her tight. "Thank you for everything, Zee."

Zee untangled herself from Jessie's arms. "Does this mean I get a raise?"

"No," Jessie said happily. "Of course not."

Colin and his ten-year-old daughter, Piper, were the next to arrive. Piper ran straight to Jessie and whispered in her ear, "We have a surprise."

Colin hadn't appeared yet, but Jessie had an idea what the surprise was. She told Piper to tell Olivia to come out to the main room. Jessie's small house was filling up quickly. Earlier today she'd set up two bridge tables and added a leaf to the dining room table. With one arm, Olivia had helped her set both tables with tablecloths and mismatched plates and utensils.

Colin came up the stairs and stepped into the main room, carrying Higgins. The kids all ran to him, and everyone huddled around the dog.

Olivia's sling prevented her from taking Higgins from Colin, but tears came to her eyes. Colin led her to the couch and set down Higgins next to her so she could pet him with her good arm.

Olivia cringed when she saw the long and winding path of stitches across Higgins's side.

Jessie was thankful she hadn't canceled payments on the pet insurance since Higgins had needed two surgeries. She squeezed a path through the kids so she could say hello to their miracle dog. Even Cecil, the cat, came out of the bedroom and jumped up on the couch to see Higgins.

Jessie's father was the last to arrive. She greeted him at the door. "How are you doing, Dad?"

"Not bad," he said as his body swayed slightly.

"Have you been drinking?"

"Just a few beers."

They stared at each other for a long moment.

"Should I leave?" he asked.

"No." She stepped close and gave him a hug, conjuring old memories before Mom left Dad and her two daughters without any goodbyes. Dad was a lot like her sister, Sophie. He'd been unable to handle Mom's absence and now spent most of his days in his favorite recliner, drinking his sorrows away.

She swallowed the sadness creeping upward, took hold of his hand, and led Dad upstairs to meet her friends.

Hours later, after everyone had had their fill of turkey, mashed potatoes, and pie, Ben, Jessie, and Colin gathered outside to talk about Dean Crawford.

"From what we've pieced together so far," Colin said without preamble, "Dean Crawford was a mix of an organized and unorganized killer. He was employed, educated, cunning, and controlled. But through the years it seems he was going through a psychological transformation. He was forced to view his beloved father's execution. We believe that may be the instigating factor that sent him down the wrong path."

"What about his mother?" Jessie asked.

"Crawford's mother has been moved to an assisted-living facility."

"Where was she when her husband was executed?"

"Not only did she get a personal invitation from the warden to watch her husband's execution, she snuck her son into the viewing room with her. We don't have the entire picture yet—that will take some time—but we've talked to people who knew Crawford and his mother when they were living in Nevada. Crawford was abused and demeaned by the woman on a daily basis. He hated her. After his father's death, they moved to his aunt's house in Folsom. We've already linked Dean Crawford to at least two murders in Nevada."

"Nevada?" Ben asked.

"Only a two-hour drive from his aunt's house," Colin explained. "Not only were we able to connect the marking Crawford carved on his victims, we found charges on his aunt's credit card for an apartment in Reno. After getting his degree, we believe he headed for Nevada to practice killing. Once he felt confident he wouldn't get caught, he began to search for victims closer to home."

"It sounds to me as if Crawford blamed his mother for his father's death and transferred that rage to anyone who helped put someone in prison." Jessie exhaled. "It's a wonder he didn't harm his mother and aunt."

"It's likely he would have killed both women long ago if his aunt hadn't been receiving Social Security checks."

"Do you know anything about his MO?" Ben asked.

"It'll be years before we know," Colin said, "but it seems his number one target was friends and relatives of inmates who had testified against them in court. Crawford's mother testified against his father. The theory is that Crawford purposely searched for and found a career inside the prison walls. That choice forced him to relive his father's last few years."

"He only made things more difficult for himself," Jessie observed.

"Exactly. Between his career choice and taking care of his elderly mother and aunt for many years, everything probably wore on him and eventually caused him to make mistakes."

"Okay," Ben said, "so he came after me and my family because I was on the stand at my father's trial. But why would he target Jessie and her friend Andriana?"

"And there's also Easton and Diane Scott," Jessie said. "Zee and I have been unable to find any connection between the Scotts and Folsom Prison. In fact, nobody in Easton's family has ever been jailed."

Colin shifted his weight from one foot to the other. "A serial killer's MO is sometimes altered to reflect changes in the killer's life. Often it has more to do with the 'how' than the 'who.' Crawford felt a need to kill. It must have been difficult for him to stick to only killing people who had testified against an inmate. So he quickly learned to branch out and go after anyone he considered to be in his way."

"Lou Wheeler only recently became Dean Crawford's patient," Ben stated.

"That's right," Colin said. "Crawford's notes about Lou Wheeler are revealing in that he sympathized greatly with the man and believed you were responsible for his incarceration."

Ben stiffened. "So I became his focus."

Colin nodded. "And anyone and everyone you associated with."

"I was able to trace the anonymous calls I received to Dean Crawford's cell," Jessie said. "But what about Lou Wheeler's murder? Do you think Crawford was involved in some way?"

"The investigation is ongoing," Colin said. "Again, no telling how long it will be before we have all the answers, if ever."

Jessie glanced at Ben. He appeared deep in thought. She had hoped Ben could at least have closure as to his father's murder. So much of Ben's life was a mystery. And now this, too, would be added to the list. Her heart also went out to Easton and Diane Scott. "If Easton hadn't hired me, Diane might still be alive."

"Don't do it," Ben said. "Don't play the blame game."

Colin nodded his agreement before adding, "It's Dean Crawford's signature that is the most revealing. Ren Howe, who you've met," Colin told Jessie, "is responsible for finding the marking on so many victims. The branding Crawford left on his victims will help us find more victims."

"You and your men should be commended for your outstanding work," Ben said.

Jessie looked at Ben and Colin. "You both played a big part in taking that man down and finding Olivia before it was too late. I'm forever indebted to both of you."

Olivia found them outside and told Jessie that Grandpa and Zee and Tobey were all about to leave. Jessie, Ben, and Colin seemed lost in thought as they headed back inside.

Ben and Melony insisted on dropping Jessie's dad off at home since it was on their way. Everyone left but Colin and Piper.

Olivia and Piper wanted to hang out in Olivia's room, and they asked Colin to carry Higgins to the bed. She and Colin sipped wine and talked as they hand-washed all the dishes. When they finished cleaning up, Jessie lifted her wineglass. "I think we should make a toast."

Colin had switched to water, but he lifted his glass. "To great food," he said with a wink. "And even better company." He smiled as he looked around. "I never thought we'd ever find time to be alone."

"To many more moments just like this one," Jessie said.

They clinked their glasses.

"Maybe we can go on a dinner date this week," Colin said. "I'll bring Piper over to stay with Olivia. What do you think?"

"I'm just not sure Olivia is ready to babysit again. I already know she'll say she's ready, but how could anyone get over something so horrific in such a short time?"

"She'll never forget what happened, but she will be fine. They don't make kids like they used to. They're stronger, smarter, much more aware. If Olivia thinks she is ready, then I'm sure she is."

Jessie took a sip of her wine, and when she looked at Colin, she realized he was staring at her. She lifted an eyebrow. "What?"

"Has anyone ever told you how beautiful you are?"

"Only you."

He took her wineglass and set it on the counter along with his water glass. Then he turned back to her and pulled her close. She rested her head on his chest and simply breathed him in.

"Olivia mentioned she was saving for a car," Colin said as he brushed his fingers through Jessie's hair. "Does that mean she's raising her babysitting rates?"

"Most likely. I really don't like the idea of her driving."

"I don't envy you," he said. "First driving and then dating, and next thing you know she'll be moving out on her own."

Jessie pulled away so she could look at him. "It all goes so fast, doesn't it?"

"Too fast."

Their gazes held for a long moment. "Have I told you I loved you?"

Jessie shook her head. "Not in a very long time."

"Well, I do."

"I love you, too." And then quickly her thoughts shifted to what Nikki Seymour's mom had told her about Ben. A bit of guilt swept over her. "I have a question."

"Shoot," Colin said.

"What if I knew something or I did something against the law, and you found out. Would you choose me or the law?"

A frown crossed his face as he appeared to ponder the question.

Jessie was quiet.

"I don't believe you would ever do anything horrible enough that I would have to question whether or not to turn you in," Colin said. "I know you and trust you wholeheartedly to make the right decision in all things, so therefore I would choose you every time." He smiled at her. "Did I pass?"

She laughed. They spent the next hour holding hands and catching up on life, enjoying their time together. The best part was just listening to his voice.

He glanced at his watch. "I better go. I promised Piper's mom I would have her home before ten." Colin stood and then pulled Jessie up, too. He leaned in for a kiss, and in that moment, everything felt right in the world. Her stomach fluttered, and she felt tingly all over, reminding her of the first time they'd ever kissed.

He pulled back slightly so that he could peer into her eyes and said in a low voice, "One of these days we're going to have sex."

"Sounds good to me."

His eyebrow shot up. "Really?"

"Definitely."

"If I didn't have to get Piper home, you would be in trouble right now."

She laughed. "How much trouble?"

"Mega trouble. If I'd known I had a chance to get lucky, I would have nudged everyone out the door hours ago."

She laughed as they headed for Olivia's room.

The girls were on the floor next to Olivia's bed. They had managed to find an assortment of makeup and had organized it into neat rows. Eye shadows first, then lipsticks and blush.

Piper had on gobs of blue eye shadow, black eyeliner, and bright pink lipstick. Olivia's eyes were hard to see through the false eyelashes. Gold glitter covered her eyelids, and her lips were bloodred. Her bruises were mostly gone now, and she no longer needed to wear the sling around her arm while she slept.

Higgins watched them from the bed. He looked sort of out of it, but his nails had been polished, and she could see that he was happy to be back home. Cecil strolled out from under the bed, his face sprinkled with gold glitter.

"Come on, Piper," Colin said, "I promised your mom I'd have you home by ten."

She moaned.

Jessie looked at Olivia. "We'll wait in the living room for you and Piper to get cleaned up and ready to go."

As soon as they were out of earshot, Colin pulled Jessie aside. "Tomorrow night. My place, say six o'clock?"

A warm and fuzzy feeling washed over her. "I'll be there."

Acknowledgments

Many thanks to Liz Pearsons and Charlotte Herscher, the best editing team an author could ask for! And to Amy Tannenbaum, I appreciate all that you do, and I'm so grateful for the advice you've given me. Thank you, Sarah Shaw and the Thomas & Mercer Author Team, for all your support. Cheers to copyeditor Karen Brown for her incredible eye for detail. Much appreciation to Brian McDougle, an amazing detective who answers all my questions quickly and thoroughly. I am grateful to my husband, Joe, for absolutely everything! Much love to my sweet sister and first reader for more than twenty years, Cathy Katz. To my daughters, Morgan and Brittany, loving thanks for being incredible media assistants. And to my readers: thank you, thank you, thank you!

If you enjoyed reading *Deranged*, read on for an exciting early look at:

BURIED DEEP

T.R. Ragan's thrilling new Jessie Cole novel, coming early 2019.
Editor's Note: This is an early excerpt and may not reflect the finished book.

BURIED DEEP

ONE

JASON

Jason slid into the back seat next to his wife and shut the door.

He exhaled.

He shouldn't be doing this. Sitting here now. Celebrating. It was all wrong. But he hadn't found the courage to tell Lacey he wanted to call it quits.

"Where to?" the driver asked.

"The Firehouse," Jason said.

Lacey leaned forward as if the driver wouldn't be able to hear her otherwise, a ridiculous notion considering she wasn't exactly soft-spoken. "It's a very special night," she told him.

The driver didn't flinch. Nor did he say a word.

"It's our eighth anniversary," Lacey went on. "Well, I mean, the actual date is a few days from now, but Jason would never be able to get a weeknight off. He works too hard." She turned his way.

Jason forced a smile as he reached for the bottle of champagne in the ice bucket. Nice touch, considering the price for a ride to the restaurant and back was more than fair, and the car was definitely not a limo. He lifted the bottle as he looked at the driver in the rearview mirror. "Thanks."

No reaction.

The foil and wire had been removed from the bottle, and all he had to do was pop the cork. Jason poured a few inches of bubbly into the plastic cups provided and handed one to his wife. She hesitated, then took a tiny sip and made a toast. "To the best life," she said.

"To the best life," he repeated.

He gulped down the champagne and refilled his glass.

He was thirty-two years old. He had his whole life in front of him. The prospect of spending another eight years with Lacey just didn't sound appealing any longer. She was cute and funny. Not the best cook, but not for lack of trying. Basically they were friends. Nothing more.

He'd never questioned her love for him. But still. He'd spent so many nights in bed, tossing and turning, unsure of how to tell her what he was feeling. But the time was never right. It didn't matter how late he came home, she always had a smile on her face. She was perky and positive, for the most part. Sure, she had her moments, but her bad days weren't like most people's. Any momentary lapses in her always-sunny disposition were more like blips on a radar screen. Fleeting.

Every morning he woke up thinking, *This is the day I'll tell her*, and every night he climbed into bed beside her and kissed her good night.

He might not be able to pinpoint the exact problem he was having with Lacey, but that didn't change anything. He knew without a doubt that, for him, she just wasn't enough.

Lacey

Lacey could hardly contain her excitement. Lately it seemed as if she and Jason never had time for each other, which was why she'd been saving her big news for tonight.

She was pregnant.

Finally.

Jason had no idea of the extreme measures she'd taken to make it happen. After they had sex in the morning, which wasn't nearly often enough, he would run off to work, and she would stay in bed and keep her legs raised high, her heels resting against the wall for hours. This was only one of the tricks of the trade she'd gotten from kindhearted people on the internet. She had tried the Espresso, Nutella, and wine diet. The no-dairy diet. Headstands and yoga.

Nothing worked until one day she simply gave up trying.

Voilà! And now they would be having a baby.

She couldn't wait to see the look on Jason's face when she told him.

Tonight would be a turning point in their marriage. She knew that for certain because Jason had seemed so distant lately. Sometimes she would catch him staring off at nothing for minutes on end. When she asked him what he was thinking about, he usually looked surprised or guilty, as if she'd caught him with his pants down. Then he'd smile and say he was simply tired, or he was thinking about an upcoming business meeting.

Lacey had talked to Jason's parents and his brother, but they'd all shrugged off her concerns, suggesting it might be time to find a hobby. Even though she worked part-time at the computer store and volunteered at the local animal shelter, they told her she had way too much time on her hands.

Jason grabbed her arm, pulling her from her thoughts. "Do you smell that?"

She sniffed the air. She couldn't smell anything, really. But that was probably because all her senses seemed off-kilter since she'd learned she was pregnant. Nothing tasted the same. She sniffed again, and this time she thought she caught a hint of something minty. No . . . no. It smelled like the bathroom cleaner her mother-in-law used.

"I don't feel good," Jason told her.

When she looked at him, she was surprised to see how pale his face had become. He was leaning back against the seat, and his face was pasty white. She took his empty cup and put her full one inside of it before placing it in the bucket. Then she loosened her husband's tie.

He closed his eyes.

Air. They needed air.

She turned to her right and pushed down on the button to lower the window, but nothing happened. When she looked at the driver, she frowned. He had a plastic apparatus over his mouth and nose. "Is that a gas mask?" she asked.

There was no answer.

For the first time since she'd climbed into the car, the driver met her gaze in the rearview mirror. His eyes were twinkling, his expression mischievous. And she didn't like it one bit. "Please open the window. It's stuffy back here, and my husband isn't feeling well." Panic didn't fully set in until she realized he meant to do nothing about the situation. It was then that she looked straight ahead through the windshield and saw nothing but trees and grassy fields for miles. *Where were they?*

Her breath caught in her throat. Her skin felt tingly and strange.

She turned back to her husband and said, "Jason. Something's not right." But Jason was out cold. She grabbed his shoulders and shook him. "Jason!"

Leaning over and gagging as if she were going to be sick, she searched through her purse for the pepper spray she always carried. And then she grabbed hold of her phone. Before she could hit the emergency button, the car swerved, and her right side slammed into the car door. Her phone dropped and slid under the seat.

With the pepper spray still in her hand, she used her thumb to swipe the lever to the left and then reached over the seat and sprayed him. Everything was hazy. She didn't care if they crashed. She needed fresh air.

He slammed on the brakes, and they skidded to a stop.

The side of her head hit the back of the headrest on the passenger side. She grunted and grabbed the door handle, trying to get out.

The door wouldn't open.

She had to do something.

Thinking fast, she reached over the seat for the device covering the driver's nose and mouth and yanked hard. The strap broke, and the mask fell to his lap.

It sounded as if he snarled at her before he opened his door and jumped out. Her heart skipped a beat when she saw him coming around to her side.

This was her chance!

She scrambled over the seats to get behind the steering wheel, clicked down on the lock, and let out a triumphant laugh when she saw the keys still in the ignition. She started the engine and felt a thump above her head as she drove off.

She couldn't see him in the rearview mirror. Where was he?

Thump. Thump. Thump.

He was on top of the car.

Cursing under her breath, she slammed on the brakes.

Jason hit the back of her seat, and she jerked forward. The lunatic driver had fallen from the roof and was now hanging onto the windshield wipers. He pulled himself up, a few inches at a time, his body sliding against the hood of the car until his face was pressed against the glass. He stared at her through the window, daring her to make her next move.

The strange fumes floating around the interior of the car were making her dizzy. She put the car in reverse and slammed her foot against the gas pedal. The car shot backward, and the man flew off.

But her reactions were slow, and before her foot hit the brake, the car swerved off the road and hit a tree. Her head jerked to the side, taking her breath away. She shoved the stick in "Drive" and hit the gas pedal again. The tires spun but couldn't get a grip.

He was charging her way.

He was only a few feet from the car when she turned and reached over the seat, hoping to find her phone.

His fist shot through the window, shattering glass and making contact with her jaw, leaving her in the dark.

About the Author

Photo © 2014 Morgan Ragan

New York Times, *Wall Street Journal*, and *USA Today* bestselling author T.R. Ragan has sold more than two million books since her debut novel appeared in 2011. She is the author of the Faith McMann Trilogy; six Lizzy Gardner novels (*Abducted, Dead Weight, A Dark Mind, Obsessed, Almost Dead,* and *Evil Never Dies*); and the first two novels in the Jessie Cole series (*Her Last Day* and *Deadly Recall*). In addition to thrillers, she writes medieval time-travel tales, contemporary romance, and romantic suspense as Theresa Ragan. An avid traveler, her wanderings have led her to China, Thailand, and Nepal. Theresa and her husband, Joe, have four children and live in Sacramento, California. To learn more, visit her website at www.theresaragan.com.